Terri,

Max & Mai

Loves you.

M Clarkexo

SOMETHING
FOREVER
M.CLARKE

DEDICATION

I dedicate this book to you!

Thank you so much for following Jenna and Becky's journey. I'm so sad that it had to end. I love them so much that it was difficult to complete this book. However, words cannot express how much I appreciate your support and for taking a chance on this series which means so much to me. Hugs, hugs, hugs!

**Special thanks to my PR-Damaris Cardinali, PA-Nicole Blanchard, cover designer-Laura Hidalgo from Bookfabulous Designs, editors-Maxine Bringenberg and Melissa from There For You, my author/friend-Alexandrea Weis. Beta readers: DawnMarie Carpintero, Vanessa Strickler, Janie Iturralde, and Kara Nichols. And to ALL my Blog friends.

**I have to thank Nancy Byers for coming up with a quote:

"You're the lighthouse to my storm. You're my beacon that brought me home."

She told me Matthew was hers. I'm so honored to know how much she loves him.

**Many thanks to Joanne Lassiter for putting together an amazing Something Forever release party. For welcoming us into your home, for creating games, for everything you have done to make it fun and exciting. I can't express enough how thankful I am.

**Extra thanks to my street team, Something Great Fan page, friends, and family. Words cannot describe how thankful I am. I'm truly blessed to have you by my side.

M. Clarke

SOMETHING FOREVER

PROLOGUE
JENNA

"Becky," I said, rushing out of the bathroom with the pregnancy test. I held it gently, as if it were a precious thing. It was plastic, for goodness sake, but it held an answer that would possibly change my life. When Becky approached me, I covered the result so she couldn't see it.

"Jenna?" Becky's eyes were wide. I had her full attention. "You're killing me. You're not smiling, so that must mean you're—"

"I'm not." I shook my head, giving her half a smile. I was both relieved and disappointed. Knowing my mom had a difficult time getting pregnant with me after many miscarriages, in a way I had hoped I was. I didn't want the same struggle she had.

Becky held a huge smile. "That's great news. You didn't want to be, right?" Looking at me with uncertainty, she sounded unsure.

"I don't know," I replied, surprised by my words. Even more surprising, tears started to stream down my face. "I know I should be relieved, but what if I can't have children? Max wants a minivan full of them." I started hyperventilating, and uncontrollable tears started to pour.

Becky set her hands on my shoulders. "Jenna, you need to calm down. Everything will be fine. This doesn't mean you'll never get pregnant. People have negative results all the time. Plus, sometimes it can take months to get pregnant. I thought you wanted to wait till after you got married, so this is great news."

Becky's lips moved, but I couldn't hear a thing. As she started to fade, I wondered if I was dreaming. "Becky." I called out for her as I bawled, but I knew my voice didn't carry. I didn't even know if the words left my mouth. I only knew I cried...until it woke me up.

Tears rolled down the side of my face and sweat trickled over the top of my forehead. Max's white T-shirt clung to my sweaty back. Wiping the tears away, I blinked to clear my vision of the ceiling above me. As my lungs expanded, I took in deep, exhausting breaths. It helped me calm down, somewhat. The splitting pain in my heart from not being pregnant lingered. After I took another deep breath, I got out of bed and headed to the bathroom.

Looking at myself in the mirror, I grimaced. My hair was in disarray, my eyes were swollen, and I looked utterly exhausted. Letting the water run until the warm water finally flowed, I washed my face to wake me up. After I patted my face with a towel, I turned to see the pregnancy test that I hadn't thrown away yet. What was I waiting for anyway? I already knew the result.

CHAPTER 1
MATTHEW

"Becca. You don't have to go, do you?" I asked, swinging my legs and arms around her to bring her sleepy body closer to mine. I was just kidding of course. Mostly. She was going to Las Vegas with her friends for the weekend. Although we had recently hooked up, it was difficult at times to spend quality time together because of my schedule.

Becca let out a loud, delicious moan. Every sound that came out of her mouth sounded sexy as hell to me. Rubbing her eyes, she yawned and snuggled against my chest. What she did next made me suck in air, hard. Her hand lifted the hem of my boxers to stroke my dick. Sweet Jesus! It was bad enough I had a morning boner, but hell, she made me harder.

"Good morning," she hummed, kissing and nipping my bare chest. "Time to rise and shine." Her voice was thick and hoarse, and way too seductive.

I had to laugh. My dick was already up. "Becca, if you start this, I'm going to finish it." My words had barely left my lips before I forgot what I had said. My head spun because my dick was inside of her mouth. Fuck! She made me feel so good. I kept my mouth shut and watched her.

After yanking off my boxers, her wet tongue slowly glided over my shaft and down. Every nerve in my body shot alive. After another lick and suck, she went in deeper and rocked faster. Holy fuck! Dropping my head to my pillow, I let her take me...stroke me...lick me...suck me...take me to the edge. My Becca did the most amazing things with her mouth.

As the urge to climax grew, I wrung a fistful of her disarrayed hair and pulled her up to kiss those sultry lips of hers. I wanted to swallow her into me, to take every part of her, because as always, I couldn't get enough. Wanting to eat her up with my tongue, teeth, and lips, I kissed her until my lips felt bruised.

Becca broke away while her teeth pulled back my bottom lip, leaving me panting like a dog salivating over a piece of steak out of its reach. "What do you want, Matt?" she asked, gazing at me with a seductive smile that said "come get me."

"You know what I want." I tugged a white, lacy, spaghetti strap off her shoulder and ran my hand down her arm feather-lightly, knowing it would give her tingles. "I told you I'm going to finish it."

Leaning closer, I gingerly kissed her shoulder and glided my tongue down to the base of her breast, then to her nipple. Becca moaned in pleasure, and I tugged the other strap off her shoulder and let my hand explore her breast. Becca had the most beautiful breasts I'd ever touched, and I'd had my hands on plenty to compare.

Becca was on fire. When I slid a hand down to rub her clit, she pushed me down and straddled me. I liked it when a woman took charge, but Becca was something else. My firecracker could always make me explode with the simplest actions.

"I'll ask you again. What do you want?" Her tone was domineering.

When I didn't answer, she shifted onto that perfect spot and started rubbing along my dick. When did she take off her panties? Holy shit, I was going to come if she didn't stop. I had dreamt of fucking her last night, and her teasing was going to drive me over the edge.

"Becca," I muttered under my breath. That was all that escaped my mouth before I realized I was inside of her.

She rode me slowly, her breasts warmed my chest as she leaned down to my face. "You're gonna miss me when I'm gone."

"Isn't that a cup song?" I asked. Then I tried hard not to bust out laughing. In the heat of the moment, and I was blowing the mood.

Becca paused for a moment, then let out a soft laugh in understanding, but thankfully she continued. She bit her bottom lip as her eyes glazed with lust and want. Planting her hands on my pecs, she started riding me again, but harder and faster this time. "I'll be singing that song for you for sure."

I grabbed that fine ass of hers to reach in deeper. It was difficult to concentrate on what she said, especially since I hovered at the point of no return. "I won't have to miss you if I don't let you go."

"We'll see about that," she said breathlessly. Sitting up with my dick still inside of her, she threw her head back and ground her hips in circles. My hands went straight to her breasts, caressing them. When I pinched her nipples, she moaned louder.

Shit. I couldn't take any more. I sat up and twisted her body under mine so fast she didn't know what had happened until she lightly bounced on the bed. With my eyes locked on hers, I slipped inside her again. Becca heaved a deep, pleasurable breath and closed her eyes. I loved watching her expression when I was making her feel good. She looked absolutely beautiful.

Becca gripped the back of my shoulders and tugged harder when I started pumping faster. "You still want to go?" I asked, banging into her with each word.

My Becca's back arched with the pleasure I gave her. She shifted her head from side to side, moaning softly. "I...don't...know." She sucked in air, breathing out one word at a time.

"What do you want?" I asked, repeating her question. However, she couldn't answer. With her bottom lip sucked into her mouth, letting out heavy breaths, she was lost in me.

Lifting both of her legs around my shoulders, I thrust deeper and cradled her ass with one of my hands while the other supported her neck. "That's it, baby. Come for me."

"Matt...hew," she murmured, rewarding me with repeatedly tiny quick breaths. "I'm...coming."

Before her moaning got louder, I planted my lips on hers and sucked as hard as I was fucking her. Her sounds echoed into my mouth, getting louder the faster I rode her. When my will had been spent and I couldn't hold back anymore, I exploded. In return, my body shuddered as I groaned into her mouth.

Lying side by side, our breaths were heavy and rapid. Becca swung her arms and legs around my body like I had done to hers earlier. "I'm still going, but this will be on my mind the whole weekend."

"Just make sure those dirty strippers keep their hands to themselves," I said sternly. "Nobody touches what's mine."

"I'm going to Chippendales. Nothing is going to happen there. It's just going to be a group of shirtless guys parading around for a bunch of women, and not directly at me." Becca laughed softly.

"So you are going to Las Vegas to check out the strippers?"

"Jea...lous?" She dragged out the word, thoroughly enjoying it. "Plus, this is my first time."

"This is your first time?" With my elbow on the bed, I propped my head on my hand to rest in order to get a good look at her. "Seriously?" My tone went up a notch in surprise.

Becca gazed at me inquisitively. "Seriously?" she scowled. "What? What kind of girl do you think I am?" Becca jumped out of bed, appearing slightly offended. She slipped on her white robe. Every time I saw her in it, I remembered the day when she practically gave me a lap dance, and also of the time when I'd visited her at her parents' house. To my surprise, she had been naked underneath it.

I never could get it. Why did girls get upset over a simple, innocent question? I was just surprised. But nooo...they had to read into words and gather absurd meanings behind them that made no sense. I hadn't meant anything by it. "Becca." I sat up and put on my clothes. I had to think of something fast. "I didn't mean anything bad. Your friend Kate got married, so I figured you took her to Las Vegas."

Becca fumbled through her drawers, looking busy, but I knew why. Her beautiful brown eyes slowly met mine, and it seemed like she allowed my words to sink in. "Oh." She paused. "She wanted to do something simple. She was pregnant."

I walked to her, anticipating her pushing me away, but she didn't. Instead, she held me tightly as if to apologize.

Moving back a little, I kissed her forehead and rested my forehead against hers. "You okay?"

"Sorry I overreacted," she sighed. "Sometimes I get moody, especially around that time of the month."

I pulled back to get a better look at her face. "Moody or not moody, I'm here. We'll work things through. We're getting to know each other. I can't read your mind, Becca, but I promise to be a good listener."

Becca held me tightly again. "You're too good to me. I think I love you."

They were the sweetest words I'd heard in a long time, and tugged at my heart. "I think I love you, too."

She gave me a bright smile, the kind of smile that made my heart warm, and I tenderly kissed her lips.

"Can you go somewhere with me when I come back?" she asked. Her brows arched while she bit her bottom lip.

Her expression was half seductive and half worried, as if I would say no to her. I wondered how to read this expression. Of course, naughty thoughts ran through my mind as I wondered where she wanted to go. "Where?"

Becca's eyes were glassy. Was she tearing up? "In two weeks, it will be the exact date my friend passed away. It's been several years. I think it's about time to visit her and wash away my guilt."

Caressing her cheeks, I stated, "Of course, I'll go anywhere you ask me to go with you. But after that, I have an appointment I need to take care of. You think we could go first thing in the morning? Would that work for you?" Little did she know I had planned to visit Tessa the same day. It was the same date as her roommate's death, but I decided not to mention it. What were the odds?

With a huge smile gracing her face, Becca nodded. She liked my answer. "Good. Then it's a date." I winked. "You know…" I licked her lips. "I don't have to go to work right away. Jenna is there, holding down the fort." I swabbed my tongue across her jawline and slid my hands down her back to her ass. I knew Becca loved what I was doing when I felt her whimper; not only that, her hands couldn't get enough of my chest.

"Round two?" I whispered in her ear.

Her head fell back. The robe slid off her shoulders to expose her naked body. "Maybe more."

I smiled and chuckled lightly at her answer. After kissing her passionately, I picked her up. When Becca anchored her legs around my hips, her breasts were at the perfect angle. On our way to her bed, I licked and sucked from one nipple to the other.

Max

Jenna's eyes grew wide and her mouth opened in shock when we entered her place. I soon found out why. Matthew and Becky were making a lot of noise in Becky's bedroom, which was just too funny and disgusting. I held in my laughter as Jenna did the same. Luckily, we had come at the tail end of it. At least this made her laugh a little.

Jenna wasn't feeling well, so I'd driven her home. I had planned to head back to work after I knew she was comfortable. However, it looked like Matthew didn't go to work today. He probably thought Jenna was there, holding down the fort. Just as I headed to the kitchen to get a glass of water for Jenna, Matthew entered. Thank God he at least had his boxers on, but he was shocked and embarrassed as hell.

"Max? What are you doing here? How long? Oh...um...were you..." he rambled, unable to finish his words, scratching his head.

I could have told him a lie and embarrassed him, but I decided to be nice, especially since I didn't have time to joke around. I needed to get back to work to get to a meeting on time.

"Don't worry. I just got here." I shrugged it off, pretending I didn't hear a thing, and I wished I hadn't. It was bad enough when I heard my parents in high school, but it was just as bad hearing my younger brother have sex. Grabbing the glass of water, I walked out of the kitchen. Poor Jenna, she must be getting the flu. It was going around in the office.

Jenna had taken off her coat and tossed it behind the chair. Placing her head down on the dining table, she seemed out of it. With her hair tousled like she didn't care, even sick, she was still sexy to me. Wearing a black pencil skirt and a red long-sleeved blouse, she looked completely edible. I wanted to do what I enjoyed doing with those buttons on her blouse: rip them off with my teeth. Jenna had to replace some of her other ones, but I knew she didn't mind. She loved it when I did that.

"Babe, drink some water." I helped her take a sip and guided her out of the chair. "Let me take you to bed."

"Is Jenna sick?" Matthew asked as Becky came out of her bedroom.

"Jenna, Max." Becky cleared her throat, her cheeks turning slightly pink. She had a long white robe on. "How long were you ..." She smothered some swear words.

Before she could turn even a darker shade of pink, I intervened. "We just stepped in. Jenna isn't feeling well, so I brought her home."

"Does she have a fever?" Becky adjusted her robe, took a few steps toward us, and then stopped.

Becky looked at Jenna strangely, arching her brows with a questioning expression. In reply, Jenna shook her head and shrugged. Then Becky gave her another scorning glare. They exchanged no words, but those looks alone told me something wasn't quite right. I swear, women could talk in secret codes with expressions alone. Then Becky gave her a disapproving look, the way a mother would scold her child.

I had no clue what they were talking about, and Matthew and I gaped at their silent communication. It was the strangest thing.

With a final shake of her head, Jenna headed toward her bedroom.

"Everything okay?" I asked Becky.

"Everything is fine."

When she nodded with a smile, I grinned to accept her answer, and headed to Jenna. However, before I did, I twitched my brows and gave Matthew a smirky grin, indicating I had heard them in the bedroom. He understood my meaning. Instead of looking embarrassed, he plastered a cocky expression on his face. Yup, that was my brother. Though he tried not to show it, he was embarrassed. He played it off, but I knew him too well to be fooled.

I didn't like how Becky had seemed to back Jenna into a corner with that questioning look, and my mind reeled with questions as to why they both appeared so intense. By the time I got to Jenna's room, she had locked herself in the bathroom. The first thought that came to my mind was that she either had the runs or food poisoning.

I knocked softly. "You okay in there?"

"I'm fine, Max. I just need to use the restroom."

After I heard the toilet flush and the sound of the water from the sink being turned off, Jenna walked out the door. "Max, were you waiting for me by the door the whole time?" She had already changed into my white T-shirt that covered her cute, tight ass. I loved it when she wore it. It reminded me of the time we went to the New York Fashion Show. I had never seen a woman get so red from drinking alcohol, and I almost took her to the hospital. It was the first time she'd worn my T-shirt to bed; the first time I had ever laid there watching a woman fall asleep. I'd known back then I was in trouble—I fell fast for her—and there we were.

I followed behind her. "You know how I am. I don't like you being sick, and I will be all over you."

"You're too good to me, Max." Jenna smiled weakly and crawled into bed. With a soft sigh, she closed her eyes. "I'm so tired." She paused. "I'll be fine. Go back to work. Becky is home. She'll check up on me." Her words mumbled in my ear.

"Jenna, I don't think you should go to Las Vegas. You might get worse."

She reached for my arm and gripped it lightly. "I just need some sleep. Then I'll be as good as new."

"Maybe I should go with you, only to take care of you. I'll stay out of the way."

Jenna flashed her eyes opened with a soft giggle. "Don't worry, Max. My heart belongs only to you, forever and ever." She showed me the engagement ring on her finger. "See, no man will come close to me. It's so big that no one can miss it. I'll tell them I'm taken by the most amazing man."

I chuckled a little. "Yes, you tell them that, and tell them if they even lay a finger on you, I'll hunt them down."

I sounded possessive, but Jenna knew I was kidding. Somewhat.

Jenna smiled, then closed her eyes again. "Oh, Max. I'm the one who should worry about all of those women wanting to get into your pants."

Caressing Jenna's cheek, I murmured, "You never have to fear about that; I promise. I'll call you later, babe." After I planted a kiss on her lips, I closed the door behind me.

Matthew had gone to work and Becky was drinking coffee by the kitchen. "Don't worry, Max. I love her, too. I'll check up on her."

Becky must have seen me staring at Jenna's door. I debated whether to cancel the meeting. Matthew would go to work, and I could have him go instead of me, but the design company was expecting me.

"Thank you. Make sure she gets lots of fluids, and make sure to call me if her condition gets worse...please," I added. Glancing at my watch, I knew I had to go. The traffic was going to be a killer.

Becky took a long sip and winked. "I will. Who do you think looked after her when you weren't around?"

I chuckled lightly. "Thanks."

Since Becky assured me she would keep an eye on Jenna, I left knowing she was in good hands. Although I didn't think it was a good idea for Jenna to go out that night, I understood. Hopefully, the nap would help her.

CHAPTER 2
JENNA

"You're driving too slowly," Becky snarled at Kate.

"Stop being a backseat driver," Kate retorted, shifting her eyes to the speedometer. "I'm enjoying the ride." Her words were smooth and slow. "I can't help it. This is how I drive when Kristen is in the car with me."

"I can't be the backseat driver when I'm sitting in the front, and Kristen isn't in the car with us." Becky snorted.

Nicole twisted on her side. "Are we almost there yet?" She laughed out loud at her joke. Her laughter was contagious, and we joined in.

Kate cranked up the volume and bopped to the rhythm. "I can't believe I'm free," she belted, then her tone went down a notch. "I mean, I'll miss Kristen, but this is the first time I'm going away. Just me, myself, and I...and of course with my besties."

"You're lucky you can trust your mother-in-law to watch Kristen," Becky commented. "I have a friend who would never leave her son with her mother-in-law. I'm glad I don't have to think about those issues."

Becky looked over her shoulder to flash her dorky smile at Nicole and me.

"Don't look at me," Nicole said. "I don't have to think of those issues. Keith and I are going to wait. If things go well, I might be able to be a stay-at-home mom."

"There's a plus and minus to that," Kate threw in.

"True, but like I said, I don't have to think about it."

"You okay?" Becky asked, looking worried.

I nodded, but the car ride was making me nauseous. Not wanting to ruin the fun, I pretended everything was fine. "That nap was all I needed."

Becky wouldn't stop staring, narrowing her eyes to analyze me. I didn't think she believed me.

"Seriously. Stop looking at me." I waved my hand, as if I could make her turn back around.

"Just checking, 'cause I have to report to my boss."

"What boss?" Kate asked. "You don't have one. You work for yourself."

Becky turned to Kate. "I do when Jenna gets sick. Max will text everyone in the universe to find out if Jenna, his princess, is fine."

I had to smile at her remark because I knew it was true. Max was overly protective when I was sick. He even came to my apartment to check on me when he was mad at me before we started dating. Thank goodness he was there, though. Luckily, I had found my prince. He was too good to me, and I didn't know what I'd ever done to deserve someone like him.

"You're fortunate Max is the way he is. You got lucky in that department. All men want to be taken care of when they're sick, but they're not good when the roles are reversed," Kate stated. "I have to be honest, Craig sucks at it. When I get sick, he'll give me medication of course, but I'm pretty sure he doesn't match up to Max's standards. Max goes beyond the call of duty."

"Beyond, beyond," Becky added. "But there is nothing wrong with that. I think it's sweet."

Our conversation had died down as we continued along the dark highway. There were no stars out tonight, adding to the eerie feeling. Luckily, there were some cars in front of and behind us, so it didn't seem like we were completely alone. Yet we drove in a tunnel of endless darkness with no finish line. It kept on going and going, and the only thing I could see was what the headlights illuminated in front of us.

The darkness reeled me back to thoughts of Crystal. Ethan stepping forward was the best thing that could have happened. I couldn't believe my eyes when he had come to our last meeting. Because of his confession about his affair with Crystal and how she'd blackmailed him, the lawsuit never made it to court. And of course I apologized for saying his balls were sagging. He'd laughed it off and told me he was glad to help. Ethan was a good guy. I was so glad he remained that way and his wife forgave him. Her support was one of the big factors in his coming forward.

"We're here," Nicole said cheerfully.

Thank God! Trying to keep my mind occupied with other thoughts beside how sick I felt, I concentrated on what was in my line of vision. The colorful bright lights brought on a whole new level of blissful ambiance. I felt like I was somewhere in rainbow city, sucked into the beauty and excitement.

"I made reservations at the Bellagio," Becky murmured, staring out the window. I was certain she enjoyed the view since it was the first time she'd been there. "Actually, Matthew made the reservations, but he confirmed it with Max. So it was both of their idea."

"What do you mean?" Kate signaled right, and then exited the highway.

I remembered Max mentioning it, and though I had told him not to go out of his way, he had done it anyway. A part of me didn't mind because it was for Nicole, but a part of me felt bad. That meant Max and Matthew were paying for the room.

"That's not all," Becky continued.

Nicole leaned closer, and slightly swung to the right when Kate turned left. "I feel so bad, but what else?"

"We have our own private limo driver."

"Really? Oh my God. Don't ever break up with the Knight brothers," Nicole exclaimed, giggling. "I have to thank them."

"We're going to parade around Vegas in style," Kate sang.

It had been a while since I'd seen Kate this jovial. I knew she loved Kristen and her husband, but I guessed she just needed her time alone.

After we valet parked, the gentleman took out our luggage, and the bellboy placed them on the cart for us.

"I'll bring them to your room," he said with a friendly grin.

"Thanks." Becky gave him a tip, and we entered the door that was held open for us.

It had been a while since I had been there, but it didn't matter. My eyes always went straight to the colorful glass decoration on the ceiling. And how could you miss all of the people snapping pictures of the garden? I loved how they changed the theme by seasons.

"I'll check in for us," Becky said, leaving the three of us standing near the waiting area.

While we waited for Becky to return, Nicole took out her cell phone. "Let's take pictures." She flipped it so that we could see the three of us. Then she took some more of the ceiling and another one of Becky walking toward us.

"Let's get this party started." Becky handed each of us our key to the suite. "This way." She led the way, and when we reached our room, we told Nicole to swipe the card. After all, this was for her. Nicole flung open the door, and I wasn't prepared for what I saw in front of me. Matthew had said he booked the Chairman Suite, but I never imagined how stunning it would look.

"Hoooly...shit," Becky murmured under her breath.

"Wow." Nicole's eyes grew wide and mine did the same. We stared, mesmerized by the grand suite.

"This place is double the size of my house." Kate started to head toward the window that took up the whole back wall. "We have a fantastic view of the water fountain. We can watch it from here."

We all rushed over. What a view! Blinking lights filled the darkness, providing a feeling of exultation. It filled me up so I couldn't help but smile and let my worries disappear. People go to Las Vegas to escape because you give up control. Reality disappeared and I got drunk on the atmosphere, the excitement, and the billboards of half-naked women and men flashing every way I looked.

"This is amazing." Nicole's breath misted on the window. With her palms and face pressed against the glass, you could tell she loved the view...and she wasn't the only one.

"Let's go check out the bedroom," Kate said.

Since Kate and Nicole headed to the first bedroom, Becky and I headed to the other one. In the center was a huge, king-sized bed with the finest and most expensive linen and bedding. I wandered into the bathroom, which was bigger than our living room, with marble trimming and—my personal favorite—a huge whirlpool tub.

The pamphlet on the powder room counter declared that not only did we get our own private check-in line, we had twenty-four-hour butler attention, VIP seating at shows, and the suite was about 4,000 square feet in size.

"I'm going to have to thank Matthew in a special way," Becky said. "This is too much, not that I'm complaining." Her fingers tapped out a text...to Matthew, most likely.

Speaking of which, I had to call Max to let him know we had arrived safely. "You're right, this really is too much."

"Let's go eat," Kate hollered from the living room.

"Feisty." Becky chuckled, grabbing her coat as we all did the same.

"Where to?" Nicole asked, placing her arm around the three of us and pulling everyone into a hug.

"Anywhere, Nicole. It's your weekend," I replied, snuggling into her hold as we walked out the door. However, food was the last thing on my mind. Thinking of it made me feel sicker to my stomach.

CHAPTER 3
BECKY

After dinner, we gambled on the slot machines; mostly quarter slots. None of us were big gamblers, so we stayed away from the tables. Since it was already past midnight, we decided to head back to our suite. We were pretty beat from work and the four hour long drive. Having a full day ahead of us, we all agreed to call it an early night, even though I wasn't tired. Jenna was one of the main reasons why I agreed we should go back to the hotel; she looked exhausted.

Scrolling through my texts with Matthew, I missed him. It had only been a little over twenty-four hours since I last saw him, but I'd never missed someone I was dating so much. Once everyone fell asleep, I sat in the living room in front of the plasma television and flipped through the channels in the dark. When my cell phone rang, I smiled.

"Matthew."

"Becca." I saw his sexy, naughty grin in my mind as if he were standing in front of me.

"You're not sleeping?" I whispered, but I didn't know why I did. It wasn't like my friends could hear me, especially since the place was huge and their bedroom doors were closed.

"I couldn't sleep. You're not next to me." His tone was pouty.

I laughed at his comment, but I loved that he was thinking of me. "Sorry. I miss you, too. I'll be home very soon."

"I know." I heard an intake of breath. "I already asked you this question earlier, but do you like your suite?"

"It cost too much, Matt, but, yes. I would be crazy to say no. I need to find a way to thank you." My tone came out flirty at the end.

"I know how you can." His sultry tone lured me in. Oh shit! What was on his dirty mind? "I want you to touch yourself."

"Matthew." I laughed softly. "You're not here."

"Just pretend I am. Have you ever had phone sex before?"

I almost choked on my own saliva. I'd heard of and done many things before, but this was a first. When I didn't answer, Matthew continued, "I can't believe I'm going to be your first." He sounded so proud. "I'm going to make you feel so good."

His words alone turned me on. Holy shit. "You mean I'm going to make myself feel good."

He chuckled lightly. "However you want to see it."

The preview porn on the television wasn't helping either. I thought about watching it, but Matthew or Max would pay the bill, and no way did I want them finding out one of us watched one. "This isn't going to work," I said. However, my hand was already kneading my breast. I imagined it was Matthew's.

"I'm stroking my dick, Becca. I'm pretending your tongue is licking it." Whether or not Matthew was really doing what he said, I didn't care. It was working for me. "Put your hand on your clit, Becca, and touch it the way I do it. Pretend it's my finger. Imagine me sucking it hard there, baby. Can you feel me?"

Holy fuck. *"Yes."* My chest rose and fell with the pleasure that built inside of me.

"Now...stick your finger inside and pretend it's my dick. I'm going to pretend I'm inside of you."

Matthew's groans brought me to another level of excitement. There was no way he could fake that sound; it was too genuine. Every moan intensified my need for him. "Can you feel me, Becca? Push in deeper."

"It's not the same," I whimpered. My body tensed. I couldn't satisfy myself, and the more I tried, the build-up became unbearable.

"Want me to finish it for you, Becca? You want me inside of you?" His tone whispered into the phone in the most delicious way. I was already losing my mind, yearning for him.

"Yes, but you're not here." I said it somewhat angrily, trying to tame the throbbing ache between my legs. I was mad at him for pushing me to the edge. My pants were halfway down, my breast exposed, and I was watching the stupid porn. How I got to that point, I had no clue. His words were magic, controlling my actions.

"I promised before that I wouldn't start something I couldn't finish. Now...open the door."

What? I pulled my clothes back on and walked to the door with the phone in my ear. "Are you serious? You're not here, are you?" I looked through the peephole. Oh my God! Before I could swing the door all the way open, Matthew reached for me. With my back against the wall, his lips conquered mine so hard you would think he hadn't seen me in months. Yet, I didn't mind. I missed him just as much.

"Matthew...how...when?" I could barely get my words out. He devoured me. His hands slipped into my PJ bottoms, feeling me everywhere he could touch. He stopped, breathing heavily against my neck.

After we both caught our breaths, Matthew cupped my face. "I assume everyone is asleep?"

"Yes."

"Come with me."

"Where?"

"Next door."

"Next door? You mean you got a room right next door?" I started laughing.

"Max did, so I followed suit." With a shrug of his shoulders, he gave me the most adorable, boyish grin...the kind I wanted to suck off his face.

Without a word, because I expected him to finish what he'd started, I let him grab my hand and lead me to his suite. When we got there, Max was standing by the door with his arms crossed. He was in jeans and a T-shirt, just like Matthew. They both looked young and playful in their casual outfits, but as devilishly handsome as always.

"What took you so long?" Max asked shyly.

He looked so guilty. It was funny to see these grown men act like children.

"Hi, Becky. Surprise." He flashed an innocent smile. "Matthew's idea," he said, then took off to Jenna.

I had to laugh at how they blamed each other. I didn't really care whose idea it was; I was just ecstatic to see Matthew. Jenna was going to be really surprised in the morning.

"Wait. He doesn't have the key to our place," I said, glancing over my shoulder to Max.

"The room is under our names, so we have a set of keys." He wiggled his eyebrows at me.

"Was that your plan all along?" With pouty lips, I gave him a playful glare.

"Maybe...maybe not." Matthew picked me up, anchored my legs around his hips, and carried me to his room. "Now, where were we before my brother rudely interrupted us?" Opening the door, he said with a wink, "Welcome to Las Vegas, Becca. What happens in Vegas continues when we get home."

Jenna

With the curtains drawn, I couldn't tell what time it was. All I knew was that I'd had a good night's sleep. No one had bothered to wake me up, so I figured it was still early in the morning.

I didn't know much about Becky's sleeping habits, but she snuggled right next to me. Not wanting to wake her, and not wanting to be face to face with her, I decided not to roll over. She must have thought I was Matthew from the way her hand rested on my hip. Trying to get out of the awkward situation, and needing a glass of water, I slowly moved my legs.

Wait a minute! Becky's leg was hairy. She wore jeans last night so I couldn't tell, but holy Jesus. Wait. It was too hairy.

I stiffened when I heard a manly groan and felt the puff of air on my neck. Oh my God! That was not Becky. Remembering the night before, I realized I hadn't done anything. I'd gone to bed first. Going into panic mode, I contemplated what to do as my heart thumped erratically. Should I scream?

I glanced down and saw that I was fully clothed. Thank God! Without looking to see who lay next to me—because I was deathly afraid to—I pushed the body beside me and jumped off the bed. It happened quickly, but my reflexes were a bit slow. When he grabbed me, I screamed bloody murder...so loud that Nicole and Kate barged through the door.

"Jenna, it's me, Max," he said, covering my mouth.

"Max?" I turned, my breath heaving and still scared out of my mind. "What are you doing here?" My eyes pooled with frightened tears as I looked at Nicole and Kate. They both had their hands on their chests, right above their heart, gaping from Max to me.

"Max?" Nicole looked confused.

"Max?" Kate repeated, seeming just as flabbergasted.

"Sorry. Everything is fine. I scared Jenna. I won't be staying. I didn't come to crash the party," Max rambled until Nicole and Kate left the room with smiles.

Max held me tightly, caressing my hair and face. "I'm so sorry, babe. I didn't mean to scare you like that. I wanted to surprise you." Max's chest vibrated against mine, and he released a small chuckle.

"You think this is funny." I pulled away, and tried to hide a smile. "You almost gave me a heart attack."

"I wouldn't mind doing CPR on you. It will be my pleasure."

I lightly socked him. "I bet you wouldn't mind. Where's Becky?"

Max bit his bottom lip with a smirk, giving me a mischievous grin. He wouldn't answer until I narrowed my eyes at him. "Next door."

"Next door?" My pitch reached its limit. "You planned to come here all this time and you didn't tell me?"

Max didn't answer. Instead, he dove in for a long, lingering, 'pulling out my bottom lip with his teeth' kind of kiss. "Jenna, I missed you."

Shoot! He started to sing. I stared at him with doting eyes. My heart levitated and his voice made me swoon. The way he sang and nibbled my neck, I couldn't even pretend to be mad at him. I had completely become an idiot.

"Max," I called softly.

"Yes, babe? Don't talk, just enjoy." He kissed me tenderly on that perfect spot on my shoulder, producing pleasurable shivers down my spine. "Let me enjoy. I'll be leaving after I have my Jenna breakfast."

Max's tongue bathed my neck and down to the base of my breast. How my buttons got undone, I had no clue. I had on a long pair of cotton PJs from Victoria's Secret. At times, I had no idea how he managed to undress me...seduce me with his eyes, his touch, and his words. Max was simply that good.

"I—" Only that one word escaped my mouth. Max pushed the blankets aside and hovered over me, shirtless. Well, that did it. I couldn't fight it, even though I had to talk to him about something important that would change our lives forever. I just didn't know how.

Max's body warmed me up, producing sensual heat all over my flesh. His kisses were soft and tender, savoring every inch of my exposed breasts. His feather-light strokes and touches drove me insane. His hands explored my body while he undressed both of us. When Max headed lower, my muscles went completely limp. I utterly lost it when he spread my legs and placed his tongue on my clit.

31

Arching my back, I moaned and let him pleasure me. Max licked, sucked, and stroked my clit until I pulled him up, wanting to kiss him. Instead, he turned my neck to the side and whispered, "Do you like your surprise, Jenna?"

"Yes," I breathed. The words barely left my mouth.

"Would you like me to continue?"

However, Max didn't let me answer. His lips pressed hungrily on mine. Our tongues danced and tasted until Max reached in deeper. He had taken control. His kiss was fierce—intense, as if we hadn't seen each other for weeks—but I didn't mind. Max wanted me. He made me feel special, sexy, and desired.

Spreading my legs a little bit wider with his knee, he teased me with the tip of his dick until I begged. That was what he'd been waiting for.

"Max, please." I panted and moaned, needing him inside me. The burning, aching, heart-pounding, intense urge was too much to bear.

"Say it, babe. Tell me what you want." His tone was hot and demanding.

Ever since I'd tied him up, and started to become more open and playful, Max had opened up to me, too. Sometimes he would say things he would have never said at the beginning of our relationship. Knowing I was open to trying new things, Max was beyond thrilled. He would never force me or put me in an awkward position, but I wanted to please him as well, so I needed to be open-minded. "I want you to take me." My eyes bore into his as I said those words. "Please, I need you inside of me."

Max's eyes showed that he thoroughly enjoyed my whimpering, begging. He knew he was in control, and he loved how he was making me feel. With his dick right on that perfect spot, he whispered heavily and hotly in my ear, "I'm going to fuck you hard."

Holy shit! His words alone made me explode, and pleasure diffused throughout me. Max entered me, slowly building me up. While his elbows supported his weight, he cupped my face and rewarded me with a loving grin. He filled me up in body and heart. I was head over heels in love with this man. He knew exactly how to turn me on.

Just when I reached the point of no return, Max pulled out. "I'm not done, babe. I'm still hungry." He lifted me up, and began carrying me. "Let's see how big this bathroom is."

Max gently put me down and spun me around. With my back to him, I faced the huge mirrors in front of and beside us over the sink. I saw our naked bodies, and it was the hottest thing. Max's eyes caught mine through the mirror. The old Jenna would have been shy and looked away, but not this new Jenna. I continued to keep my eyes locked on his, and watched his hand caress my body.

Even when he thrust inside me, I watched his hips in motion. Holy Jesus, I was watching Max and Jenna porn. I had never seen porn before, only the previews from the hotel television. Damn, it was hot, and I was losing control.

"I like to watch you watch us," Max panted, pumping faster. "Don't we look good together?"

"Yes." When Max started grinding harder, deeper, I let my head fall back to his shoulder and closed my eyes. "Oh God," I yelped when Max went faster.

"No one can hear you, babe. Scream all you want. Let me know how good I'm making you feel."

I didn't hold anything back after that. Familiar sounds escaped my mouth, the types of sounds that screamed pleasure. "Max," I called his name as I gripped his hands. "Oh God. Oh God."

"Open your eyes, Jenna. Look how beautiful you are," Max demanded as he pumped deeper with each word.

I did as he instructed, staring at the wonderful man who showed me things I refused to see before—me, being beautiful; me, being desired; me, being loved the way every woman should be loved.

Max pulled out again and laid a towel on the sink counter. Placing me on it, he entered me again. "I love you, Jenna," he said tenderly, caressing my cheek with his lips.

"I love you too, Max," I replied with conviction.

With a satisfied grin, Max held me tightly in his arms and gave me all of him until I couldn't take it anymore and his will had been spent. Panting and breathing hard, Max's head rested on my shoulder. His hot breath escaped against my skin.

"I like my surprise. You can surprise me like that any time," I said weakly. Utterly drained, I leaned against Max.

Max's body slightly shook when he let out a soft laugh. "I will. I go wherever you go." He paused. "I better let you get ready. You girls have a long day planned?"

"Yes." I nodded. "Tonight is the real party. Some of Nicole's friends will be there, too."

"Just be careful. And you sure you're feeling better?"

"Yes. I just needed that nap."

"Good, but nothing else is on your mind? You seem pre-occupied at times. The only time you're not is when I'm inside of you."

I flushed with warmth from his comment. "That's not true." I pouted, giving him my most sexy smile with my finger in my mouth.

"Geez, Jenna." Max raked his hair back and looked away. "I'd better go before I lock us in the bathroom and don't let you out."

"Wait." I grabbed his arm. "Thank you for everything. For this room, for the limo."

"Only the best for you. And you can stop thanking me."

I had lost count of how many times I'd texted Max thanking him for everything. Max walked out of the bathroom and I followed, watching him put his clothes on. The way his muscles flexed when he slipped his shirt over his head, the way he tucked it inside of his jeans, and the way he slicked his hair back was too dreamy. I could just stare at him doing this all day.

"Where are you going?" I asked, slipping into the covers naked.

"Matthew and I are heading back home. I came by to make sure you were feeling better."

"You didn't take my word or Becky's?"

Max slipped on his shoes. "I did...just thought I'd give you a surprise visit."

"Are you driving back home?"

"No. We took the plane."

"Spoiled," I commented playfully, with a light laugh.

"I offered you the plane, but you turned me down."

"Next time, I won't. That was a long drive."

"See, I'm always right."

I frowned because most of the time he was.

"Call me later. And please be careful." Max leaned down and kissed me. Then he did it again. This time, he punctuated each spoken word with a peck on my face. "Don't...talk...to...strange...men. People...are...crazy...here."

"Understood, Mr. Knight. I'll call you later."

Max looked over his shoulder, winking one last time before he closed the door behind him.

CHAPTER 4
JENNA

"So glad we had VIP passes. Can you imagine standing in that line?" Nicole asked, and took a bite of her smoked salmon.

I glanced at the line again. From where we sat, we had a clear view. "The buffet lines are crazy. I don't remember it being like this the last time I came here, but then again, I was in high school and I came with my parents. We always ate early to beat the rush."

"We did come around the time when everybody heads to the restaurants. It's brunch time." Kate looked like she was going to bust out laughing. "Some of us wanted breakfast, and some already had breakfast in bed." She cleared her throat.

Becky and I looked at each other and our cheeks turned the same color. "Sorry," Becky said sheepishly. "I had no idea Matthew and Max were going to throw us a surprise visit."

"That's okay." Nicole adjusted the veil attached to her plastic tiara. The back of the veil read *Bride to Be*. It was Kate's idea. She also gave us T-shirts that read *Bride's Maid*, which were decorated with pink trimmings. Though it was something I'd normally never wear, we did it for Nicole and for the fun of it. It made Nicole happy, and that was all that mattered.

"So, here is the plan..." Becky started to say between bites of her toast. "We're going shopping after we eat, catching an early show, and going to dinner. We'll be meeting some of Nicole's friends, and we'll all be out together for a fun night."

"Sounds good," Nicole agreed, glancing at me. "Jenna, how are you feeling? You look a little out of it."

"That's because she has something to tell you." Becky nudged me underneath the table to reassure me.

I couldn't hold on to the news any longer. I should have told Max when I saw him that morning, but knowing how he felt, I chickened out. The fact that he had traveled miles to surprise me was even more reason not to dampen his visit. However, these were my best friends, friends I trusted. Why couldn't I just say it? I was embarrassed.

I'd sworn I would never be pregnant before I got married, so what had happened to the promise I'd made to myself? Max happened. He gave me pleasure beyond anything I could imagine, and he gave me love that far surpassed the pleasure. I shouldn't be embarrassed. It was out of love that I was carrying his child.

I had to admit that a part of me exulted. Never knowing if I could have children because of my mom's history, I was thrilled when I found out I was pregnant. I could still recall the day I'd told Becky.

"Becky." I rushed out and almost ran into her waiting just outside the door.

"I'm right here, Jenna. Where would I be? I'm nervous as hell for you right now." Becky looked as if she was the one who had to tell me the news, like she was holding her breath. I could almost feel her heart pounding hard against her chest, like mine.

Holding out the stick with my shaky hand, I said, "I'm not sure how I feel right now, but for whatever reason...this happened.

I'm pregnant." I bawled in front of her, not knowing if I was happy or upset over the news.

Becky reached for me and held me tightly. "It's okay, Jenna. Things will work out. Max will embrace his baby."

Nodding to agree, I cried harder. After I let it all out in Becky's arms, I wiped my tears and gathered myself. "Sorry, Becky. I'm happy that I can get pregnant, but I'm also worried. Even if Max and I were married, he didn't want to have children right away. He wanted us to travel the world and have an adventure before we started a family."

Holding my hand, Becky led me to the sofa. "You don't always get what you want. Sometimes, life happens and you have to make new plans. Nobody can prepare for the unexpected. Max will be a great father. You're already engaged, so there is no reason to be ashamed about this news."

Sniffing, I wiped my tears. "To tell you the truth, I think I'm excited, but at the same time I'm really scared. This is a life changing moment." I paused and ran my hand down my face. "How do I tell my parents? They are going to flip."

Becky leaned closer to me. "Your parents are cool. Give them some credit. Plus, you said your mom had a difficult time conceiving you. Maybe she'll be relieved that you can get pregnant."

I smiled to let her know I agreed. Part of me knew my parents would be okay with this, especially since Max and I were engaged. Peering down at my huge, sparkling diamond ring, my mind went back to the day he proposed to me. Thank God he had. If he had asked me afterward, I would've thought he was asking me out of obligation.

"So...what's the news?" Nicole asked.

"Are you moving in with Max? Wait." Kate looked confused. "You practically live with him, so that can't be it."

"Hurry, Jenna. You're driving me crazy. You know I'm not good with waiting." Nicole laughed, but she was serious. She leaned from the opposite side, staring at me as if she could read the words on my face.

"I'm pregnant." There, I said it. I finally said it.

Silence.

More silence.

Kate stared at me like I'd said I was an alien, and Nicole simply looked dumbfounded.

"Oh my God! Jenna, I'm so happy for you." Kate finally opened her mouth, but her tone betrayed her words. She appeared more worried than happy for me.

Nicole looked like the news was finally sinking in. "That's wonderful...right?" Her words confirmed my expression wasn't a jovial one.

"Yes, of course it is," Becky intervened. "It's all good. Kate was pregnant before she got married."

"Max proposed to you even before knowing, so that's great," Kate threw in. She got up and walked around to give me a genuine hug, and so did Nicole.

Kate raised her glass to toast, but stopped. "Wait, does Max know?"

"Not yet. I planned to tell him when I got back."

Silence.

"You didn't tell him?" Kate whispered. "I mean...you're going to tell him, right?"

"Of course she is." Becky sounded upset. She glanced at Kate with her brows raised, questioning her choice of words.

"Sorry, Jenna. I didn't mean to ask so many questions. It's just that I remember being so nervous to tell Craig. He didn't take it well at first, but he came around. I'm sure

Max will be different." She smiled, but it didn't reach her eyes.

I hoped so.

CHAPTER 5
BECKY

All dressed up—in high heels and dresses that turned guys' heads—we were ready to party the night away. Getting into our limo, we took pictures and sent them to Max and Matthew to thank them. I even sent a picture of just myself to Matthew. He texted me back, telling me to change into sweats, and I had to laugh at that. In reply, Matthew sent me a picture back of his frowning face. It was too adorable.

I'll be there tomorrow, I texted.

Waiting for you. Have fun and be safe. I'll be hanging out with my boring one and only brother.

No surprise visit tonight?

You didn't know I had a secret side job, did ya?

What? Lol!

I'm one of the Chippendale dancers. It's my shift tonight. I'll dance for you.

Hahaha!

You hurt my feelings. You don't think I could be one?

You have the body for it.

Good answer.

You can dance for me privately when I come back home.

I can't wait. I won't even take money from you.

I'm not sure what I did right, but I couldn't believe Matthew and I were together. Not that I didn't deserve a guy like him, but a guy like him was hard to come by.

Never would I have imagined finding a guy so good looking, with a great career, and who knew how to treat a woman. He was a fabulous package, one that I hoped to keep forever.

Looking at us with teary eyes, Nicole passed out the champagne glasses to toast. We all had alcohol in ours except for Jenna. Hers was filled with apple cider. "Thank you to my best friends. My life wouldn't be the same without you. You fill my heart with happiness. When I need someone to lift me up, you are all there for me. And for that, I thank you from the bottom of my heart. Love you all to pieces."

"Love you, too, Nicole," Kate said. "May you and Keith forever hold on to the happiness you both deserve."

"Ditto," I bellowed. Kate had taken the words out of my mouth.

"I can't wait for you and Keith to finally get married," Jenna said. "Only a month away."

After we toasted, our limo driver blasted the music for us. We were headed to dinner to meet Nicole's friends.

"Whoo hoo!" Nicole shouted. "I'm going to get blasted tonight." She gulped down her drink and asked for another. Nicole was good at holding her liquor, so I didn't worry.

Jenna looked a little spacy, so I nudged her. "You okay?"

"Just a little nauseous. I hope it doesn't get worse." She took a few more sips of her drink. Poor Jenna, she'd hardly eaten during brunch. I knew it was worse than she let on; she was always that way. She was worried that she would ruin the fun, so she tried her best to hide how miserable she felt. I knew her best...Nicole and Kate had no clue.

"Look." Jenna showed me her phone. Max had sent her a picture of himself frowning just like Matthew had done. I laughed out loud and showed Jenna the picture I'd gotten from Matthew.

"They're having dinner together," I told her, but she already knew that. "If you need to leave early, don't be afraid to let me know. I can tell you're not feeling well."

Jenna took another sip and gave me a sideways hug. "Don't worry about me. I'll let you know if I can't handle it. I could use a little distraction." Jenna started laughing, shifting her eyes to Nicole and Kate. They sang, moving to the beat of the music, and laughing like crazy. I couldn't help but laugh, too.

"And people think I'm the loud one," I said to Jenna.

"They just don't know you like I do," she replied.

Jenna was right. Not only did I get lucky in the "finding the right guy" department, I was lucky in the "finding a best friend" department. No one knew me the way Jenna did. I hoped I was as good a friend to her.

Getting out of the limo, Nicole and Kate gave us a show, giggling and saying funny things that made no sense whatsoever. Jenna held onto Kate, while I held onto Nicole. Thank God I didn't drink—I had my own reasons not to—because I couldn't imagine Jenna taking care of the three of us.

Nicole's friends were already waiting for us at Taos. I had heard of this place before. The ambiance was amazing, decorated with Asian culture items and fixtures. I felt like I was dining in one of the finest restaurants in China. Our large group was seated at a corner table. Luckily, the space allowed us to have some privacy.

After the introduction and greetings, we ordered our food and held small conversations. Nicole was smiling and having a great time. I was so happy that everything was going as smoothly as planned. I had worried about how we would fit in with her other group of friends, but they were nice and friendly. It made the gathering that much more pleasant. Kate checked her phone now and then, most likely checking on Kristen.

After dinner, we all hopped back in our limo, including Nicole's friends. I took a bunch of pictures with my cell phone. When one of Nicole's friends took out stacks of dollar bills, we started laughing like crazy.

"I'm ready for tonight," she said, fanning them in front of her.

Shoot! Bringing dollar bills hadn't even crossed my mind. I knew Jenna didn't bother to bring any, so I didn't even ask. However, looking at me with the most innocent smile, she handed some to me. With my eyes practically popping out, my jaw on the floor, I laughed out loud.

Jenna shrugged her shoulders. "I didn't know if you'd brought any."

"It didn't cross my mind. I heard about it, but I figured tonight was for Nicole, not me. I can't believe you went out of your way to get all of these dollar bills."

"Actually, Max gave them to me."

"What? Seriously?"

Jenna let out a small chuckle. "He wanted me to think of him every time I used one."

"Max, Max, Max." I shook my head, but I loved it. He showed his possessiveness in ways you couldn't get mad at him for. I was surprised Matthew hadn't done the same thing.

By the time we passed through traffic, everyone was tipsy except for Jenna and me. Our group talked loudly as we stood in line, and we were even louder when we got inside.

It was crowded. I had never seen so many women in the same room all at once. When the show started, not only did loud music fill the air, but women's screams and shouts for the men strutting along the stage echoed all around us.

It was hard not to stare at the muscular men with nicely defined pecs, grinding their hips and posing to the music. Women ran to the stage and looped their dollar bills around the men's G-string thongs. Some men came out as doctors, firemen, or businessmen, but fully clothed. Then they stripped their way down to their very toned asses.

One of the strippers went directly to Nicole and tossed her plastic wedding veil off her head. Laying her down on the table, he pretended to be fucking her. It happened so fast, but he held us spellbound...we didn't know what the heck was going on. Oh my God! Women around him seemed to want to drop their panties.

I had to admit, he was beautiful. With a toned body and ripped muscles that would be found on a perfect man, he was the complete package. Lifting Nicole's hand, he placed it on his chest and ran her hand down to his thigh. I swear I heard Nicole whimper and gasp hard. She'd dream of this tonight...if she was sober enough.

Looking at the women watching as their eyes grew wide, I was pretty sure they wanted to be in Nicole's place. When I turned to Jenna, her expression was the same, but she stepped behind me when the stripper looked directly at her. I didn't blame her; she probably thought he would go to her next. And sure enough, he got off Nicole and headed toward Jenna, but one of Nicole's friends grabbed him. He gladly took the willing participant instead.

As much as I enjoyed being with my friends, now that I was dating the man of my dreams, it didn't seem right. Though I wasn't participating, or screaming and lusting for these men, a part of me felt guilty. I wouldn't want Matthew to be in a room full of almost naked women parading around for him to lust over. Now I understood why he didn't want me to go.

Chippendales weren't all that they were cracked up to be, not that I expected much in the first place. If I were single, the experience might have been different. Nicole and her single friends had a blast, and that was all that mattered. After the show ended, we dropped off Nicole's friends at their hotel and went back to ours.

CHAPTER 6
JENNA

We finally arrived home late the next afternoon. When I opened the door, the sweet fragrance of roses wafted out. I thought my mind was playing tricks on me until I saw a couple of vases full of the fragrant flowers on our dining table. Not only there, but also in the kitchen, on the coffee table, and in our bedrooms. I was just glad the fragrance of them didn't make me want to vomit.

"That was so sweet of them," Becky gushed.

While Becky texted again, most likely to Matthew, I dropped my purse on the dining chair and searched for a note. There it was. I took out the note addressed to me and read it.

My dearest Jenna,
Hope you had good time.
I missed you liked crazy.
I wanted to welcome you home,
but I didn't want to be overbearing
so I thought roses would do the trick.
I'm trying to seduce you through this letter.
Come to me!

TKLS,
Max

My lips spread into a huge smile. I looked up to see Becky's doing the same while she read her note.

"I'm going to Max's place," I said, caressing the rose petal. Their silky softness always put me in a state of tranquility.

"You're going to tell him, right?" Becky gave me a reassuring smile and plopped on the sofa.

"Yes. I'm going to tell him." I felt bad that Nicole and Kate knew before Max. Who else would find out before he did? Knowing Kate and Nicole, they probably would tell their significant others. "I'm going to give him a surprise visit and one hell of a surprise he won't be expecting."

"It'll be fine, Jenna."

"I know," I agreed, but I really wasn't sure.

I opened Max's front door with my set of keys. Before I pushed it open, the door swung so fast I almost fell. Actually, I did fall...into Max's arms. I let go of my bag and allowed Max to hold me.

"I knew you would come." Max started kissing me all over my face. "I missed you."

"I missed you, too, Max," I said between his lips on mine. "Maybe I should go away more often."

Max gave me a strange look. If his expression could speak, it would say 'hell no'.

Taking my hand, he led me to the kitchen. I stood by the entrance while he went straight to the stove. "You came just in time for dinner." Max stirred the pot's contents with the wooden spoon. "Did you eat? I'm making beef stew."

"You made dinner? You know how to cook?"

"I know how to, I just don't do it that often."

There was something indescribably sexy about seeing a man cooking. Watching Max brought out a strong sexual desire within me, especially when Max took the spoon out to take a sip. His lips smacked and then his tongue slid across his lips. Even though he wasn't trying to be seductive in the least, I saw it that way.

Little did he know food was the last thing on my mind. I'd heard of morning sickness, but whoever thought of the name should reconsider calling it pregnancy sickness. Morning sickness should mean only being sick in the morning. Hell, I felt sick all day. Pregnancy was not fun at that point. Regardless, I had to pretend to feel well, at least until I told Max the news.

"I ate a little," I lied. "But I can eat with you."

Max turned away from the pot to look at me. He made cooking so sexy. With his disarrayed hair, comfortable cotton shorts, and plain white T-shirt that framed his toned chest, I wanted to eat him. Forget about food!

"So, what did you do while I was gone?"

Max raised his brow flirtatiously, and when he spoke, his playful tone was hot and heavy. "If you want to know, come here and get your answer."

"Maybe I don't need an answer," I teased back.

"Then maybe I had tons of women at my place and I stripped for them. Not only am I a great singer, I can dance, too."

I frowned. Although I knew he was joking, I didn't like the idea at all. "Maybe I let one of the dancers touch me."

Max's lips formed into a straight line. "Not funny, Jenna." He turned away.

Was he mad? Jealous? Surely he knew I was playing around. I didn't know what had gotten into me. Maybe the pregnancy hormones were acting up, or maybe I simply missed him more than I would admit. Whatever the reason, I had to have him now.

"Max." The words drew out seductively as I started to unbutton my sweater and wiggle out of my jeans. When Max stopped stirring, I knew I'd gotten his attention. "It's my turn to surprise you. I promise I didn't let anyone touch me."

Max didn't breathe a word. In fact, I wasn't sure he breathed at all when he saw me with nothing on but a black lace bra and a G-string. Walking to him seductively, I placed my hands on his chest, and that was all I needed to do.

Max turned off the fire, lifted me up, and set me on the counter. Sliding between my legs, he pulled me into him. My whole body blazed from our bodies pressing together. "Nobody touches what's mine," he growled with heated breath. The intensity behind his words and his hot breath on my skin sent chills down my spine. His possessiveness toward me always turned me on.

"Want a taste of my delicious beef?" His lips curled up into a sexy smirk at the double entendre.

He slid his finger in my mouth and slowly pulled it out.

"You're a great cook," I commented, letting my tongue glide across my lips while savoring the taste of the sauce.

"I'm good at a lot of things," he said, watching my tongue move across my lips again.

"Aren't we confident?" I teased, leaning back enough to push my breasts toward him. I needed his touch.

"Arrogant," he said. "I can be very arrogant. And I am damn good at making Jenna feel pleasure."

Max dabbed a splat of sauce on my neck. "I think I'll try some Jenna sauce." Oh God. His tongue worked perfectly on that spot on my neck. My breath heaved and quickened when he dripped some more sauce between my breasts.

"Delicious," he mumbled on my flesh. Then he yanked my bra just enough to allow his mouth to suck from one nipple to the other.

"Max." I shuddered, unable to take anymore. Pulling his head back, I gave him the look and knew he understood.

Anchoring my legs around his hips, he pressed me against the kitchen cabinet while his hands ran along my thighs. He slammed his lips into mine and sucked all of the breath out of me. While kissing me, he managed to take off his shorts, then let me down to remove his T-shirt and the rest of what I had on. He was fierce, hot, and ready...and so was I.

Max lifted me up again and planted my back against another cabinet door. I didn't know where he got his strength, but he was unstoppable. Heavy gasps left my lungs when Max entered me. He felt so good the room spun, and I was intoxicated by the pleasure he gave me. Max had no mercy as he pumped, sucking the nipple conveniently right in front of his mouth.

"Jenna, you're so wet. I love how you're wet for me," he panted. "Did you miss me the way I missed you?"

"Yes," I whimpered. His hips ground his dick deeper inside of me.

My head spun even more when Max swung me to the kitchen island. "Say it louder, Jenna." His words seethed out of his mouth.

With my back against his chest, he entered from behind; one hand teased the hell out of my clit, the other hand kneaded my breast. Max stimulated every sensitive area on my body that would make me explode even harder.

Max shifted me around and took me to the sofa. When he entered me, he cupped my face and gazed lovingly into my eyes. Every nerve in my body awakened, every muscle in my body quivered, and every inch of me felt his love and my pleasure.

"Welcome home, babe. Thank you for my surprise." Then he gave me all of him. Little did he know he had another surprise coming.

After dinner we got ready for bed. My stomach knotted and my heart pounded too fast for me to keep up. I only had to open my mouth and tell him, but at every opportunity I had lost the courage.

When we got into bed, knowing it was my last chance for today, I told myself everything would be fine. Though the lights were turned off, I could still dimly see his face from the night-light we had decided to use when I bumped my head finding my way to the bathroom.

"Max." I snuggled closer to him, and pressed my head against his chest.

"Yes, babe." With his eyes closed, he wrapped his arms around my waist.

"I need to tell you something, but I'm scared."

Max shifted to turn on the lamp and instantly sat up. "What is it? Is everything okay?"

I squinted in the sudden brightness. "Everything is fine." My old habit came back again as I fidgeted with my thumbs. It was so difficult to look at him. "I have something growing inside of me." Max didn't let me finish. He started to freak out.

"Jenna, what's growing and where? Do you have cancer? Did you go see a doctor? I know the best doctors. We'll fix this. Nothing is going to happen to you. I won't let it." His words came out so fast I couldn't stop him.

Before Max lost it, I had to calm him down. His eyes went straight to his cell phone on the nightstand. He was about to spring out of the bed and call someone, perhaps a doctor, in the middle of the night. Resting my hands on his shoulders, I looked him squarely in the eyes. "Max, I'm pregnant."

He sunk back on the bed and stared at me as if I had spoken to him in Chinese. "Max...did you hear what I said?" I gulped, anticipating his words.

Max leaned into me. We were sitting upright, facing each other. "Did you just tell me you're pregnant?"

"Yes." I nodded to confirm.

There was clearly one expression on his face: he had been given the shock of his life. "I don't understand. How could this have happened? I mean...we were careful. I mean...I thought you were on the pill. I used a condom except that one time."

He answered exactly how I had predicted, but hearing them hurt me more than I had imagined. It had sounded and felt differently in my mind when I played out the scenario. Max got out of bed. While he paced around the room, he looked at the ground, then at the ceiling. I could imagine what was going through his mind, possibly the same questions I'd had.

I answered before he could ask. "I think it happened when you tied me up on the stairs."

Max froze and focused his eyes on the floor again. I could tell he was thinking of that night, when he'd thought

I was going to leave him. The same night I thought I had lost him.

"I didn't come inside of you," he mumbled under his breath.

Anger flashed through me. "So this is all my fault? You think I planned this? That I purposely got pregnant. You knew I hadn't had sex in three years. Why would I be on the pill for no reason?" Tears started to blur my vision, but I would not let them fall. I didn't want Max's sympathy.

Confused, Max glanced at me. "Jenna, I didn't think that. I'm sorry. I'm trying to…" Max raked his hair back. "I'm trying to…understand. Are you sure? Did you take a pregnancy test?"

I understood what he was going through. After all, I'd had more than a week to take in the news and adjust since I first found out from the home pregnancy test. I had enough time to come to terms with it, but he'd just found out. Of course he would act shocked and confused. He must have millions of thoughts running through his mind, just as I had.

"Yes. I saw a doctor to confirm." I recalled the appointment that I'd gone to several days ago.

The door creaked open. "Ms. Jenna Mefferd," Anne, the petite nurse I saw once a year, greeted me.

I headed to her with a smile. Even knowing what the test result would be, I needed to confirm with my doctor. I doubted the pregnancy test was false, but I needed to see the doctor to make sure everything was fine.

Once inside, Anne became casual and talkative. "What brings you here today, Jenna? Just the annual pap smear?"

I didn't know why, but I was embarrassed to tell her. It was the fact that I wasn't married. It was the fact that I was a straightforward type of girl. I had everything planned: the age I would get married, when I would have kids...preferably after marriage. However, this...this was never in my plan.

Unable to look her in the eyes, I said, "I took a pregnancy test. It was positive. I'm here to double check and see what I need to do." I purposely made sure to flash my engagement ring.

Anne smiled at me. She was genuinely happy for me. "Congratulations. I see that you're engaged."

That was not the response I had expected. I should be happy, too, just like her. I was supposed to glow, like how I read in an article. It said that pregnant women glowed, but I was sick...utterly wanting to throw up sick. There was nothing pleasant about this.

"Dr. Howard will be here shortly." After she jotted down stuff on my file, she closed the door behind her.

When the door opened, I snapped out of my thoughts. "Hello, Dr. Howard." He looked tired today.

"Hello, Jenna." He got right to the point. "Why don't we take a test, just to make sure? Home pregnancy tests are pretty accurate, but we like to confirm." He handed me a cup. "Urinate up to the line. Lift up the metal door, then stick this cup inside it."

"Thanks," I said, and did as instructed.

After about ten minutes, Dr. Howard came back. "Jenna, good news. The test came out positive. Congratulations."

Dr. Howard and Anne were happy for me — and part of me was, too — but a part of me wished this was a dream.

"How are you feeling?" Max asked, breaking me out of my thoughts. He didn't let me finish as he stood at a distance. I could tell his mind was still reeling from the way his eyes flickered, searching for words. "You weren't feeling well before you left to Vegas because...I understand now. You should have told me, Jenna." I didn't like his scolding tone at all. "I can't believe you didn't tell me until now."

"How could I when I needed to come to grips with this news, and I didn't know how you would feel?"

"How long did you know?"

"Little more than a week."

"More than a week?" Max gripped his hair in frustration, then took my hands into his. "You should've told me right away. We are responsible adults. We created this child together. I have to be honest with you, I want to have lots of babies with you, but not right now."

My blood pressure shot up and my heart thumped erratically. "What do you mean? You...you don't want our baby?"

"No, Jenna. That is not what I meant. You know what my plans were." He paused, running his hand down his face. "I just need some time to adjust. This is a big, life-changing factor. I think...I think we should also get married as soon as possible, but only if you want to."

"I don't want you to feel like you have to marry me right away because of this child."

Max caressed my cheek. "Babe, look at me." When I did, he continued, "I'm the one who wanted to get married as soon as possible, remember? Everything will be fine. We are going to have many bumps along the road, but we'll ride them together. I'm just glad you're fine. For a minute there, I thought you had cancer. At least we know now you can get pregnant."

Max took it better than I had imagined. Initially, I thought he was going to lose it and stay that way. However, I wondered if he was hiding how he truly felt. For my sake, I knew he would try. I wished he had been more thrilled about the news. It would have made it more acceptable for me.

Max knew how worried I'd been about not being able to get pregnant because of what my mom went through. He was right, though. At least we knew now that I could. I just wished Max was really happy for us. Turning away from him, I couldn't help the tears as I snuggled against my pillow. It was the first time I'd slept with my back toward him.

CHAPTER 7
BECKY

There was a soft knock at the front door about an hour after Jenna left, which was faster than I'd expected. I knew who it was, and I couldn't wait to see him. I had texted Matthew that Jenna was going to Max's place. After looking through the peephole to confirm it was him, I twisted the door handle. Before I opened it all the way, Matthew shoved the door open and almost knocked me down in the process.

"Becca." Matthew's tone came out low and thick, and his eyes focused on me hungrily. Before I could speak, he conquered me in his arms and claimed me with his lips. "I...missed...you," he said between kisses, slamming us against the wall.

"I...missed...you...too." I breathed the words between returning his kisses and tearing off his clothes. We bumped into each other while we tried to undress. It would have been easier if we both took a step back, but we couldn't. We needed to touch each other, and even a second apart was too long.

Matthew took me to my room and gently placed me on top of my dresser. Slowing things down, he kissed me tenderly while his hand ran down the length of my body — he didn't miss a single spot. Every place he touched, heat blistered each nerve in my body. Though I should have been enjoying his gentle caress, it was a torture. I needed him inside of me. It had only been two days, but it felt like a week.

"Matthew." I took a fistful of his hair and pulled him up. His tongue teasing my clit drove me insane. Taking his lips on mine, I kissed him with desperation. I pulled away, practically bathing his neck with my tongue. "I need you inside of me," I demanded, nibbling his ear. Matthew's moan was an indication he wanted the same.

"Not just yet." With his wet tongue, he slithered down from the tip of nose, down my neck, to my collarbone, over my breast, and sucked the hell out of my nipple. Then he went down to my belly button, to my thigh, and to the tip of my toes. Holy fuck, he was sucking my toes. No one had ever done that before, so I never knew it could be so stimulating. Hell...it was over. I had gone over the edge.

"Matthew. Now." I jumped off, taking him with me. He landed flat on his back on my bed. Matthew chuckled, thoroughly enjoying seeing me like a wild animal. Well, he was going to get exactly what he asked for. Straddling him, I pinned his arms over his head. He held a sexy smirk while he let me take over. Matthew and I both heaved in air and made eager sounds when I positioned his dick to slip inside of me.

"My wild Becca." His words were barely audible. I ground my hips into him so hard and fast that I was the one in control. Matthew tilted his neck back with his eyes closed. Seeing him come apart made me feel powerful, knowing I was giving him as much pleasure as he had given me.

Then Matthew flipped me over with a growl. He hovered over me. With his elbow supporting him so he wouldn't crush me, he caressed my hair back. His eyes pierced mine with affection; it was overwhelming to see that he cared for me as much as I did for him. I could tell from his expression he was searching for the right words to say to me.

"Becca," he called my name softly. "I really missed you. And I'm not saying this casually like it's no big deal. I don't think I've ever missed anyone this much before."

Shocked by his sincerity, I blinked in surprise. No guy had said that to me before, and it was hard to grasp that someone I cared about felt the same way about me. Always the asshole magnet, a part of me expected something to go wrong. He would break up with me because I wasn't good enough for him, or he would turn out to be one of the assholes I'd been attracted to. Yet, he was turning out to be a true prince.

"I missed you, too," I said, giving him a coy smile.

"How much?" His eyes got dark and greedy again. I could tell he was aroused by my tone, and hell...he already had me on fire. I wanted him to stop talking and give me all of him.

"More than I thought I would," I replied, and gasped when Matthew entered me again.

"More than you thought you would?" He sounded disappointed. "Next time I'll do a lot better to make you miss me even more." With each word, he pumped me harder. Lifting my legs over his shoulders, he reached in deeper.

"Oh God," I yelped, grabbing his arms. My body moved to the rocking motion of his fine rock hard ass.

"Becca," he murmured my name when he came. Out of breath, he dropped next to me, breathing heavily. Giving me the most adorable killer smile, he said, "Welcome home, Becca. I told you what happened in Vegas continued when we got home."

Max

Jenna is pregnant! Those words played in my mind like a broken record all freakin' night. Tossing and turning, I thought about the what-ifs. Shit! It was my fault. I'd always used a condom to be extra cautious, even if my date was on the pill. I had assumed Jenna was on the pill and I hadn't used one with her a couple of times. She told me she hadn't had sex for three years. I guess that should have been my sign to ask her about it. Too late.

Leaving a note on my pillow for Jenna, I went to work early that morning. Having a difficult time sleeping, I decided it was best for me to clear my head without her around. I hoped Jenna understood.

Jenna,
I need to take care of things before the meeting.
I'll see you at work.

Love,
Max

Jenna being pregnant was slap to the face shocking. I knew the questions I'd asked were idiotic, but being that surprised, I said whatever came to mind. Thank goodness I hadn't asked her a stupid question like, "Is the baby mine?" I knew Jenna. Of course it was mine.

I had to admit, knowing she didn't have a tumor or cancer was great news, but I never expected this. Having a baby was life-altering. I wanted to show Jenna the world, get married, and then start a family. Fuck!

Raking my hair back, I stopped pacing around in my office and sat down. I turned on the computer, replied to a couple of emails, and then swirled my chair to face the window.

People streamed in and out of the building. All those people down there had to deal with shit that happened in life every day. I was one of the lucky ones who didn't have to worry about how to feed my family, pay the bills, take care of a sick loved one, or other issues. I should be grateful. So what did it matter that we had to delay our trips around the world? We had each other, and we were healthy. For Jenna's sake, knowing how worried she was about having a difficult time getting pregnant, the news should be a blessing. What the hell was wrong with me?

I needed time. I had to process the news and figure out how to embrace it. I prayed I hadn't made Jenna feel like shit. I hoped she'd understand I needed some space to get used to the idea. After all, she'd had more than a week. I could understand why, but at the same time she had waited so long. Because she knew I would flip. Damn it! I did exactly what she thought I would do. No wonder she had waited.

Picking up my phone, I called my secretary. No answer. What time was it? I had forgotten it was seven in the morning. I thought about calling Jenna, but she might be sleeping. I texted her instead.

Good morning, babe. I'm in the office. I'll be out all day. Let's talk tonight.

Thinking about her made me feel like shit. Though I couldn't remember exactly what I had said to her, I thought I might have said stuff I shouldn't have. Did I? Considering how I felt, it dawned on me how Jenna must be feeling. She was the one who had to carry our child for nine months.

Her body would be going through changes, not mine. She had to make physical accommodations, and maybe even mental ones, and here I was thinking of my selfish, greedy wants. I was an asshole.

I knew what I had to do. First, I needed to give her peace of mind and let her know I was there with her every step of the way, then the rest would have to follow. Second, I needed a drink.

CHAPTER 8
JENNA

Stretching and yawning, I turned over to find Max, but he wasn't in bed. Rubbing my eyes, I propped myself a bit to look for him. When I didn't see him, and instead discovered a note, my heart dropped. At first I thought it was a note telling me he didn't want to be with me anymore. Being the carrier of not so good news had made me paranoid, but my heart rate quickly subsided when I read the note.

Max had never gone to work that early before. In fact, I knew his schedule better than he did, maybe even better than his secretary. He didn't have a meeting until ten. This proved that he needed time alone. I understood, but why did it hurt so much?

My vision of how I would feel pregnant was nothing like the reality—I should be ecstatic, my cheeks should be glowing, but I felt neither. Being pregnant had become a dark cloud over my head and I felt utterly depressed. Releasing a long, heavy sigh, I got ready for work.

The first thing I saw when I stepped inside the office was Matthew's smiling face. He stood by the whiteboard, glowing with happiness. It was good to see him this way. He was the only one in the office. I assumed the others hadn't come in or were out and about somewhere in the building.

"Good morning, Jenna," Matthew greeted, giving me a warm hug. "Max came in early today. Does he have an early meeting or did you kick him out?" Matthew let out a light chuckle. I knew he was joking, but I panicked at first.

"How did you know he was here early?"

"I swung by his office to drop off a document."

"Oh. I see. And by the way, I kicked him out," I joked back, trying to hide my worries.

"And I deserved it."

I flashed my eyes to where the sound of the voice beckoned me to surrender. Standing there with his arms resting on the door hinge, he took my breath away. It was the element of surprise, and seeing my beautiful man all suited up in a Hugo Boss suit, formed to his toned body, had me spellbound. But his words and his presence startled me. My heart did a funny flip. It was the love at first sight kind of flip, and at the same time one that stung, like I was seeing an ex-boyfriend I still loved after a break up.

"You deserved it?" Matthew asked, narrowing his eyes with a question, and turned to me. "Want me to kick his ass for you?"

Max didn't hear what Matthew had said; his eyes locked on mine. Taking one careful step at a time, he came for me.

"Jenna and I have a meeting in here. Now," Max stated without even a glance at Matthew. His words were final.

"Maybe I should leave." I thought that was what Matthew said. From far away, I heard the sound of the door being closed.

"Don't you have a meeting to go to, Mr. Knight?" I cleared my throat. The way Max looked at me with those predatory eyes made me nervous. I remembered that look he used when he was pursuing me. "I got your text that you would be out at meetings all day."

Placing his hands inside of his pants pockets, he took another step toward me. "I have one with you right now. I was worried about you. I know you're not feeling well. I read on the Internet about all the possibilities of what you might be going through."

"Sometimes I feel like vomiting, depending on what I try to eat. Sometimes I feel nauseous for no reason."

"Do you feel like that all day?"

"Thank God, no. I feel best in the morning and it progressively gets worse toward the evening, but I think I'm starting to feel better. At least I'm able to eat a little. A bit more than I could a week ago."

"That's good." Max nodded, then slid his hand across his strong jaw. After he cleared his throat, he spoke again. "I have to be honest with you, I didn't have a meeting this morning. I needed some time to think. That was the reason I left early."

"And I have to be honest with you," I said. "A part of me thought you left me, or were thinking of leaving me."

Max tilted his face with a look of hurt in his eyes. "You think I would leave you because you're pregnant? You think that I could stop loving you even for a second?"

Max loomed in front of me, and I gasped at his proximity. He had stood in front of me many times before, but I was extremely shy today. Perhaps it was anticipation. Being able to read his body language better than before, my body reacted to his. Heat spread to the depth of my core, and I could already feel his hands all over me.

When I didn't answer, he continued, "Jenna, I can't even breathe without you. Every second you're on my mind. Every happy thought is of you." Max lowered his hand to my stomach. "Now, every thought will be of the both of you. I'm sorry. I was a little...weird last night. I just needed some time to take in the news. I promise to the both of you, I'll be there every step of the way. Our baby is going to be the luckiest baby in the universe."

Tears blurred my vision. As if a brick had been lifted off my shoulders, my body relaxed, and I could breathe again. "You...want this baby...our baby?" I'd heard him clearly, but I needed confirmation.

"Of course." Max pulled me to his chest. "I've always wanted us to have a van full of kids together. We're ahead of schedule, but that's okay. Life is unpredictable. We have to go with the flow or we'll drown in fear."

My eyes set on his with a coy smile. "You're very wise, Mr. Knight."

"I became a wise man when I first looked into your eyes and fell in love with you. I didn't think you would date a foolish one, so I had to shape up."

I pressed into him, fluttering my eyelashes. "I'm glad you did."

"Ms. Mefferd." His words came out tender, affectionate. Max stroked my cheek while his other hand cupped my ass. "I missed you this morning." I didn't get a chance to speak; his tongue bathed my neck in a slow, circular motion. "You're wearing my favorite easy access skirt," he murmured as his lips continued down. With his teeth, he popped a button without breaking it. Thank God! "These are pretty strong buttons," he said against the base of my breast.

"Mr. Knight," I whimpered, shivering and feeling a strong urge to unzip his pants. "We're at work."

Bending lower, Max ignored me as his hands started from my thigh, and moved ever so softly up to my ass while scrunching up my skirt. Thank goodness I'd worn a nice, sexy pair of panties instead of the "granny panties", as Becky called them.

"I love what you're wearing." He purposely purred a hot breath right at that perfect spot, making my thighs quiver.

"Max, I'm serious. Someone will walk in." When I started to push him away, he seized both of my hands behind my back.

Holding onto me, he started to walk us backward. "Don't worry, Ms. Mefferd. Matthew locked the door behind him. He's headed to your department meeting, but it's okay...you're allowed to be late, so says the boss."

"I'm late?" I repeated, but the words barely escaped me. Matthew locking the door behind him meant he knew what Max was up to. Not only was I blushing from what we were doing, but also knowing Matthew knew.

Max carefully laid me down on my desk. I had no idea how I got there, but that was the way it was with Max. Once he had his hands on me, my mind and body surrendered to him. I had no energy or will to push him away.

Hovering over me as his lips gently pressed on mine, he said, "Don't talk. Just enjoy. I'm going to make it up to you. I'm going to make you forget that I left this morning. I'm going to make you forget you have morning sickness. I'm going to make you feel so good, Jenna." His words left his mouth hot and heavy. I already tingled from the rush of the excitement. "Every time you come to your office and see your desk, you're going to remember what I'm about to do to you."

Sliding his hands down on my legs, Max lifted them up and anchored my heels on the desk. Moving my legs apart, he lowered his lips to my panties. With his tongue, he slipped inside the fabric and...Oh heavens, he sure was making up for the grief he'd given me.

"Max," I cried softly, digging my toes into the tips of my high heels. He didn't respond. He was thoroughly enjoying himself making me come undone. I had no idea why I called his name, besides wanting something that I knew we shouldn't do.

When I felt myself losing control and I burned for him between my legs, I managed to pull him up to face me with a fistful of his hair.

"What do you want, Jenna?" He curled his lips into a wicked, satisfied grin. Devouring my lips with his, he sneaked a hand between my legs and rubbed, flicking my clit.

Arching my back from the intense pleasure, I tugged on his silver tie. "Max," I begged. "I need you inside of me." I pulled away from his lips, panting.

A buzzing sound stopped me. It was Max's phone. The sound of his phone brought me back to reality, shaking me out of the daze. I had forgotten where we were.

Max let me slip from under him. Straightening out my skirt, I tried to compose myself while the fire between my legs begged for more. Hearing Max growl while looking at his phone, I knew he wasn't happy.

"Babe." He embraced me. After kissing my forehead, he fixed the strands of my hair back into place. "What time will you be home tonight?"

Smiling, I was lost in thought, unable to believe what had just happened. Though we'd had sex in his office before, this was different. His office was private and sound proof, whereas I shared one with other employees, including Matthew. Oh God, how was I going to look Matthew in the eye? "I should be home around six."

"Good. I'll be home a little later. We'll continue this meeting there. It seems as though I can make you forget how sick you are. If I have to do this all night long, then I will." Max winked. He looked so proud that he could make me feel better. I was sure it fed his ego. "Meanwhile..." Max conquered my lips again, kissing me harder and deeper. After pulling back, he grazed the tip of my nose with his teeth. "Something to remember me by. Remember how I made you feel right now, not how you felt this morning. See you at home."

With that, he strutted out the door. Standing there feeling dazed, I knew I had something to do. What was it? Shoot! I had a meeting to go to. Flipping my compact mirror out of my purse, I made sure I looked presentable and put it back. I checked the memo to see which room the meeting was held in and headed there.

CHAPTER 9
MATTHEW

"Welcome to our meeting, Jenna," I said as I shuffled my file folder to place inside of my workbag.

Jenna looked flustered and out of breath as she glanced around at an empty room. "Was...there a meeting?" Her eyebrows pinched in the center, doubting her question.

"It was a very short one. The meeting is over." Sitting back down, I smiled at her. With my hands clasped together, I swirled my chair from side to side. My soon to be sister-in-law was too adorable when she looked all confused. Being a tease, I wanted to have fun with her and make her blush. After all, that's what brother-in-laws were for. "Would you like to come in and get debriefed on the meeting you missed?"

"Sure." Jenna tugged at her skirt. From my perspective, it looked like she was making sure she was presentable.

I chuckled to myself, getting ready to interrogate her in a playful way. She had no idea what was coming. I cleared my throat. "How was your meeting with Max?"

Pulling out a chair next to mine, Jenna's eyes grew wide. Without eye contact, she murmured, "Great. It was...short." Jenna reached inside of her bag and removed a folder and pen. She was all ready.

"Short?" I questioned. "Max usually takes his time, making sure every section of the meeting is covered." I emphasized the word *every*. "He likes to take his time, making sure he is diligent in every sense of the meeting. At least that's what he told me."

Jenna's cheeks turned slightly red. "He does...I mean..."

When she paused, I continued, "After all, meetings can get boring if it's the same topic over and over. Sometimes we need to present standing up, behind, or perhaps on the desk."

A small cough choked out of her mouth. Finally with eye contact, she gave me the slyest smile as she caught on to what I was doing.

"I have to agree with you. Who wants to be in a boring meeting? You can make it even more entertaining by getting down on your knees."

Holy shit. Did she say what I thought she said? Jenna confirmed it when she turned away shyly. I succeeded in making her blush, but I wondered if she saw my cheeks flare up?

"You know," she continued. "After you open the meeting, if you give it the right tender, loving strokes, you can make the long, hard meeting pleasurable."

Fuck! I would never in a million years have thought those words would come out of her mouth. Jenna did have that feisty, wild beast in her. I was completely blown away by how our conversation had taken a twist. She was making me blush big time.

"Well...I'm happy to hear that you had a successful meeting this morning." At that point, I had no idea what I was trying to say.

"Will that be all, Mr. Knight?" She gave me a warm smile with a soft laugh.

I let out a chuckle. "Yes. This was quite interesting. I was very surprised by your...choice of words."

"Oh, you have no idea. Your brother brings out the beast in me." Jenna winked and headed out the door. Twisting the knob to turn, she looked over her shoulder to me. "Thanks for locking the door when you left." Her words came out bashful and tender. With a warm smile, she left.

Jenna

Heading back to the office, my mind reeled from my conversation with Matthew. He wanted to toy with me and make me blush big time, but it backfired. That sneaky Matthew. I had to admit, it was fun surprising him with my comebacks. Yup, I really like the new me.

When I got back to the office, my eyes went straight to my desk and heat infused my cheeks. Recalling myself sprawled on my desk with Max licking me, I felt the twinge of pleasure right between my legs. How just the thought of him made me feel aroused like that was beyond me. Max said I would think about what he had done to me every time I saw my desk, and he was right.

After I greeted my co-workers, I checked my agenda and emails. The buzzing from my work phone snapped me out of my concentration on the layout on the screen. I was just about to approve by clicking on the format of page ten for Knight Magazine.

"This is Jenna Mefferd," I answered without looking at the caller ID.

"It won't be Jenna Mefferd soon. You're better off calling yourself Mrs. Knight. You might as well get used to it."

"Max." I lowered my voice, trying not to catch anyone's attention. With the phone resting between my shoulder and ear, I refocused on the screen. "How can I help you?" I sounded way too formal, but I was at work after all.

"I know how you can help me." His tone came out way too flirty.

He'd gotten my attention for sure. Smiling, I said, "Really? And what is it that you need?"

"Are you sitting in your seat?"

"Yes," I answered, clicking away. I had a deadline to meet and Max was a huge distraction.

"Did you think of me when you walked into your office and saw your desk?"

"Yes." I started to feel hot and flushed, recalling how good he'd made me feel.

"Good. Then I know—"

"Actually, I think I forgot." I interrupted him with something he wouldn't expect. That got his attention big time. His ego must have deflated because he was silent for a second, probably contemplating whether I was teasing or being serious. I smiled, proud I had stumped him a little.

"Really?" He sounded quite surprised. "I'll help you remember tonight."

He didn't have to tell me that; I already felt tingles down to my clit from his words. His flirty, sexy tone always got to me and made me feel like I was in his arms.

"I'll see you tonight, Mr. Knight." With that I got back to work, but how was I supposed to work when all I could do was think of what Max had done to me on my desk? When I heard a small cough, I looked up. I didn't recognize the woman standing in front of me, so I glanced at Matthew, who'd just walked back into the office after a meeting, then back at her. Matthew shrugged. He had no idea why she was there. She had a nametag on her shirt and held a box, indicating she was there to deliver something to me.

"Hello. May I help you?" I asked.

"Are you Ms. Mefferd? Soon to be Mrs. Knight?"

I smiled at her words. Max was up to something. He'd probably told her to ask that question. "Yes, that's me."

She handed me a box with a blue and pink ribbon tied neatly into a bow. "I'm from Café Express. I was told to deliver this to you."

I reached into my wallet and handed her a tip. "Thank you so much." After she walked out the door, I opened it. Inside of the box were some salted crackers, a heart shaped Rice Krispy Treat, a pink cookie that read, 'Maybe a girl?' and a blue cookie that read, 'Maybe a boy?' Happy tears dampened my eyes. I wiped them away before they could fall. Max filled my heart with joy and made me feel so light, like I could levitate off the ground from being so happy. He was too good to be true.

I picked up the note inside.

Jenna,

The crackers will help ease the queasy stomach. Make sure to eat a little throughout the day, and also drink a lot of water. Whether a boy or a girl, I promise to love our child and I promise to be the best father and husband.

TKLS,
Max

Jenna

Since our schedule didn't allow us to have dinner together, and Max was coming home after me, I grabbed a quick bite to eat at work. I wanted to surprise him. I thought about dressing in his favorite lingerie and sitting next to the running bath, or wearing nothing except his silver tie and draping myself across the bed. All of those naughty thoughts ran through my mind while I drove. I couldn't believe I was thinking like that. After all, I had to find a way to thank him. He sure was making up for leaving me in the morning with a broken heart.

The smell of roses whiffed through my nose when I entered our place. Baffled by the smell, I turned on the lights and dropped my stuff on the sofa. Oh my God! Vases of roses were *everywhere*. I saw red every way I looked. Seeing a note on the table, I picked it up.

Soon to be Mrs. Knight,

I told you I was going to make it up to you for being an ass. Follow the rose petals on the floor so I can finish what I started in your office. I was thinking of you all day.

TKLS,
Soon to be your husband and a father

With a huge smile on my face, I shifted my eyes to the floor, and sure enough, a line of rose petals led to the next room. Following the trail heading upstairs, I started taking my clothes off. The rose petals led me to the bathroom. Glowing lights reflected from inside. What was Max up to?

Candles of different sizes filled the bathroom: on the counter, on the floor, and even around the bathtub. My eyes grew wide at the beautiful, serene ambiance. Off to the side of the bathtub were two glasses and a champagne bottle.

Soft instrumental music filled the air and rose petals floated on the water. Steam rose off the bath, so he'd recently filled it. It was no wonder he'd kept texting me when I was on my way home. "Max?" I called softly when he was nowhere to be found. Almost all the way undressed, I prepared to take off my underwear and bra to get into the tub.

When I felt a warm pair of hands capturing me from behind, I gasped lightly and melted into Max's chest, especially when he rubbed his dick on my ass. The feel of his flesh brought me to another level of excitement.

"Let me help you with that," he whispered in my ear. He unhooked my bra and allowed the straps to slip off my shoulders ever so slowly with his help. His feather-light touch was driving me insane. "And let me help you with this one."

Max came around to the front of me and got down on his knees. After he gave me that sexy grin, he tugged my G-string with his teeth and pulled it down to the floor. Starting from my toes, he licked his way up to...oh my God! I sucked in air when his tongue circled around the sensitive spot at the junction of my thighs.

Wanting more, I spread my legs for him. His deep, satisfied growl, proved Max knew I was enjoying myself. When his tongue moved higher, passing my stomach to my nipple, I crumbled. My legs became weak, and got even weaker when he gathered my arms behind my back and sucked the daylights out of my breasts. Holy Jesus, I was already climaxing.

"I hope you can forgive me," he breathed. He didn't give me a chance to respond. The room spun when Max lifted me up. Thank goodness he had...I wanted to drop to the floor from sensation overload.

"Thank you for my goodies." I wanted to tell him before I forgot.

"This is just the beginning." With one careful step, we lowered into the water. All of my worries faded in the perfect temperature, like the way the petals drifted away. It was just the right amount of warmth. Having my back against Max's chest gave me the support I needed. Leaning my head against his shoulder, I exhaled a deep breath as I watched water waving back and forth across the length of the tub.

"I forgive you, Max," I said, closing my eyes.

Max pulled my hair to one side; his lips caressed my cheek. "I don't want you to forgive me just yet."

I opened my eyes, suddenly feeling a little dread. "Did you do something else?"

Max's chest vibrated with suppressed laughter. What was so funny? There was no humor in Max doing something I didn't like.

"I wouldn't dare." Max extended my arm out of the water. With a single rose petal, he lightly rubbed my arm. The fragrance of roses grew stronger being surrounded by them. "I think you should forgive me after I show you how sorry I am. But before I do, we need to talk."

I nodded, knowing Max was right. He was more of a problem solver, and I was the one who wanted to run away from them.

"We should tell our parents," he continued. "I'm going to assume you haven't told yours. And I think we should get married before our baby is born. It's a good thing I proposed to you before you got pregnant. You can't use that excuse that I only wanted to marry you because you're pregnant. Women are so complicated. Damned if you do and damned if you don't." Max chuckled, shaking his head. "Don't you agree with me?"

I turned around to face him. My wet hair was pulled back as he softly massaged my head while talking. Max wiped away the few drops of water trickling down my face. It always made me smile when he took care of me.

Leaning back against the tub, I peered at him through the steam rising to his gorgeous face. His body spread out naked was a beautiful sight. Tilting his head back to slide a little lower, his lips curled into the sly, sexy grin that made me crazy for him. When he raked his hair back, a few beads of water trickled down his firm, sculpted arm and the side of his forehead. It was a mouthwatering sight. Max in the bathtub, just like this, was going to be framed in my mind...forever. Arousal bubbled up, and I anchored him with my legs on either side. "You're probably right." Picking up a rose petal, I started to caress his cheek with it.

Max guided his hands to my ass and left them there. "I'm glad you agree. I thought you were going to fight me on getting married earlier than we had planned."

"I want to be Mrs. Knight," I said against his lips. After slowly gliding my tongue across his lips, I slithered inside of his mouth.

Max's mouth engulfed mine, kissing me back harder and deeper, and then he pulled back. "Good, because we have a family dinner next week at my parents' house. Matthew is planning to bring Becky. We should both tell our family the wonderful news."

"Okay," I replied with a pouty face in the sexiest way I could muster for one word. "No more talking. It's my turn. Just enjoy." Max's eyes grew dark and greedy at my words.

Kissing down his chest, I dunked myself underwater to his dick.

When he'd had enough, he guided my head out of the water, most likely knowing I couldn't stay under too long. After grabbing a towel, he lifted me out of the tub and carried me out of the bathroom.

"It's my turn," he whispered hungrily.

CHAPTER 10
BECKY

Dressed in my form fitting sweater dress with the black high heels Matthew loved, I got to the restaurant a bit early. Flipping through my messages on my phone to pass time, I waited for Matthew to meet me for dinner. It was one of our favorite Mexican restaurants that we went to on a regular basis. Halfway between his workplace and my apartment, it was a perfect place to meet when neither of us had decided to spend the night at each other's house.

Matthew was usually on time, but for some reason not today. Wanting to make sure I hadn't missed his call or text, I checked again. When I didn't get a message from him, I called...no answer.

"Will Matthew be joining you?" our usual waitress, Donna, asked, refilling my cup. Too busy with my wild imagination, I didn't realize I had gulped it down. It was easy to drink that fast with a straw.

I started fidgeting with the menu. "He's just a little late."

"Oh, no worries, hun. There was an accident about an hour ago, miles from here. They had to close off two lanes. That's what I've been hearing." Donna glanced around. "Everybody who just came in was complaining about it. I'm sure he's stuck in traffic. If you'd like to order first, let me know. I'll be back."

"Thanks." Donna's words gave me goose bumps. I tried to calm myself by thinking Matthew was late because of a meeting he couldn't get out of, but he would have called to let me know. Then I thought Matthew must be stuck in traffic. His cell phone had run out of battery or he'd forgotten his phone at the office.

Looking at my phone again, I realized he was half an hour late. Yup, that did it. My heart pounded hard against my chest with ugly thoughts. I panicked and dialed Max. *Please pick up, Max.* There was no answer.

Just as I was about to dial Jenna, the phone rang. The caller ID flashed an unknown number. I debated picking it up, but did in hopes that it was Matthew. The tension in my shoulders disappeared when I heard a male's voice. I let out the breath I was holding when I knew it was Matthew for sure.

"Matthew," I greeted him with relief.

"I'm so sorry, Becca. You must have been worried."

I laughed. "I was. Actually, I was about to call the police and say that someone kidnapped you."

When Matthew didn't laugh, I knew something was wrong. "Becca, I don't want you to worry, but I'm at the hospital. They finally let me call you."

"What?" I think everyone in the restaurant heard my desperation. "Are you hurt? Are you okay? What happened?" I fired out a bunch of questions at once. I needed answers and I wanted them now.

"I'm fine. I got into a car accident. Can you pick me up at the hospital? I'll tell you everything. You can even take good care of me." His tone was flirty at the end, but I didn't respond. My heart had taken a dive off a cliff and was trying to find its steady beat.

"I'll be right there. Which hospital?"

"General Hospital."

After I explained to Donna what had happened to Matthew, she confirmed that he was most likely involved in the accident that people were talking about.

"Can you drop me off at home, Becca?" Matthew asked, gazing out the passenger's window.

Matthew looked so tired and worn, but he was still sexy in his suit. I loved it when he wore dark gray. Looking so sleek and all business-like, he made naughty thoughts run wildly in my head. "Sure. I can do that. How are you getting to work tomorrow?"

"Max will take me to work. Since my car is in the auto shop, he is going to take me to rent a car."

I signaled and turned left. "I could take you. You know you can ask me."

Matthew turned to me. "I know. It will be easier. I can go to the office with Max since he lives above me. You'll have to go out of your way."

"I don't mind."

Matthew slipped his hand into mine and continued to look out the window, deep in thought.

"So...want to tell me what happened?" I tried to bring humor to the situation because it was dead silent in the car. "Were you too busy looking at a pretty girl walking down the street that you forgot to look at the road ahead?"

Matthew chuckled lightly and gave me a suave, sexy grin that made me want to pull down my panties for him. "Yeah...I thought that pretty girl was you. I only have eyes for you, Becca."

That was pretty smooth, and I couldn't help but smile. However, I needed answers so I changed the tone of the conversation. "How bad was the accident? What happened?"

"The other driver had a red light. Instead of stopping, he decided to go for it. What a stupid idiot. I can't stand people who drive like that." Matthew scowled as if he was reliving the moment. "It was a green light for me. I headed for the intersection. By the time I saw the car, it was too late. I tried to swerve around it. It happened so fast that it was impossible to stop the collision. You know what makes me mad? The man was driving under the influence of alcohol. I smelled it on his breath when he got out of the car to talk to me."

"Did he get arrested?"

"All I know is that the officer was testing him. I'm sure he was arrested. Luckily, the officer was nearby so it only took him about five minutes to get to us. Someone had already called the ambulance, too. Since my car was really trashed, I called the tow truck. After the cop got my information, I left. The accident happened right in front of the hospital. How convenient." There was sarcasm in his tone. "I went inside to call you. My cell phone is somewhere in the car. I couldn't find it.

"You know what makes this situation worse? His friend. He didn't reek of alcohol, but he didn't say a word. He should have been the designated driver. How stupid is he?" Matthew started getting fired up again. "You do not get in the car with a wasted person, and you do not let your friend drive drunk. I don't care what that asshole said to his friend to convince him he was fine. That is just fucked up. I don't understand people."

With one of my hands on the steering wheel, the other began rubbing his arm for comfort. I exhaled a long sigh. "Maybe his friend didn't know he was out of it."

"Either that or he's just a dumb fuck."

"Well, I'm glad you're safe."

"Me too. The right side of the car was smashed in. I got really lucky."

"Nurse Becca will take good care of you."

Matthew smiled at me with a twinkle in his eyes, like he was envisioning a scenario with the both of us in it. "Nurse Becca, I hurt everywhere. I'm going to need a lot of tender loving care."

"Nurse Becca is good at making her patient, Matthew, feel better...everywhere."

Matthew batted his eyelashes at me. I couldn't help taking a quick look at him when he leaned to my side. Thank goodness we were at a red light. "Would you like to start tonight?"

I let out a small chuckle and playfully rolled my eyes. "You feeling up to it? You want me to stay the night?"

Matthew's bottom lip curled down and gave me a lost puppy look. He looked so adorable. I wanted to eat him up in the car. "Please...I'll beg if you want me to."

When he leaned even closer, my body succumbed to his proximity. It didn't matter where we were or what we were doing, his body being that close to mine gave me electrifying tingles. Erotic heat spread through every part of me. Of course he didn't have to beg; I had already planned to stay the night.

CHAPTER 11
BECKY

Matthew lived in Max's penthouse complex on the floor below Max. I wondered if Jenna was there. It was getting harder to see her on a daily basis; she was either at Max's or I was at Matthew's.

For a man's place, Matthew kept it pretty clean. It did help that he had a maid do his laundry, go to the dry cleaner for him, and tidy things up for him. Spoiled. His place was decorated with modern yet elegant furniture. The back wall, which was nothing but glass, gave an amazing view of the city lights below.

We swung by a restaurant, picked up Chinese takeout, and ate at his place. After dinner, we washed up and settled in bed. Matthew picked up a magazine from his nightstand to read. With his back against several pillows, he finally looked relaxed. I felt his eyes flicker to me, then back to his magazine. Matthew was acting adorable. He wanted my attention, but he tried not to show it. Seeing me engrossed in a book, I assumed he didn't want to bother me.

At first my book sucked me away, but I was aware of Matthew's movement no matter what I was doing. I took a peek of him from the corner of my eyes; I couldn't help it. I wanted to see what he would do next to get my attention.

Matthew shifted, cleared his throat, and turned the page again. It took every ounce of self-control to keep from giggling. Playing along, I turned away from him slightly so my back was to him. When he released a small growl, I knew he was annoyed.

Suddenly, Matthew slipped his arms around my waist and spun me around. His legs anchored over mine, and he snatched my book away, imprisoning me with his hands. His lips were a breath away from mine. "I don't think you need that."

"Hey! That's not nice. I was reading."

"The book is getting more attention than me." Matthew curled his lips into his sexy pout. I wanted to eat him up, but I controlled myself. "I don't like it when your book boyfriends steal you away from me. Who is it this time?"

I played along. "His name is Mason."

"Really?" Matthew's eyebrows pinched at the center. "So you're admitting you have a book boyfriend? What's so special about Mason?"

"Is this a trick question? 'Cause you know I read for a living, right?"

Matthew's hand ran through my hair. "I do. I know many things about you, like where you like to be kissed." With a gentle twist of my neck, Matthew opened his lips and ever so softly started sucking on the tender spot right below my earlobe. Then he stopped and looked at me. "Well...you haven't answered me."

Feeling dazed, I blinked my eyes back to him and tried to remember what he had asked. "Ummm...Mason is a demi-god. He can shoot electricity bolts from his hands."

"Now I understand why the book is called *From Gods*."

"And you know what else?" I started to giggle, baffling Matthew. I was sure my eyes sparkled from the excitement of telling him about the story. "There's this part when he places his hands on Skylar's stomach and gives her erotic tingles everywhere. How awesome is that? I bet he can make her climax with a simple touch. What an amazing power. And of course he can kick ass and electrocute the monsters they call vultures."

"Seriously? You like to read stuff like that?"

"It's called a young adult paranormal romance. And yes, I do."

"You know what I like to read?" Matthew's tone became flirty again.

"Boring business magazines," I replied, trying to push him away just to be a pain. Although I liked being in his arms, I wanted to give him a little challenge. I liked it when he fought back. I knew it was childish of me, but it gave me the satisfaction of knowing that he would fight for me.

"Nope. You're so wrong." Matthew shifted his body weight over me, pinning my arms above my ahead against the pillow. "I like to read stories about Becca." His eyes pierced into mine with heat and lust. "I'm going to read you like a book, and lick every word off your body. From chapter to chapter, I'm going to tease you and then leave you hanging like a cliffhanger. I might even give you a teaser to the next book if you beg."

Holy shit. That was one of the sexiest things Matthew had ever said to me. My heart thumped faster, my blood pressure rose, and I lusted for him. My lips gravitated toward his, which were inches away, but he pulled back.

"Pretend I'm Mason," he said. "I'm going to give you one hell of a shock. You're going to feel the power of my electrical bolts that I'm going to shoot through you, but not just with my hands...I can do it with my tongue. When I'm done with you, book boyfriends will never cross your mind. Real boyfriends can make you feel things book boyfriends never could."

Fuck! I was wet and ready for him. When Matthew gave me a satisfied grin, I knew he saw the look in my eyes. I wanted him...now! No matter how many countless book boyfriends I had, Matthew topped them all. He continued to prove he was the perfect model of what a book boyfriend and real boyfriend should be.

"But before I do," he continued, "a couple of things. We're having dinner with my parents this Friday night. I want them to meet the woman I would do anything for." He paused. His eyes glistened. My heart became full at that moment, expanding as I took a deep breath from his loving words. I didn't know what to say, so I just smiled. "Then you can have me all Saturday morning, but I have to go somewhere in the late afternoon. Now...no more talking."

Rewarding me with a sexy grin, Matthew spread my legs with his knee. His animalistic wild beast side took over as he practically yanked my clothes off. Matthew's kisses were passionate, yet filled with hunger. He nipped and sucked roughly at my lips. I thought he was going to swallow me up.

"I can't get enough of you, Becca," Matthew growled as he continued to bathe my neck down to my nipple.

I yelped in pleasure when he opened his mouth and took a mouth full of my breast while his other hand tenderly caressed the other.

"I'm going to electrify every inch of your body," he groaned.

With his teeth, he grazed ever so slowly down my stomach, causing all sorts of tingles to every nerve, every fiber of my being. With the tickling sensation added to the pleasurable feelings, I was beyond ready for him. When I dug my fingers into his shoulders, he got the message to spread my legs. And what he did next...oh my *God*.

Matthew wasn't gentle that night. He sucked the hell out of my clit, harder than he had ever done before. If he wanted to prove real boyfriends were better than book boyfriends, I would have to agree: at least Matthew was.

Jenna

"I don't know what to wear," Becky said, pouring hot water and freshly made dumplings from the local Chinese restaurant into the strainer. Little did we know we could order them in frozen bundles...many thanks to Max and Matthew for giving us that information. I should be starving since I had hardly eaten all day, but it didn't look appealing like it used to, before morning sickness.

"What to wear as in...when we go to Max and Matthew's parents' house?"

"Yes," Becky said, fanning the steam with her hand. She looked over her shoulder to me when I didn't respond. I was too worried about how Max's parents and my parents were going to respond to my pregnancy. After all, we weren't high school kids. We were responsible adults with careers. Maybe we'd messed up on the responsible part, though.

"Well?" Becky narrowed her eyes at me. I knew she guessed my thoughts, as usual. "I hope you're not thinking about whether Max's parents are going to approve of this early marriage and the baby. They already know Max proposed to you, and he told you they were happy about it. You even had dinner together."

"I know," I sighed lightly, handing her two plates. "They were happy about his proposal, but having a child before marriage...I'm worried about that. Knowing them, I'm sure they'll be fine. I don't know why I feel so nervous."

After running cold water on the dumplings, she used a ladle to scoop them up and place them on the plates. "Not that many," I said. "I'm still nauseous."

Becky nodded in understanding. "I know why you feel so nervous."

"Why?" My eyebrows arched, already knowing what she would say.

"Because...you are a good girl. Getting pregnant before marriage is frowned upon. It's something an irresponsible person would do, and you're not that at all. Somehow you see it as something you did wrong, and not Max. That is the kind of person you are. You're putting the blame on yourself when the finger should be pointing at the both of you. To tell you the truth, nobody really frowns upon pregnancy before marriage any more unless you're a teenager."

Becky was right, but I wasn't ready to admit it. Taking the plates to the table, I said, "I know. Maybe you're right." I went back to the kitchen to get glasses of water and walked back out with Becky, who brought out a dish that she'd heated up in the microwave.

Becky put the dish on the table and sat down. "They call this Chinese broccoli. I love this vegetable."

"I had that before with Max. I call them long, skinny trees. But they don't look appetizing right now."

Becky let out a short laugh and placed some on my dish. "Try...for the baby's sake."

"Okay, Mom," I joked.

I didn't know if she heard me, but she looked at me as if she realized something. "You didn't tell your parents, did you?"

I stabbed a fork through one of the dumplings, dipped it into the soy sauce, and took a nibble. "No, not yet. I wanted to see how his parents would respond first. My mom is going to want to know how they reacted. She'll want to know that they have embraced the news so that it will make it easier for her to do the same. My dad is pretty easy going, so I'm not worried about what he will say."

Becky took a sip of water and nodded. "I understand. I really do. Just don't think that this is your fault, and don't think there is any fault to being pregnant. You told me before that you were so worried that you couldn't. Well..." She swallowed the bite she'd just taken. "Embrace it. You're supposed to be glowing. It's not good for the baby to be sulking. Happy Mommy makes happy, healthy baby."

"Thanks." I smiled at Becky. She was right. I just needed to hear it.

"When's the due date?"

"November. A week before Thanksgiving day."

Becky's eyes twinkled with delight. "See," her tone went up a notch, "a Thanksgiving baby." She let out a hearty laugh. "Even your baby is trying to tell you something."

Smiling at her enthusiasm, I looked down at my stomach, which would be growing soon. "Yes, my baby is." I looked up at her again. Becky's mouth was stuffed, and she chewed as fast as she could while trying to tell me something. Nodding, chewing, and pointing a fork in the air, she mumbled a few incoherent words. All I heard was "...dumplings are so good..."

I had to admit it, they were. After I nodded to agree, I spoke again. "I'm going to answer your question that you asked me earlier before you changed the topic. I think you should wear whatever you want. You'll look beautiful no matter what."

Becky's head tilted in a shy manner with a smile, but it was more of a thank you gesture. She was never shy, or at least not that I knew of. When she finally swallowed, she asked, "What should we take? This is my first time."

"Since you're driving us there, we can stop by the bakery and the floral shop. We can take a bouquet of assorted flowers and stop by JJ Bakery. They make the best cake. Their frosting is the best, not too sweet. The cake melts in your mouth."

"From your description, sounds like you're craving a piece," Becky said.

"Maybe my baby wants cake."

"Baby must have food first. Eat some more. You hardly ate."

"Yes, Auntie Becky."

"Auntie Becky. I like the sound of that. I promise to be the best auntie."

My eyes started to pool with tears. "Thanks, Becky. That means a lot to me. Blood is not thicker than water for sure."

"Nope. I love you as if you were my own sister. You mean the world to me. Don't you ever forget that."

Becky's words made the tears I tried to hold back fall. Wiping them away, I said, "I won't."

Chapter 12
Becky

My heart thumped faster than its normal beat; sweat dampened under my armpits. It was difficult to concentrate on the road ahead. The closer the GPS indicated we were to Matthew's parents' house, the faster my blood pumped through me. What was the matter with me? I'd never been so nervous in my life.

"Becky...you missed the exit." Jenna laughed out loud. The bouquet of flowers she was holding in her lap practically blocked my view of her so that I had almost forgotten she was there.

"Oh shit. I'll get off at the next one and just go local." I paused to look at the time. "Oh no, we're going to be late."

"Becky, it's okay. I already texted Max to tell him we were running late."

My shoulders immediately relaxed. I exhaled a deep breath I didn't realize I was holding in.

"We're here. Turn right at the light," Jenna directed. She must have noticed that I wasn't even looking at the GPS. I was in my own world...again. I had to snap out of it, or I was going to make a big fool out of myself.

When we got there, Jenna rang the doorbell. I knew Matthew's parents were well off, but holy crap! They lived in a mansion, the kind you would find in a magazine that you could only dream about. For some reason, this made me even more nervous.

Before the door opened, I quickly ran my fingers through my hair, straightened my sweater dress, and asked Jenna if I had anything on my teeth. Her lips pinched together, trying not to laugh. "Don't worry, Becky. They'll love you."

Just as she said her last word, the door opened.

"Hello, Jenna," a lean, well-dressed lady, wearing black trousers and a magenta cowl neck sweater, greeted us. She had beautiful blonde, shoulder-length hair and was a little bit taller than Jenna. After she gave Jenna a hug, she turned to me and offered one, too. "You must be Becca. I've heard so much about you." I had to smile at that. I wanted to tell her my real name, but decided not to. After that hug and seeing her beautiful friendly smile, I relaxed.

"Mrs. Knight, it's such a pleasure to meet you. I've heard so much about you from Matthew and Jenna." Even though I really hadn't other than the fact that Jenna told me she was really sweet, I fibbed. Matthew and I mentioned our parents, of course, and the topic of them came up, but we never went into details.

Mrs. Knight's cheeks flushed a little. "Call me Ellen, and please...come in." She stepped aside.

I tried my best not to gawk, but I couldn't help it. The foyer was absolutely beautiful. From the crystal chandelier, to the table that held a tall vase, and the double staircases, I couldn't wait to see what the rest of the house looked like. Having been on her yacht, I already knew she had elegant taste.

"These are for you," I said, "but we'll help you carry them to the kitchen."

"Thank you. You shouldn't have." Her eyes beamed with happiness. "Max and Matthew are in the backyard. They don't know you're here. I wanted to say hello first."

After we set the dessert and the flowers on the counter, I was re-introduced to Carlos. He clearly remembered me from Valentine's Day. His friendly greeting and smile indicated that he did. I didn't know why I felt so embarrassed. Maybe because he knew Matthew and I had sex on the yacht.

"You can go out this way." Ellen opened the door for us with a smile. Before we had a chance to take a step, a tall man appeared. At first I thought it was Max, but it was Mr. Knight. The resemblance was uncanny. With salt and pepper-colored hair, he was dashingly handsome. If Max looked like that in his older years, Jenna was very lucky.

"Jenna." Mr. Knight smiled broadly. After giving her a hug, he turned to me. "And you must be Becca. It's a pleasure to meet the first woman Matthew has brought home in a very long time." Mr. Knight reached for me with uncertainty, but when I leaned toward him, he embraced me warmly.

"It's nice to meet you, Mr. Knight," I said, still in his arms.

Mr. Knight released me with a grin. "The pleasure is all mine. Please, call me Rob."

I smiled at that and turned when I saw a body from the corner of my eyes. Knowing it was Matthew, I diverted my attention away from Rob.

"Becca." Matthew planted a quick kiss on my lips.

Matthew kissing me in front of his dad made me blush. He didn't smother me; it was just a peck. I felt bashful around his parents, such a well-known couple. I'd admired and read about them in the newspaper.

"Good to see you, Becca," Matthew said, his eyes piercing mine, bringing me back to attention. I saw so much affection for me in those eyes. Sometimes I wondered if he was real. Did I really get lucky this time? Was this forever?

"Time to eat," Ellen said, walking out of the kitchen back door with Carlos.

Matthew seized my hand and took me to the table where Jenna, Max, and Rob were already seated. Had Matthew and I been staring into each other's eyes that long? Time seemed to stand still when he looked at me that way.

The backyard was bigger than I had imagined it to be. With a swimming pool, tennis court, basketball court, and a section for golf, this could be a mini vacation place, especially when the palm trees and the décor made you feel like you were on a tropical island.

Most of the dishes were already displayed on the table. Carlos brought out the last one and headed back in. There was more than enough to feed the six of us. I was very grateful that they would go out of their way for Jenna and me, to make us feel welcomed.

"Please, help yourself and eat plenty," Ellen said, handing the plates to us.

Matthew took the initiative and started scooping food on my plate. No guy had ever cared enough to put food on my plate before. This wasn't the first time Matthew had done this, but every time he did made me feel even more blessed and special. Seeing Max doing the same thing for Jenna made me respect him as well. When I saw Rob doing the same for Ellen, I knew Max and Matthew must have learned this simple but meaningful gesture of love from their dad.

"Thanks," I said softly.

"Becca," Rob started to say until Max interrupted.

"Dad," Max chuckled. "Becca's real name is Becky. Matthew likes to call her Becca. I thought you should know."

"Oh. Sorry." Rob leaned back into his chair, looking slightly embarrassed, then took a sip of his wine.

"That's okay," I said quickly. I glanced at Matthew with a small laugh. "I'm getting used to it. I kind of like it."

"Then, Becca it is." Rob clapped his hands happily with a smile and crossed his arms on the table. Leaning forward, he looked like he was dying to ask a question. "Your job seems very interesting."

I stopped myself from placing a piece of steak in my mouth. "I love my job. Though sometimes it can be stressful, much like any job, I get to read stories created by many talented potential authors."

"Is there any particular genre you like to read?"

"Young adult paranormal romance," Matthew blurted, then shoved a broccoli in his mouth. He had no idea everyone was gawking at him since his eyes were on his food. Until it was so silent that he finally figured it out and looked up. "What?" He chuckled. "I don't read that stuff. Becca told me about them." He shrugged and got back into his food.

After laughter was shared at the table, it became quiet as we dug into our food.

"Jenna and I have good news to share with everyone," Max said into the quiet. After he'd gotten all of our attention, he spoke again. "As you all knew, Jenna and I are engaged. We've decided to move up the wedding date."

"That's fantastic." Ellen's eyes sparkled. "When?"

Max held Jenna's hand, kissed the back of it, and gave her one hell of a sexy wink. She smiled nervously back.

Then he turned to his parents. "We didn't plan this, but we're happy about the news I'm about to tell you."

"What is it?" Rob asked impatiently. "Max, you're killing us. Stop rambling."

Ellen's eyes were watery. Her hands covered her mouth as if to stop saying what she wanted to say. She definitely knew what was up. When Jenna hung her head down, I knew she'd seen Ellen's reaction. I was nervous for her. Please let Ellen's expression be a happy one. It was hard to tell.

"You're going to be grandparents soon," Max announced.

Silence.

Matthew squeezed my hand so tightly, I thought he was going to break it. Or was I holding his hand tightly? He smiled at me, letting me know everything was going to be okay.

Dead silence.

Ellen burst into tears. Rob stood up, looking baffled.

Oh shit. If they said anything negative, I would lose all respect for them. My fear vanished when Ellen dashed toward Jenna and embraced her. "I'm going to be a grandmother!" Ellen squealed. Tears escaped her eyes, falling over her cheeks.

Jenna got out of her chair, looking surprised and happy. With tears flowing down her face, she gave Ellen a proper hug.

"Congratulations, Max," Rob said, with a hug. "Finally, we'll have grandchildren before we get too old."

"Thanks, Dad."

After the tears were wiped, everyone settled back down. Ellen looked at Matthew and me. "I'm going to assume we're the last ones to know."

I smiled and kept my mouth shut.

Matthew shrugged. "I'm his brother and you're our parents. You said parents before friends."

"That's right. No matter how old you are, we are your parents first, then friends." Ellen turned to Jenna. "My dear, soon to be mother of our grandchild, you have nothing to worry about. I understand what you must have been thinking. I assure you, we will embrace our grandchild with loving arms." Ellen slipped her hands into Rob's. "We were so busy as working parents that we missed too much of Max and Matthew's childhood. It's going to be different for our grandchildren. I promise." Ellen started tearing again.

"Let's toast," Matthew said, raising his glass. "To Max and Jenna's wedding and their child."

With a clink of glasses, everyone took a sip.

"When's the wedding? We have to hurry and plan. Many vendors get booked up so fast. Sometimes you have to wait for a couple of years," Ellen said.

"Jenna and I already discussed having a small wedding with our family and close friends. Becky is going to be her maid of honor and Matthew will be my best man. That is all," Max said. "I've already spoken to Pastor Sam. He agreed to marry us. We would plan this wedding sooner, but one of Jenna's closest friends is getting married in three weeks. We also need to get ready for the fashion show in Australia."

"There's so much to do," Ellen said. "I can make some phone calls. We can...oh my...we can...can we?" I could tell Ellen was running with thoughts in her mind from her smile and her sparkling eyes.

"Mom," Max chuckled. "Slow down. I think I read your mind. And yes, Jenna and I thought it might be a wonderful idea to have the wedding at our favorite getaway. The Grand Del Mar in San Diego."

"San Diego, here we come." Ellen nodded her head in delight and slipped her hand around Rob's arm. When she snuggled closer to him, he kissed her forehead. It was the sweetest sight. "I'll make some phone calls for you, Max." She turned to Jenna. "Please, let me help you. With my connections, they will treat you like a queen and cater to your needs."

"I can use all of the help I can get," Jenna said with a smile. "We don't have much time."

"Perfect. I'll make an appointment for your wedding dress. We need to contact the florist. Decide on the flavor of the cake. Oh, the invitations. We need to get those out. There's so much to do. The list goes on. I'll contact you as soon as I talk to the manager at Del Mar."

I wasn't sure how long the list would be, but it had taken Nicole at least half a year to prepare everything for the wedding and the reception. With Ellen's connections, I was sure Jenna was in good hands.

CHAPTER 13
JENNA

"Hi, Jenna," Mom greeted from her phone.

The sound of her voice got my heart thumping so fast, I could hear it beating as Mom waited for me to answer. "Hi, Mom."

"How are you? Is everything fine?"

There was a little pause before I spit out what I needed to say. Before I could change my mind, I blurted, "I'm pregnant."

"I'm not sure if I heard you correctly. Did you say you were pregnant?" I knew it. Her tone was concerned and I could just imagine her disapproving expression.

I inhaled a deep breath and swallowed before I spoke. "Yes." There was a stretch of silence. I thought I heard a soft cry, but I wasn't sure. "Mom? Are you there? Before you get mad, Max and I are in love. We're going to get married. And—"

"I'm so happy for you, baby," Mom blurted out, loud and fast. I could still hear the tiny gasps from her cries. She was making me cry, too. "I'm so happy that you don't have to go through what I went through, years of misery of miscarriages and false hope. This is wonderful. And we can't wait to be grandparents. I can't wait to tell your dad. I know he will be so happy for you. We hoped you and Max wouldn't have to go through what we've been through."

"Thanks, Mom." Her blessing meant the world to me. And hearing my mom's reaction, I knew dad would feel the same for sure.

Matthew

Jenna walked into the office elegantly dressed in a dark gray dress suit. Her hair was neatly pinned up with some loose strands by the sides. However, what caught my eyes after her outward appearance was how drained and pale she looked. Max had told me about Jenna's morning sickness. If I felt the need, I was ordered by Max to send her home even if she disagreed. Easier said than done. Knowing Jenna, she would fight me. And knowing myself, I would probably give in to her.

"Good morning, Matthew," Jenna greeted me with a smile. After she acknowledged the others, she sat in her chair and turned her attention to the computer.

Jenna had no idea I watched her from the corner of my eyes. She had an amused smile when she looked at her desk, as if she were recalling a memory. She chuckled to herself, then got to work.

Oh my dear brother, Max...something happened on that desk. I snapped out of it when Jenna called my name.

"Matthew. You can stop staring at me. Did Max tell you to watch me like that?"

Shit! She caught me. "Max? What makes you think that?" Forget this. I could be honest with her. I scooted my chair to her and whispered, "Jenna." I waited for her attention. "Max told me about your morning sickness. If you don't feel good, you can work at home. Please let me know if you feel the need to go home."

Jenna lowered her voice. "I haven't told anyone in the office. Wouldn't it seem odd if I went home often?"

"You might as well start telling people; you can't hide your pregnancy forever."

Jenna let out a snort. "True. But you know the rules, don't you? Pregnant women never announce pregnancy until after the first trimester...just in case. Anything can happen in the first trimester."

"Oh," I said, taking a pause to think. Those thoughts had never entered my mind; that was how little I knew about pregnancy. Then again, that was far from what I needed to know at this point in my life. "I'm sure everything will be fine. Just think happy thoughts." I had no idea what I was saying, but it seemed to work.

"Thanks." Jenna smiled and some color returned to her cheeks.

"Max told me he acted like an asshole when he first found out."

"He did?" Her eyes lit up with embarrassment.

Shit. I didn't mean to bring up the unwanted topic, and I certainly didn't want to embarrass her. I had to fix this.

"He did. And I'm pretty sure most guys would have responded in the same way. If Becca told me she was pregnant, I think I would have flipped. I mean...not that I don't want children with her, but because we just started to get to know each other. Having a baby would complicate things. Becca and I haven't even spoken about marriage yet." I was rambling, trying to make Jenna understand Max's actions from a man's point of view.

"I understand." Jenna nodded.

"Have you told your parents about it?" Another slip of the tongue. This was none of my business.

"Yes." Jenna nodded with a smile. Finally, I saw a pinkish glow. "They can't wait to be grandparents, my mom especially."

"That's fantastic. I'm so happy for you."

"Thanks."

"Now...don't take this in the wrong way, Jenna. You don't look so well. Go home. Take a nap. You already turned in your formats. We can take it from there. This isn't a suggestion. This is an order from your boss."

Jenna released a small smile. "I'm going to listen to my boss today. I haven't been able to eat much, and I've been so tired lately."

"For a very good reason," I added. "It looks like you've lost some weight."

"Don't worry. I'll be gaining as soon as my morning sickness is over."

"Why do they call it morning sickness anyway? Are you only sick in the morning?" I was really curious about this.

Jenna's smile got bigger. "I wish I knew."

I was glad to temporarily help her forget her nausea. Little did she know a big surprise waited for her at home. I was glad I didn't have to twist her arm to get her to cooperate. Jenna agreeing to go home only indicated how much her sickness affected her. I felt so bad for her.

When I had first found out about women's monthly cycles, I was glad I wasn't one. Now, watching Jenna and what she was going through, and knowing what she would be going through, I was most certainly glad I wasn't a woman.

Jenna

I stepped into the apartment, dropped my workbag next to the sofa, and draped my coat on it. I was so tired and exhausted, my insides felt like they were doing somersaults. A bitter taste lingered in my mouth and though I was hungry, the thought of food made the feeling worse. The strong need to vomit took over, so I rushed to my room.

Seeing a figure from the corner of my eyes, I screamed for dear life as my heart leapt out of my chest.

"Jenna, it's me." Max ran to me and held me until I was able to calm my shaking body.

I pulled back. "What are you doing here? I mean...I'm happy to see you." I gripped his white T-shirt tightly. "Don't scare me like that ever again." My voice was stern. I didn't mean to sound irate. I was already aggravated from not feeling well.

"I'm sorry, babe." He kissed my forehead. "I wanted to surprise you."

"You surprised me all right. Is that the reason Matthew wanted me to go home so badly? He was very convincing, you know, but he didn't have to try too hard. I don't feel good today. Sometimes I think I'm getting better, but then days like this happen." I sighed.

"I know, babe. It's the reason why I took today off. I cancelled my appointments so I could take care of you. You've lost weight and you look drained. You're making me worried. I'd like to go to your next appointment with you."

"You would?" I sounded surprised.

Max arched his brows and cupped my face. "Of course I would. Why wouldn't I? I told you I would be there for you every step of the way, and I meant it."

Wrapping my arms around the nape of his neck, I hugged him tightly in response. He knew my answer by my gesture...he always did.

Max released me and held my hand. "Let's get you something to eat. I didn't take off work so I could scare you."

"I'm not hungry," I fibbed. Somehow I found the strength to not act as sick as I felt in front of Max. He made me too happy.

One of his eyes narrowed at me while his lips pursed. His forehead creased. It was one of his hottest expressions that made me melt. Yup, he could make me do anything with that look alone.

"I don't believe you." He tugged me to the kitchen. "I made you homemade organic chicken soup with organic onions, carrots, celery, and fresh made noodles." Max opened the lid and the smell of something delicious filled my nostrils. Why didn't I smell this mouthwatering aroma when I first walked in?

Hunger pangs struck me like they had never done before, then tears started pouring. My pregnancy hormones were kicking in strong.

"What's wrong, babe? You don't have to eat. I'm sorry. Shit...I didn't mean to be so demanding," Max rambled. His hands reached for me, then stopped. He looked confused on how to comfort me.

Wiping my tears with my back to him, I turned to him with a smile. "These are happy tears. Thank you. You're so good to me. I would love to have some soup now."

Max took me to the dinner table and, though he didn't need to, helped me settle in my seat. He came back with a bowl of soup and crackers. I didn't even know they made organic crackers. Leave it to Max to find me some.

"Only the best for my family." With a smile, he handed me a spoon. Finally, he got a bowl for himself as well and sat next to me.

Warmth soothed my throat and down to my empty, achy stomach at the first sip. The more I ate, the fewer pangs I felt in my stomach. I couldn't eat it all, but I ate enough.

"I guess our baby was asking for Daddy's chicken soup," I commented. Feeling satisfied, and with the nausea fading, for the first time I felt just a little bit better.

Max finished his last sip. "I have to say, I make one hell of a chicken soup."

I nodded to agree. "Yes, you do."

"I made a large pot for you." Max winked.

"Thank you so much," I gushed, gazing into his eyes while caressing his cheek. Max leaned into the palm of my hand and kissed it.

"Time for you to rest and time for me to work." After taking me to my room, Max helped me out of my clothes into more comfortable ones. He lifted the covers and helped me into bed. When he'd cleared the dishes away, he laid next to me with the computer on his lap.

"Are you staying the night?"

"I'm right here, babe." Max gave me a kiss on my cheek and shuffled the blanket closer to my body. "I'm not going anywhere. We'll have chicken soup for dinner unless you want something else. I'll have to go to work tomorrow, but I'll be back."

"I should go to work tomorrow."

"Only if you think you feel up to it. Matthew told me the layout was finished. He can take it from there. You need to take care of you and baby first. So whatever you need, it will be taken care of."

"Thank you." I sighed, feeling full, loved, and gratified. Then sleep came quickly to my peaceful mind.

CHAPTER 14
BECKY

"You ready, Becca?" Matthew leaned against the frame of the bedroom door. With a form fitting black sweater and jeans, he looked like a GQ model on a shoot. And his sexy grin was enough for me to want to rip the clothes off him.

"I'm not sure." I walked up to him, and running my hands across his ripped chest, I flirted with my eyes. Tantalizing him with my smile, I licked and sucked on the lollipop that was already in my mouth.

A sexy, slow growl escaped Matthew's mouth. His hot breath brushed against my ear. "You're such a tease, Becca. I love that about you." His tone was low and smooth.

Changing the subject, I ran my finger across his supple bottom lip. "I really like your parents."

Matthew gently nipped and licked my finger. With a fast yank of my hips, he pulled me closer. His eyes shifted from my eyes to my lips. "They like you, too...but I like you even more."

Twisting my lollipop, I said, "I was so nervous they wouldn't like me."

Matthew licked his bottom lip, mimicking what I was doing. "Of course they did. Why wouldn't they?"

Hell, I was turned on the second I saw him, but now he was driving me insane. While one of his hands gingerly rubbed my ass, the other one unbuttoned my jeans. I cleared my throat, feeling the need between my legs building. "You know...the whole 'she's not good enough for my son' kind of thing."

Matthew's tongue licked my lips from bottom to top with one long stroke as if I was his lollipop. Holy shit. I was supposed to be the one playfully seducing him, not the other way around. "My parents aren't like that. And if they were, it wouldn't stop me from wanting to be with you. I'm all or nothing, Becca. You should know that by now."

"We haven't gone out that long. How do I know?" I swallowed.

"I practically stole my parents' airplane, went to a book convention where I had to endure all that book boyfriend shit, and forced Jenna to tell me where you were. I think that proved it."

I closed my eyes and enjoyed Matthew's soft kisses on the side of my neck. "I guess." I chuckled lightly, knowing he was right but not wanting to admit it.

Matthew's kisses trailed down to my shoulder, up my back again to my jaw, and then to my lips. "What flavor is it?" he asked when I wouldn't let his tongue slip into my mouth. He pulled back to look at me with a frown.

I sucked on it harder to tease him. "I'm not going to tell you."

"I want to taste it," he demanded with a hiss.

With a soft laugh, I pulled out my lollipop. Maneuvering my tongue ever so slowly, I licked from bottom to top, taking my time and giving him the show of his life. Then I glided it in and out of my mouth while I bored my eyes into his. I had a huge smile on my face until Matthew pinned me against the wall where he had stood a second before. It happened so fast, not only did I suck in air, I also bit into my lollipop and broke it in half.

"You want to tease me, Becca?" he seethed through his teeth. "I can tease you right back." With hungry eyes, he dove in for a kiss while his hands held tightly to my hips. Not only was his tongue playing with mine, he licked and tasted the broken lollipop in my mouth, too. "Cherry, my favorite."

"It comes in all different flavors." I managed to say the words between his lips devouring mine.

"I'd like to taste every single flavor just like this," he murmured, slowing down. "But now...it's in the way." Matthew pulled the stick out and continued to kiss me. Then he placed his hands on my cheeks and pressed in deeper.

I had no idea how he moved us without me knowing, but the next thing I knew he tossed me on our bed. How I got completely naked and not him, I had no clue. When I looked to make sure the door was closed, just in case Max and Jenna decided to pay us a visit, there was a trail of clothes on the floor. Somehow, I'd gotten so lost in his arms that I couldn't recall what had happened a second before or how I got to that position.

"Matthew," I moaned. "Take off your clothes."

"You're my lollipop, Becca. And I'm going to lick every inch of you. I'm going to tease you like you teased me."

Matthew did not disappoint. He practically bathed me with his tongue. He started from my face, down to my collarbone, to my nipple. Then his tongue glided down my stomach to my clit. Begging him to stop did not work. I tried everything to take off his clothes, but he would not budge. I couldn't believe how much self-control he had. When it seemed like his will had been spent, he stopped.

Taking a deep breath, Matthew stood up, raking his hair back. "Time to go, Becca. We have a schedule to keep."

He tried to look calm and collected, but I could tell by his chest rising and falling rapidly that he wasn't.

Spread out, shamelessly naked and short of breath, I tried to tame the torturous yearning between my legs. I lay there unable to move or say a word. I was utterly drained from being licked like a lollipop.

"But mine was just a lollipop," I whined, running my hand down my face. "You're bad...terrible." I shook my head with a naughty thought circulating my mind. Two could play at his game. Before he could walk out the door, I called his name. Licking my fingers, I placed them on my clit and started rubbing myself. With the other hand, I fondled my breast and squeezed my nipple. "We have time for a quickie," I teased, making pleasure sounds he could not ignore.

Matthew's eyes grew wider than I had ever seen before. I loved knowing I could turn him on that way. The last thing I heard before he stripped off his jeans and sweater was the word, "Fuck."

After flipping me over with one swift move, he pulled my thighs to him so that my feet touched the floor. My back was toward him and my arms tucked underneath me. Spreading my legs with his knee, Matthew lightly pressed his chest on my back and entered. I was already climaxing from all the build up he had inflicted on me.

When Matthew wrapped his arm under my thigh and started rubbing my clit while he was rocking me, I climbed to another level of ecstasy. Oh my God! It felt so freakin' good. I didn't want this to be a quickie. Just when I thought we were done, Matthew flipped me over to face him and lifted me onto the bed.

Anchoring my legs over his shoulders, he pushed down, making my knees bend. Gazing lovingly into my eyes, he said softly, "I'm all in. You've got all of me. Now you're going to pay for your teasing." He gave a wicked grin.

The way he had me positioned gave him a deeper access to me. I felt him to the depth of my core. His words and actions made me utterly weak. I surrendered to him, allowing him to take me, all of me. He felt so amazing and I didn't want him to stop as I climaxed again and again.

"I want to live inside of you and never come out," Matthew murmured against my ear. With a low groan, he fell over the edge.

"Then live and breathe inside and never come out," I managed to say before I completely came undone. Matthew and I had climaxed together. He dropped down next to me, panting like he had run a mile. Out of breath, I turned to him with a smile. With our eyes locked on each other, we fell into a deeper level of connection...a deeper level of understanding...a deeper level of us.

Matthew

"You want to talk about your friend?" I asked, holding Becca's hand with one hand while the other held the steering wheel. She had been quiet for quite some time and I could tell something was on her mind. We were headed to her friend's gravesite, and I knew there was more to her story than she had shared with me before.

Becca looked at me for a second, then focused elsewhere. "Her name was Amber. She was my best friend and roommate."

I waited for Becca to tell me more, but she stopped. "And?" I dragged out the word. "You already told me that. Tell me something I don't know."

Becca released a deep sigh. "She died in a car accident."

I signaled left, turning when it was clear. "You already told me that, too." It was like pulling teeth whenever I asked for more information regarding her friend.

"There isn't much to tell," she sighed. "My friend drove drunk and killed herself. I tried to stop her, but she didn't listen. I probably should have tried harder, but I was out of it myself. I was a shitty friend. Friends don't let other friends drive drunk...remember?" Becca rambled quickly. Her tone was harsh, but I could tell there was a lot of self-blame.

I pulled her hand to my lips and kissed it, then placed our joined hands on my thigh to rest. "It's not your fault. She should've known better. I'm not passing judgments. I've done stupid things myself. At least she took only her own life. It would have sucked if she'd taken someone else's life, too." I was thinking of Tessa at that point. A drunk driver had taken her life, something that could have been avoided.

Becca stiffened and pulled her hand away from mine. "I didn't mean—"

"I know," Becca cut me off. "It's nothing."

When we stopped at a red light, I examined her from the corner of my eye. She was not her usual friendly self. In fact, she was jumpy and fidgety, as if hiding a secret. The sound of plastic crinkling from the bouquet of flowers irritated me. Becca couldn't stop messing with it. Looking deep in thought, she had no idea what she was doing until I took her hand away from it.

"Sorry. I was just thinking," she said when she finally realized her repeated gesture.

"That's okay." I paused to turn right. "We're here."

I didn't know why, but going to gravesites filled me with both dread and serenity. Many graves held fresh flowers. It indicated that their loved ones had visited recently.

"Turn left, up ahead," Becca said. "I think that's it."

After I did as instructed, I parked. "Here?" I asked.

Becca glanced around and nodded. "Yes. I remember those two trees. It's been a while, but I never forget those trees."

I had no idea what she meant. "Those trees" she was talking about looked exactly the same as any other trees. Women, go figure. Opening the passenger's door, I helped her out of the car. Becca looked up to the sky before she took a step. I looked up, too—curious as to why she did—but all I saw were puffy clouds. Perhaps she was saying a little prayer. Who knew? However, that was not the time to ask what she was thinking. I could guess because I had been in the same situation before. The first time coming back to the gravesite after the funeral was always the hardest, no matter how many years had passed.

Following Becca on the grass, I stopped when she did. Becca didn't know that I had planned to come here late that afternoon to meet up with Tessa's sister, Teresa. Visiting Tessa at her gravesite was my plan, but Teresa had called that morning asking to meet with me. I had put off telling Becca because I knew how distraught she was about coming here. I didn't want to add any more stress on her plate.

"This is Amber," Becca said, looking at me for direction. She appeared uneasy.

I weaved behind her and held her lightly from the back. My hands slipped around her waist and bent lower to rest my chin on her shoulder. "Say hi. She can hear you." Could she really? Who knew? Regardless, talking to Tessa as if she was there helped me, and I knew it would help Becca, too.

"Hi, Amber. I brought Matthew with me." Becca's tone became shaky. After she cleared her throat and her shoulders lifted from taking in a deep breath, she continued, "I'm sorry that it took me so long to come see you. I was a chicken shit." Becca let out a soft laugh; that made me smile. "Amber used to call me chicken shit," Becca informed me.

"Nice friend," I commented sarcastically while rolling my eyes. "Go on."

"I have a new roommate, but you probably already knew that. Her name is Jenna. We were like two opposites, but now I think her goodness rubbed off on me. She doesn't call me chicken shit. She actually influences me to be a better person. I'm not saying anything bad about you, but we did some crazy, wild things together."

"Really?"

Becca nudged me with her elbow, gesturing me to keep comments to myself. "We were in college," she said quickly. "That's the time to experiment."

"True." I kissed her cheek and squeezed her a little bit tighter on her waist.

Becca grunted when she felt the pressure. Releasing a sigh, she continued, "Matthew, who is a leech on my back right now, is the best thing that has ever happened to me. You'll be happy to know Matthew is not an asshole and I am officially not an asshole magnet any longer."

I rocked us from side to side, letting her know how much I appreciated her words. "I'm glad you don't think I'm an asshole," I added quickly.

"Shhh. I'm still talking." Becca laughed. "I wish you could meet him in person. He's truly a gentleman, more than I could ever have expected. Sometimes I don't think I deserve him." She paused. "Matthew is really good to me, unlike any of the guys you've seen me date, but fate took you away so soon. And I'm so sorry that I didn't force you to get out of the car. I should have yanked you out...or taken your car keys, anything to stop you from driving."

Becca's hand reached for her face to stop the tears from falling. Seeing her like this not only made my heart ache, but made me sad for her. However, I also knew that once she passed this stage, she would learn to forgive and let go. There would be closure, and no one understood that better than me.

"It's not your fault, Becca," I whispered in her ear. Switching positions, Becca faced me, her whole body engulfed in my arms.

"It is my fault," she muttered into my sweater. "I could have prevented it. I could have done so many things differently, but I didn't. It's my fault. Amber didn't die alone."

At this point Becca was sobbing. I could tell how much she was hurting from the guilt and the loss of her friend. Her pain traveled inside of me. Whatever she felt, I felt it, too. That's how much I cared and loved her. That's how much she meant to me. I would do anything to mend her pain and hurt, anything to make it right for her.

Then something stone cold struck me. My heart started thumping harder against my chest and my muscles became stiff. I couldn't move. Becca's last words felt like a slap on my face. *Amber didn't die alone.* My eyes shifted from the ground to the headstone. I hadn't paid attention to what was written on it since I was standing behind Becca, trying to give her some privacy.

When Becca had told me her friend passed away on the same date as Tessa, I thought, 'What a coincidence'. There were billions of people on this planet, surely many people died on the same date. Yet when I traced Amber's full name with my eyes, I thought I was going to drop dead. Amber James echoed in my mind. Surely it couldn't be the same person. Could it?

I didn't know what came over me, but tears blinded my eyes. My grip on Becca loosened. I dropped down to my knees. Oh God! Please don't let it be true. I needed answers fast, but not there.

"Matthew...Matthew...what's wrong?"

I felt my body shake and my name echoed in my head until I finally came to. "Becca, I need to take you home. Now!"

CHAPTER 15
BECKY

I wasn't sure what had triggered Matthew's sudden anger, but I didn't want to add to it, so I kept my mouth shut and got in the car. Matthew didn't even look at me or say a word. In fact, the drive back to my place was dead silent. I wanted to ask him questions, but the stone cold look on his face made me so nervous that I dared not say a word.

Replaying the words I had said to him didn't help make me understand his actions. Matthew had been so loving and supportive while we were there until he saw something or remembered something, causing him to drop to his knees. Flabbergasted, I tried to remain calm and steady my heartbeat, but my stomach turned nasty somersaults, and the acid feeling inside of my chest built.

"Matthew, what's wrong? What happened back there?" I finally asked, starting to feel a little ticked off seeing him pacing back and forth in deep thought. His lips were parting and closing; he was trying to tell me something, but it never came out. Now I was beyond annoyed. Sitting uncomfortably on the sofa, I stared at him hard, as if that would make him snap out of it. I had never seen him like this before, but enough was enough. "Matthew, what the hell happened? You can't just shut down on me like that."

Matthew stopped in front of me, peering down at me. Either he looked really concerned or really scared. I couldn't tell which. "What happened the night your friend died?"

Where was he going with this? "I already told you. She drove wasted and died in a car accident. I was—"

Matthew dropped to his knees to meet me at my eye level and interrupted, "You're hiding something. You didn't finish the story, did you?"

My eyes flickered back and forth; I couldn't look at him. "I'm not hiding anything."

"How did Amber die?" Matthew's tone was calm, but I felt goosebumps up my arms. It was the way he had asked, like he knew. Surely he couldn't have guessed.

"I already told you. What the fuck, Matthew? What is wrong with you?" I stammered, standing up to walk away, but Matthew gripped my arm.

"Sit down." His tone was cold and demanding.

Under other circumstances I would have told him to screw himself and walked away, but I listened. Clearly something was bothering him. When I sat, Matthew sat on the floor with his knees tucked in. "Please answer with the truth. What do you mean 'she didn't die alone'? Did your friend, Amber James, kill someone the night of her accident?"

How could he possibly freakin' know? Not even Jenna knew. And there was no way Jenna would spill the beans if she did. Regardless, I needed to tell him the truth. Oh God! I remembered. My tongue had slipped at the gravesite. Maybe it would do some good to get it off my chest. Matthew would understand. Amber was right. I had always been a chicken shit.

Inhaling a deep breath, I let it all out. "Not a day goes by where I don't hold this guilt inside of me. It has been eating me alive. There are days when I'm fine and days when I feel so much remorse that I wish it was me. I could have prevented this."

Matthew lowered his head. Taking a deep breath, his chest expanded. With a puff of heavy air, he looked at me again. His hands gripped the sofa and he seemed thoroughly pissed off. "Tell me. It's a simple word. Yes, or no?" His words seethed out of his mouth in a way I'd never heard before. He was right. It was a simple answer, one word that was hard to say.

I looked away shamefully. "Yes. Amber killed someone. She killed herself and someone else. So that makes me responsible for two deaths. Is that what you want to hear?" Tears started pouring down my cheeks.

Matthew ignored my tears, unlike before. He had a motive, but why? "When and where did it happen?" Matthew leaned in closer, as if I would speak faster.

"It was raining hard that night. We were at a party, somewhere near Santa Monica. Amber took off. From the police report and what her parents told me, she ran a red light on 7th Street. I think—" I stopped talking when Matthew's face turned pale.

"No...no...no," he repeated, gripping his hair tightly. Standing up, he stared at me like I was his worst enemy. I was not prepared for the cold look he gave me. That alone killed me, stabbing my heart a thousand times.

I had no clue what the hell was the matter with him. "Matthew. What's wrong?" When I took a step to him, he jolted back. He didn't want me near him, and that action twisted painfully in my heart. Tears began to fall again.

"Did you know?" He took another step back.

"Know what?" I wrapped my arms to my chest to hold my shaky body together. "Please, I don't understand." I felt like I was losing him and I had no idea what I had done.

Matthew raked his hair back and turned his back on me. He stepped closer to the door. "Amber...killed...Tessa. Tessa's car was hit on 7th Street, and she died the same night your friend died. She...killed...my...Tessa." Matthew's tone was soft, but I could feel every stabbing pain.

Dead silence filled the air. I stopped breathing. This wasn't happening. Not my Matthew. Not the man I wanted forever with. What should I say? There were no words for comfort and no words to apologize. I tried to take a step to him, but my body was too stiff—too much in shock. I let the tears flow and searched for the right words...but nothing.

"Matthew." I swallowed, hearing my voice crack. "I swear to you I didn't know. I never knew the name of the person. I never wanted to know her name. The guilt was already too much, and I thought if I didn't know her name then it would be as if it never happened. I know it's probably not right to think that way, but it was the only way I could go on."

"Her name was Tessa Young," he gritted through his teeth softly, but sternly, as if I should have known.

"I'm sorry, Matthew. I really didn't know." Tears kept flowing, and no matter how much I tried to stop them, I couldn't. Although Matthew was physically present, he was long gone. I'd lost him. I knew it when he wouldn't look at me, even after I apologized, even after telling him I didn't know.

I found the courage to stand next to him and place my hand on his shoulder. "Matthew, please say something."

"Becca," he said, inhaling a deep sigh, "I need some space right now." Without looking at me, he walked out the door with his head down.

I dropped to the floor where he left me and sobbed into the palms of my hands. My pounding heart hurt like hell, traveling through every nerve, bone, and muscle in me. Matthew was simply gone. He said he needed space, but he might as well have said goodbye, because that was how it felt. All of my energy had been spent pouring out the gut-wrenching ache through my tears. I sat there crying until there were no more tears to be shed. When they ran out, I cried more empty tears.

Matthew

I could not believe what was happening. Fate had fucked me big time. What the fuck? What were the odds of Becca's deceased roommate killing my Tessa? Through the shock, I couldn't remember what I had said. I had needed air; to get away to think and soak the news in.

With keys in my hand, I was already at my front door. I had no idea how I got home. Pouring myself a drink, I wondered how I was going to remain calm while visiting Tessa with her sister. It would feel like I was hiding a secret. Though it wasn't Becca's fault, the connection was just so freakin' weird. I was dating the best friend of the girl who killed Tessa.

I sat on the sofa, tilted my head back, and spread my legs. Grabbing a sofa pillow, I hugged it tightly, as if it would help get rid of my frustration. I held it so tightly that I could see my veins protruding. This wasn't happening. It felt like my whole world was crumbling. Not only that, it felt like Tessa had died all over again.

It was bad enough knowing the name of the girl who killed Tessa, but it was worse when Amber somehow became more than just a name I cursed. I didn't know anything about her, but she began taking a physical form. I never knew or wanted to know what she looked like, but now I could see her standing next to Becca even though she was dead.

"Fuck!" I hurled the pillow across the living room so hard that it made a loud thump as it bounced off the wall.

If Becca and I were to get through this, I had to suck it up and try to get Amber out of the picture. I just needed time to wear off the shock. Too tired to move or think, I decided to call Becca tomorrow. I was pretty sure she needed time to take in the news, too.

CHAPTER 16
JENNA

"Becky, you look beautiful in that dress," I said when she came out of her room. She smiled, but it was forced. A week had passed since Matthew walked out, and he hadn't called. Becky tried to hide that there was something troubling her, but I knew Matthew was the reason when I saw the same look on his face at work. Finally Becky confessed and I tried to comfort her the best I could, but no amount would suffice.

Though it was none of my business, I had asked Matthew why he looked so out of it, and he said he had a lot on his mind and was busy getting ready for the Australia fashion show. That was true because our department was working overtime, but Matthew worked mostly out of the office. I wondered if he was avoiding me or needed time alone.

"I told Max to meet us there, so I can drive," I said, standing by the door with my coat and purse. "Ready to go?"

Becky grabbed her coat off the sofa. "You don't have to drive me there. And you don't have to feel like you need to stay with me. I'm fine."

She really wasn't. Not just her eyes, but her whole face looked puffy. The bags under her eyes made her look twice her age and she'd hardly put on any makeup. She looked like she was going to a funeral instead of a wedding rehearsal.

"Max has a lot of work to do anyway, so don't worry." I turned the doorknob. "And plus, that way I can stick around longer."

Becky's eyes scanned my body. "How's the morning sickness? Any better? You're still skinny. You need to start eating more for the baby."

Why was it that people who had no idea about pregnancy made comments as if they knew what they were talking about? "Actually, I started feeling a bit better today. And don't worry, I'll become fatter by the second trimester."

"Okay, sorry. I didn't mean anything by it. I don't even know what I'm talking about. In fact, I really don't want to go tonight." Becky started tearing. "I'm so sorry. It's just that..."

Seeing Becky like this reminded me of when we were in college. Reaching for her, I held her tightly in my arms, and I couldn't help my own tears. I didn't want her to see me crying, too, so I did my best to hide them. "It's okay. I know you're hurting. Matthew needs time. He didn't say anything to me, but I can tell he's also hurting. He just needs to wear out the shock." I had no idea if it was true. I hoped I was making enough sense for Becky to understand. "He loves you. That's why he's hurting. Everything will work out in the end."

Becky nodded and let go. As we both wiped our tears, we walked out together.

After the wedding rehearsal, the whole party went to the restaurant located inside a hotel in Beverly Hills. Nicole was glowing with happiness and Keith looked relaxed as they sat near the head of the table. The rectangular table was long enough to accommodate the whole party, but we had to lean forward to see the people toward the end.

Max texted me, letting me know he was in traffic, then the next text I got was to meet him by the lobby. When I got there, Max was nowhere to be seen. I pulled out my phone and texted him back.

I'm here, but you're not.

I'm here.

I glanced around again. This lobby wasn't that big. Where was he?

Are you sure you're at the right hotel?

My beautiful view tells me that I am. And may I add how I love you in that red dress.

My husband to be bought it for me.

What a lucky man.

I'm very lucky to have him.

Maybe I'll get lucky tonight and steal you away from him.

View? I peered up to the second level. No sign of Max.

Were you on the second level?

I was a second ago. You're too slow.

Laughing to myself and shaking my head, I texted back. *You better show yourself or I'll leave.*

Go back. I'll be right there.

Got it. Going.

As I headed back to the restaurant, I made a quick stop in the restroom and started the long walk down the hall. Suddenly, I was snatched from the side.

"Max," I screamed, feeling my heart leap out of my chest.

Max's arms around my body calmed my nerves. I thought I was going to have a heart attack. We were in a secluded corner, so no one could see us if they walked by.

"Sorry, babe. What took you so long? I thought someone kidnapped you." He grinned.

"I stopped by the restroom."

Max's brows twitched. "Anyone in there?"

"Max," I squealed, knowing what he was implying. "Why are you hiding in this corner?"

"I just want to see you privately before I go in there with you. I haven't seen you in four days. You're torturing me."

"I missed you, too, but Becca is so miserable. I couldn't just leave her by herself."

Max's naughty hands roamed all over me while his lips tenderly kissed me gently on my face and neck, as if to savor this moment and me. "I know. I understand. Matthew told me what happened, but I think what Becky is telling you and what Matthew is telling me are two different stories. Becky needs to stop being stubborn and answer Matthew's phone calls."

"What?" I pulled away. "What do you mean? Becky told me Matthew wanted space."

We both looked confused. Max's brows crinkled. He had no idea how sexy he looked. "Matthew did tell Becky he needed space, but he called her a couple of days later. She wouldn't answer his phone calls. He even went to your apartment and there was no answer."

None of this made sense. Who was telling the truth? I would bet my money on Matthew; Becky liked to punish herself. That was how she dealt with guilt. Now I knew the whole picture.

"We need to get back," I said, tugging him out of the corner.

"Not so fast. I didn't get enough. I need a little bit more."

There were no words after that. Max let me know how much he missed me. I was getting to the point that I wanted to drag him to the ladies room with me or even the men's room; I didn't care which one. His hard passionate kisses and his hands touching every sensitive area got me completely unglued.

Tilting my head back, I gave Max easier access. "Max, there's no one in the ladies' room right now." I had no idea what had come over me. There was no way I would have ever suggested that before.

Max's eyes lit up with a wicked grin. "Are you sure?"

"I want you," I purred. "I want you inside of me right now, but make it quick."

There was no need to convince him further. He was already hot and ready. Taking my hand, we snuck into the restroom. Max took me to the last stall and turned me to face the wall. After he unzipped his pants and pulled down my panties, he was in. They said that pregnancy hormones would not only make you horny but also extra sensitive. Oh hell yes. I was already climaxing, but Max didn't know how much. Having to hold in my cries of pleasure only made me breathe harder.

"I want to rip your dress off you," he groaned into my hair.

I moaned and tilted my head sideways. Max's tongue took control and conquered my mouth, inside and out.

Max held me tightly. I could feel his hot breath against the side of my neck as he pumped faster and harder. "I'm going to have to end this soon, babe. We'll continue after dinner. This is no good. I need to touch your skin. I want every part of me touching you."

With a soft groan and growl, Max had his climax. Looking pleased and contented, he kissed my lips. He nudged my nose lovingly with his and gave me one more kiss before we took off, laughing like teenagers.

After the introduction and greetings, Max took his reserved seat next to mine. I tried to ignore the looks Nicole's friends and relatives gave Max, but it was evident in their sparkling eyes and flirtatious smiles. It was something I had to get used to. Max was not only good looking, he took good care of his body. And every inch of him showed it.

When he took off his suit jacket, his form fitted white dress shirt that curved to his ripped chest was drool worthy. Besides the young ladies, even Nicole's mother and mother-in-law-to-be stared. I had to remind myself that I didn't need to be jealous. I was going to be Mrs. Maxwell Knight soon, and the mother of his child.

Dinner was delicious and the conversation was light. Everyone seemed to be having a great time, and surprisingly, even Becky. She flirted with a guy she was paired up with to walk down the aisle, and he was heavily flirting with her as well. I knew she was enjoying the attention, especially with what was happening with Matthew. She was trying to forget him.

"Who are you walking down the aisle with tomorrow?" Max whispered into my ear.

"His name is Andy and he's sitting right across from you," I whispered back.

Immediately, Max let go of his hand from mine and wrapped his arms around my shoulder. Pulling me closer, he planted a kiss on my lips that made the other women gawk with jealousy. Max had no idea they were drooling; he was too concerned about letting Andy know I was his.

"Max, what are you doing?" I asked softly so that only he could hear.

"I'm letting Mandy know that you're mine." Max nibbled my ear.

"His name is Andy...Andy," I stressed. Max had a habit of making up names. Laughing to myself, I played into his game. "You're just jealous because he gets to walk me down the aisle first."

Max snarled. Thank goodness everyone was holding small conversations, so hopefully no one heard, but I knew Becky did when she flashed her eyes to Max. "Mandy, Sandy, I don't care what his name is. I don't like the way he looks at you, and I don't like the way he smiles at you. And you're right. I don't like the thought of anyone walking you down the aisle besides me." Max leaned forward, smiling, pretending our conversation didn't take place.

"He's just being nice."

"He better be nice to you, but not in a way I wouldn't like." Max guided my left hand out across the table, letting my engagement ring shine against the candlelight, making sure Andy got a clear sight of it. Andy had already seen my engagement ring during the wedding rehearsal, but I didn't stop him.

I loved how Max was being jealous. I was the one who observed how women gawked at him, but Max seemed to never notice...either that or it didn't faze him. He didn't care. Seeing how he acted around other women when they tried to get his attention only confirmed that I could trust in his love for me, that it was genuine. I was the lucky one, the one who was carrying his child. I couldn't be happier.

Matthew

As I washed up to get ready for bed, I looked up from the sink to see a tired face in the mirror. What happened? Becca and I were so happy one minute, and the next thing I knew, we were apart. I couldn't believe I was at this low point again. This only confirmed how much Becca meant to me. How much I'd fallen in love with her in such a short period of time.

Becca still wouldn't take my calls or texts, nor would she open the door when I came by her apartment. When I used the spare key, the other lock was set and I couldn't get in. I'd made a big mistake when I left her. Knowing Becca, she had taken it the wrong way, but in that heated moment, I was not thinking clearly.

At first I thought I should give her space, but that wasn't what she needed. She needed me to comfort her, to make her feel less guilty, to show I still loved her. Now, it seemed as though she didn't want anything to do with me.

It was the night of Nicole's wedding rehearsal, and I got no call from Becca to remind me to be there. Even when I texted her asking about the location, she didn't respond. This confirmed that Becca didn't want me in her life, and that hurt me more than anything. I'd hurt her big time, and I had no idea how to fix this. I also knew guilt was eating at her. She was most likely thinking that she'd killed Tessa, and that she and I shouldn't be together.

Recalling that day, I should have gone back to her place and patched things up, but when I met up with Teresa, she gave me the shock of my life. Then I'd needed a couple of more days to myself; a little more time to grieve...a little bit more time to let go and heal so I could give Becca all of me again.

"Matthew, I have to tell you something," Teresa said.

I snapped out of my thoughts of Becca and focused my eyes on Tessa's gravestone. I didn't say a word; instead, I waited for her to continue.

"Tessa didn't want to tell you. You were both so young, and she knew you didn't...the reason she insisted that you get married so quickly..." Teresa let out a heavy sigh. "I promised I wouldn't say a word. She was supposed to tell you the day she was in the accident. I'm not telling you to make you feel guilty. I know how much you loved her."

My heart skipped a beat and my blood pressure shot up. I had this gut feeling I knew where this conversation was headed, but I didn't say a word. Hoping that I was wrong, I let her finish. Oh God! Please let me be wrong!

"I debated for a long time if I should tell you, and I didn't tell you earlier because I didn't want you to have more guilt, but I can't do this anymore. It's eating at me, but I think you can handle the news I'm about to tell you. You have the right to know. Tessa was pregnant. It was the reason why she wanted to have the wedding a lot earlier. I'm so sorry, Matthew. She's gone and there's nothing you can do. I want you to live your life and find someone who was meant for you."

Our conversation took me back, and now it seemed obvious why Tessa was in a hurry to get married. We were so young. I wouldn't have been ready to be a father back then, but that wasn't the point. I'd not only lost Tessa, but my child as well. It hurt like hell. I felt robbed by this girl I'd hated for the past several years. And not only that, she turned out to be Becca's friend. What the fuck?

I wondered what my life would have been like with Tessa. We would have had a daughter or a son; our child would have been about the age of two. However, that was then and I lived in the now. No way would I let Amber get in the way of my happiness again. This time, I was going to take ownership of my destiny.

Enough was enough. I'd given Becca space; it was time for me to take charge. We had a huge bump in the road, but it was time to get back on track. If we couldn't get through this, then we wouldn't be able to get through what life threw at us, and I was sure there would be plenty of other bumps ahead. I loved Becca, and she needed to know. How to get her to see me, though? I didn't want to get Jenna involved, but I was desperate. Just as I was about to text Jenna, there was a knock at the door.

"You look like shit." Max pushed the door wider and walked in.

"Thanks. It's good to see you, too." I rolled my eyes.

"Hi, Matthew." Jenna smiled, seeming unsure if she should be there. Her eyes were full of pity. Did I look that bad? She followed Max. Since they were both dressed up, I figured they'd stopped by before heading to their place. Sometimes I regretted living a floor below Max, especially at times like this.

"Come in," I said after the fact. "It's kind of late for a visit, don't you think?"

Jenna and Max had made themselves comfortable on the sofa, all snuggled up in each other's arms.

"It's kind of late to drink, don't you think?" Max added.

I shifted my eyes to the half-empty glass. "It's never too late to party by myself." I slid the drink closer after I took a seat across from them. "So, how was dinner?" I took a sip.

"Dinner was interesting," Jenna said, glancing at Max with pursed lips. Max must have done something that I would have done. I'd bet he made sure Jenna's partner was fully aware that Jenna was his.

"I'm sure it was." I twitched my brows, twirling the cup to hear the sound of ice cubes hitting each other. Then it became awkwardly silent. I cleared my throat. "So...are you all set for the wedding?" I glanced from Max to Jenna.

"Getting there," Jenna said. "Your mom is fantastic. The wedding invitations have been mailed. She's already made a lot of appointments for me. I have my final fitting for my dress next week. I'm glad she's taking care of so many things for me. I've only had to answer her questions like 'What color? How many? What design?' I've been so sick that it was nice to have your mom take care of so many of the details."

"Yeah. Mom's great, but don't let her push you around. She's good at getting things her way."

"Most moms are. Though it would have been nice to have my mom help me with decisions for the wedding, I'm better off without her help. She would have driven me crazy. Your mom, on the other hand, has been giving me advice but accepting our decisions. My mom wanted to fly down and help me, but I told her that I had all the right connections from your parents."

"That's good." I nodded.

"Have you spoken to Becky yet?" Max asked. *That* came out of nowhere.

I looked away. "She won't talk to me."

"You going to sulk in your apartment, or are you going to do something about it? If you wait too long, it might be harder to fix it."

Max always looked after me and gave me words of wisdom. I guess that was what big brothers felt like they had to do. I nodded to let him know I heard him.

"If you love her, then don't let the past get in the way. The past is just that...the past. Fix what is now to have a better future," Max added.

"I know. Becca won't see me, so I need your help." I stared at Jenna. Her eyes opened wider. Was she glad I was finally going to do something about it?

"I thought you would never ask," Jenna said happily. "What's the plan?" "I'm not sure. It will have to be something she wouldn't expect."

After we came up with a plan, they went to Max's place. Though I still sulked, it was good to see Jenna and Max. It was great to have family support. I was glad Jenna was willing to help me out. Most women stuck to themselves and blamed the fight on the men.

CHAPTER 17
JENNA

"I now pronounce you husband and wife. Ladies and gentlemen, introducing Mr. and Mrs. Keith Hunt," the pastor announced.

The clapping echoed inside of the church as Keith and Nicole walked down the aisle. Nicole's white dress swayed with her steps. She looked stunning with just the right amount of makeup and her hair up with loose, curly strands along the side.

All of the bridesmaids and groomsmen followed the wedding couple after the ring bearer and the flower girl. On my way, my eyes shifted to my right, knowing exactly where Max sat. It didn't matter how many times he winked at me, it always felt like the first time, melting me to my core. I wanted to be in his arms—but the beautiful décor of flowers on every other pew and the lace that dangled along side by side distracted me—and I couldn't wait for our wedding day.

After we were announced at the reception, we all took our seats. Since we didn't sit in a traditional style, I was able to sit with Max. Pale lavender linen covered the tables, and topped with clear vases holding white and pink flowers. At each setting was a party favor—a little white box with a lavender bow that tied the box together. The box was printed with a picture of Nicole and Keith, and inside were assorted chocolates.

"Did I tell you how beautiful you look?" Max brushed his lips against my ear.

"I believe not enough." My lips curled into a crooked smile as I sliced the salmon into bite size pieces. I was craving steak, but I decided to feed my baby salmon instead since it had Omega 3. I read that it was good for the baby's development.

Max let out a soft chuckle and gave me a slice of his steak. He must have seen me drooling over his. "The lavender dress looks great on you, and you can't even tell that you're pregnant. But you look beautiful in any color...actually, I'd prefer them off you."

"Would you now, Mr. Knight?" I took a sip of my water.

Max nodded after taking a bite of mixed vegetables. Pressing into my ear so only I could hear, he said, "Anywhere and anytime. It's my pleasure to take care of my wife to be. I'll be your slave. I can do as you will, but be warned...I will give you pleasure beyond what you can handle."

Holy Max! His words were hot enough, but when his hand slid up to my clit from the front slit of the dress, I almost choked on my water.

"You better watch it, Mr. Knight, I might just end up getting under the table and taking you on." I couldn't believe I had said that, but I was having so much fun flirting with Max. And he made it so easy, it came out natural for me. I also knew Max loved this new side of me. He claimed he was the cause of the new Jenna, and I would let him know every time that he was right.

Max jerked a little when I glided my hand, which was already resting on his thigh, to his crotch. "Okay." He guided my hand out on the table. "I think we'd better stop or I'm going to have to cover myself if I need to get up."

I couldn't help but laugh, but one side of me felt guilty for being so happy. Becky sat with her matched up groomsman at a table adjacent to us. I wondered why she was sitting there. Surely Nicole would have sat us together. This made me wonder if she asked Nicole to seat us at different tables.

Becky was getting tired of me asking her questions about Matthew. It was like talking to a wall when that conversation came up. Knowing how stubborn Becky could be, I understood I wasn't going to win this one. Matthew and I had already conceived a plan. It had to be something sneaky. Something Jenna, the old me, wouldn't have done for sure.

"I'm so glad you're feeling better these days," Max said, placing broccoli on my plate.

"Me too." I was grateful it hadn't lasted too long. I'd read that morning sickness lasted during the entire pregnancy for some women. How awful.

Max held my hand underneath the table. "It hurt me to see you like that. I wanted to take it away for you. And if I could have taken your place, I would have."

I knew he would; my wants and needs were always first with Max. Giving him a warm smile was my reply to thank him. "Max, stop giving me your food. I'm not that hungry. You need to eat, too."

Max chuckled. "Sorry. I can't help it. You're eating for two. I can't wait to see your stomach grow."

When Max had told me he would be there for me, I didn't guess to what extent. I'd had a glimpse of his promise in action when he was there for me during the hardest time of my morning sickness. Although I never doubted him, he confirmed his commitment at that moment, and continued to confirm it with every new experience and every roadblock. Actions always spoke louder than words, and Max's actions were very loud.

After the father-daughter and mother-son dance, it was time for all of the groomsmen and bridesmaids to dance. Max growled softly when Andy took my hand.

"Have fun with Mandy," Max whispered quickly before I was whisked away.

I looked over my shoulder and mouthed, "Be a good boy."

Max gave me a shy, adorable grin.

That silly, funny, adorable, hot Max...how he turned me on.

Andy was a perfect gentleman the whole slow dance, but I would be too if I had someone staring at me the way Max watched Andy. I couldn't help but smile. Every time I looked at Max, he would wink and blow me a kiss. I was glad he didn't come and cut in to exchange places with Andy.

The wedding and the reception went smoothly, without a hitch. The planning and organizing paid off. Nicole had done a fabulous job, along with her helpers, including myself. Being overly fatigued, I decided to leave earlier than I had planned. Since Kate promised to look after Becky and take her home, Max and I left the party.

Becky

I walked out of my bedroom and saw Jenna sitting on the sofa, folding her laundry. She had gone to Max's place last night from the reception, so I figured she would stay today as well. "Jenna? You're home."

"I came home an hour ago," she replied.

I headed toward her, wondering if she'd come home because of me or if she'd had a fight with Max.

"What did you do for lunch?" Jenna asked as she continued to fold her laundry. "I called to see if you wanted to have lunch with me, but you didn't answer your phone, text, or email."

"Oh." I plopped down next to her on the coach. "I went out to eat."

"With Matthew?" Jenna's tone got a bit too excited. She even stopped to look at me.

"Nope. With Tanner." I started folding a towel from her basket.

"Tanner?"

"You forgot his name already. Tanner, my groomsman partner."

"Oh." Jenna sounded disappointed. "Did you have a nice lunch with him?"

"I did. He's very sweet. I like him a lot. I like hanging out with him. He's so funny, too. When I'm with him, he makes me forget my worries. Did you know he has a place in Paris? He told me that if I ever visited there, I could stay at his place."

Jenna gave me a half smile. "That's great, but what about Matthew?"

"I told you that we're done." I took a deep breath to keep myself from tearing up. Changing the subject, like I always did whenever Matthew came up, I asked, "Nicole's wedding was beautiful, wasn't it?"

"Yes," she agreed. "Did you stay till the end?"

"Yes, pretty much."

I changed the subject again and hoped Jenna would stay off the topic of Matthew. "I can tell you're feeling better. Your cheeks are glowing and you're eating more. I'm so relieved for you."

"Thank you." Jenna picked up her phone to text. "Do you have plans for dinner tonight?"

"No."

"Good." Jenna texted again, then slid her phone to the side of her so I couldn't see who she texted. "Dinner will be on me." After closing her eyes, she opened them again. I knew when she opened her mouth many questions would be pouring out. She had every right to ask. This was going to affect our entire circle of friendship. I wasn't ready to answer questions a week ago, but now I was. "You're going to be at my wedding, right? It's a little over a month away."

"Of course. I wouldn't miss it for anything." I smiled to reassure her.

"Matthew will be there."

"I know." I looked away. "Don't worry. I'm sure by then Matthew will have moved on, if not already, and we will all be fine."

Jenna took a deep sigh. "Matthew loves you and you love him."

Oh God. This was too hard. Talking about Matthew only made me miss him more; the wall I built to try to forget him was crumbling down. "Jenna," I swallowed, desperately trying to hold back my tears, "Matthew hurt me. You should have seen the look on his face. It's etched so deeply in my mind that that is the only thing I see."

"I understand, I really do, but you have to understand he was in shock. You knew about his past already and how much he was hurting. Then you came along. You were the only person he wanted to have a relationship with. I know he tried to call you. I know he tried to see you."

I rolled my eyes. "Matthew told you?"

"No. Max did. Matthew is hurting a lot, too."

A part of me felt good that he hurt, too, but that didn't mean a thing. "He walked out on me." I paused. "I can't do this, Jenna. You know my record with guys. I just added Matthew to my list." When I stood up, the towel I was supposed to be folding dropped into the basket. Not wanting to show Jenna my tears, I headed for my room.

"Becky." Jenna froze me in place when her tone didn't sound as sweet as usual. I turned to see her standing. "You know damn well that Matthew does not belong on that list. People have their own way of dealing with things. I've always respected your ways even when I disagreed with them. You need to hear Matthew out. He at least deserves that. Then you can make up your mind."

"Okay," I sighed. Even though she was right, I only said that to get her off my back. Jenna had no idea how much I missed him and ached for him. Not a second went by that I didn't think of him and wish he was there with me.

"Okay?" Jenna sounded surprised.

"Okay."

She grabbed her purse and started walking toward the door. Her laundry was still spread out on the sofa.

"Where are you going?" I asked. She was acting strange. "It's almost dinner time. Are you trying to tell me I should follow you now?"

Jenna ignored me and opened the door. I froze. My heart took a dive right out of my chest at the first sight of Matthew's body. Unable to look him in the eye, I turned away. When I heard the door close, I knew Jenna had left.

That sneaky girl. I didn't know she was capable of such treachery.

From that one-second glimpse of Matthew, my stomach fluttered in the familiar way it always did when I saw him. This made the ache even more painful. He looked so tired and worn, I wondered if he lacked sleep like me.

"You can at least say hello to an old friend," Matthew said, heading to the dining area. He pulled out a chair and sat in the same position as when I had done a lap dance for him. Recalling that incident made me laugh inside, but I would not let that affect me.

"Hi. What are you doing here?" My tone was cold, but I didn't care.

"You wouldn't take my phone calls, answer the door, or even text me back, so I had to reach out to my last resource."

"Consider your last resource no longer your resource for anything. After the stunt she just pulled, she's no longer my friend," I snapped, though I didn't mean a word I said.

"You don't mean that." Matthew leaned forward. I jerked back, thinking he was coming for me, and I bumped into the doorframe.

Ignoring him, I changed the subject. "It was nice of you to stop by, but I'm busy right now."

"You're lying and we need to talk. I'm not leaving until you hear me out," he said sternly. I knew he meant it by the look on his face. "Come sit next to me and let's talk like mature adults."

I narrowed my eyes at him. I knew I was being stubborn, but this was the only way I knew how to deal with problems. Running away had always been the easiest way out. "Fine. But I'll stand here."

"Okay." Matthew nodded. "I'll go first. Why didn't you take my phone calls?"

"Because there is nothing to talk about. We were broken the minute you walked out the door."

"I told you I needed space. I didn't say we were done. Don't put your words in my mouth, Becca."

For some reason, my anger grew. It boiled inside of me with every breath. "You thought I knew that my friend killed your precious Tessa, and that I kept it a secret from you," I huffed. I couldn't tame my emotions any longer; the hurt and anger poured out. "You blamed me for her death. You walked out on me even knowing how devastated I would feel." Oh shit! Tears were coming.

"Asking you was a natural question, and I didn't blame you for her death. Why would you think that?"

I couldn't hold back the tears any longer. "It was the way you looked at me. And then it was the way you wouldn't look at me. It was the way you said her name, and the way you said mine. It's what you believe in...friends don't let friends drive drunk. How could you even want me after what's happened? What I did? You could have been with her. You would have been married by now, living happily ever after. I can't believe—" I stopped. The words had flowed out of me so fast, I had allowed myself to be vulnerable for that second, but no more.

Matthew rushed to me and placed his hands on either side of the door. I had nowhere to go as he prisoned me like before. Oh God! I was going to lose it. Feeling dizzy from his proximity, I turned my head away.

"Becca," Matthew gripped my arms. "Look at me." When I refused, his voice got louder. "Look at me!"

Tears flowed against my will when I did. Seeing his eyes red and teary pained me, too. "Damn you, Becca. Stop punishing yourself. This isn't your fault." Matthew pulled me to his chest. The smell of him intoxicated me to the point I wanted him. It took every ounce of will power in me to stop myself from kissing him when his lips inched toward mine.

Though Matthew's grip was too strong, I managed to create a space between us. Wiping my tears, I said, "It doesn't matter if it's my fault or not. Every time I look at you, I see her. You and I will never be the same. Her death came between us. Her death is fate telling us we don't belong together."

"I'm so sorry I hurt you. I was in shock. You can't blame me for being in shock, Becca. If the roles were reversed, you would have been the same way. And you're wrong. Tessa's death opened the road for our paths to cross. Don't think of it as a negative thing. Fate screwed me once before, but it made up for it when I met you. My heart was empty and you filled it up with hope. You are the reason I found love again. You're the lighthouse to my storm. You're the beacon that brought me home. You can stand there and tell me how wrong I am, but I'm not giving up on us. I'm not going to let you go that easily, Becca. I love you, and I know you love me, too."

Oh God! What could I say after that? I wanted to tell him I felt the same. However, I loved him so much that I would rather push him away. When he walked out on me, he'd crushed me. I felt a constant stabbing ache in my heart that never stopped bleeding. Once I felt the raw ache of what it was like to lose him, I didn't know if I could go through it again. "You're wrong, Matthew. In fact, I have a date tonight. So I think you should leave. He'll be here any minute."

"Tell me I'm wrong after this."

I had no idea what he was talking about until I felt his hands on my cheeks. Matthew conquered my lips without my permission. I was in so much shock that I let him at first. This was the very thing I wanted to avoid, but I had no will power. It fled completely the second his lips touched mine. Missing Matthew had killed me the past week. At the first taste of him, I lost it. I utterly freakin' lost it.

My heart pounded faster. I wanted to rip off his clothes and feel him inside of me, to have him stay there forever. Tears poured as fast as my panting breath while I kissed him back with passion and hunger. The pain and anger subsided, until I remembered why we had fought in the first place. Then I heard Matthew's words echoing in my mind, "Her name is Tessa Young," as if to remind me how much he loved her and that I was just a replacement.

Managing to pull away, I wiped my mouth, disgusted at myself. "I want you to leave," I said breathlessly. "I need to get ready."

Matthew let out a laugh. What was so funny?

Since I wouldn't look at him, he leaned down to me and whispered in my ear, "I know you still care, Becca. I felt it in your kiss. I'm going to prove to you that we're meant to be together. I'm going to leave you now since that's what you want, but I'll be back. I'm not giving up. By the way, I know you don't have a date. Jenna texted me to let me know you were free."

I closed my eyes and cringed after Matthew kissed my cheek and left. My heart softened a little bit and my guilt lessened, but it was still there. It felt wrong to kiss the man I loved when he should have been with someone else, and would've been had it not been for my poor judgment and careless ways.

CHAPTER 18
BECKY

I had no idea what Matthew had meant by showing me how much he cared for me, but if the number of roses were any indication, his love for me was more than I could measure or comprehend. Vases of roses began arriving at our place. Jenna kept going to the door and bringing back more and more. At first I thought they were for her, but they were all for me...except a couple of them.

Jenna wore a huge smile. "See how much he loves you? Don't punish yourself and him. Take him back, Becky."

Feeling overwhelmed, I inhaled the sweet fragrance and took it all in. I tried not to smile, but I couldn't help it. No one had ever apologized to me so grandly before. Matthew could have said, "Screw you," and walked away, but he didn't. I needed some time. If he could give me a little bit more, then I might be able to move on with him.

"Your phone was ringing." Jenna passed it to me and headed back to the kitchen. She was filling the vases with water.

"Thanks." I scrolled through it to see who had tried to reach me. One call from Tanner, and another one from Matthew. I texted Tanner first and let him know I was considering visiting him since I was planning to attend the London book convention. I could take the train and swing by his place after the convention. I scrolled up to find Matthew's.

Just in case you didn't read my messages on the cards, I'm texting it to you. Each petal on all of the roses is how many times I'm saying I'm sorry for hurting you. Each petal on all of the roses is how many times I'm saying I miss you. And each petal on all of the roses is how much I love you. Call me when you're ready. I'll be waiting.

Tears streamed down my face and my heart lit up in ways it hadn't for weeks. "I miss you, too," I mumbled under my breath. My fingers itched to text him those words, but I couldn't. When I looked up, Jenna was right beside me.

"Hey." With tears in her eyes, she smiled at me.

Then I lost it. I embraced her and sobbed like crazy in her arms. I needed her comfort. I needed for her to tell me that everything was going to be fine, but she had no idea what I was going through. Nobody knew. I had never told her about my condition.

"It's okay. Let it all out." She rubbed my back, holding me tightly. "I don't understand why you are doing this to yourself, but I do understand why you feel guilty. The first step is telling your friends how you feel. The second step is talking about it and working things out. I'm not in your shoes, so I don't know what it's truly like. I'm not judging you, but you deserve all the happiness life presents to you. Don't let it slip away. I'm sorry, but Tessa had her chance. God took her away, not you. You didn't kill her, Becky. It was just her time to go. Someone better was meant for Matthew."

I nodded, letting her know that I'd heard every single one of her wise words, and I'd needed to. Pulling back, I wiped my tears. "Thank you. I needed to hear that."

"I can't believe you didn't tell me. All these years you kept this bottled up. It was eating up your heart and soul,

Becky. I don't care about Tessa. She is only a name to me. But I care about you. You're a wonderful person who deserves Matthew more than anyone else does. Don't think you deserve anyone less. If Matthew was an asshole, I would tell you to forget him, but look around you. This place is filled with his love for you."

I glanced around, still unbelieving. Everywhere I looked was a reminder of Matthew. "Okay." I nodded. "I'll talk to Matthew, but I need to take one step at a time. He's going to have to give me space. We can't just jump into where we were."

"I understand, but Matthew is going to Sydney this weekend for the annual Australia Fashion Show."

"Oh...I'll be going to the London Book Fair the same week. Then several weeks later is your wedding." Seeing Jenna's worried eyes I jumped in again. "Don't worry. I'll be there, even if Matthew and I can't work it out. I wouldn't miss it for the world."

Jenna rubbed my arm with a caring smile. "Just do what your heart tells you to do. That is what you always told me. Now I'm giving you the same advice back. Your heart won't lie to you."

"I love you, Jenna." I pulled her in for a tight squeeze. "What am I going to do when you get married?"

Jenna sniffed into my sweater. "I'll always be here for you." Her voice cracked. "I'm just a phone call away. When you and Matthew get back together, you'll be a floor below me."

I knew she was saying those words to make us feel better, but we both knew that once she got married things would be different. It already was since she got together with Max, and it would get worse when she married him. I wouldn't have it any other way for her. She deserved all the happiness. Me, on the other hand, I didn't know.

Maybe Matthew and I would work things out, and maybe we wouldn't, but that was all up to fate. Before I decided to do anything, I needed to take a trip to the doctor's office again. If my predicament was what I thought, then I was in deep shit.

After the doctor's visit I went to Starbucks near my apartment. With a hazelnut coffee in my hand, I settled into my favorite corner table where the sun shone just enough on my back to give me warmth. As I took a sip, it soothed my throat and blocked out my troubles.

I had an important decision to make, but the question was should I take care of it on my own? I didn't want to trouble anyone. It would have to wait till after Jenna's wedding. How would I tell Matthew? Either way, I was screwed. Surprisingly, I was calm...too calm. Maybe I was in shock. I jerked a little when a body brushed against mine. A part of me wished it was Matthew. Reminiscing on our last encounter there, it made me miss him. I didn't know why I thought it was Matthew, but I glanced up with a smile.

"I was wondering if this seat was taken?" a tall, good-looking guy asked.

Feeling disappointed, I was about to tell him that it was when someone else spoke for me.

"Actually, this seat is mine." His tone was territorial.

I flashed my eyes in the direction of that familiar voice, and saw a sexy smirk across his face. My heart thumped mercilessly from just the sight of him. Our eyes finally met, then he turned away and stared hard at the guy who was still standing there waiting for my answer.

"Uh," I started to say, but no words came out of my mouth. However, I didn't have to say anything as Matthew pulled out the chair and sat. The guy scowled and left.

"Hello, Becca," Mathew said. "You're not working today?"

I took a sip to give myself some time as I tried to decide if I should tell him the truth. "I just got back from a doctor's appointment and I decided to stop by here."

"Is everything okay? Are you sick?"

I shook my head and took another sip. "Everything is fine. Just a routine check up," I lied. Biting my lip, I forced myself not to cry. I wanted to jump in his arms and tell him the truth, but I couldn't. "Why are you here?" I diverted the subject.

Matthew leaned forward on the table with his arms crossed. "I came by, hoping you would be here. You told me you needed space and I'm trying to give it to you, but I miss you. I miss us." Matthew paused. "I was going to sit at the opposite corner table and watch you, but then I saw that guy checking you out. I wanted to punch him."

"Matthew," I said softly, but my high pitch made some heads turn.

"He was lucky we were in public," he added. "I came here because I wanted to be where we shared our very first not so friendly connection." I laughed, recalling that day clearly. "It's the day you stole my heart, and you never gave it back." He leaned forward, piercing me with his eyes. "It's still with you."

When Matthew reached for my hand, I let him take it. "Becca, let me in. Let me help you. Whatever you're feeling or whatever your worries are, I'll take it away. I'll fix it. I promise you. If the roses don't show you how I feel, at least hear my words. Let me make this right."

He had no idea how much I wanted to say yes and jump into his arms, but not until I got more results, so I had to think of something fast. "Matthew, let's talk when you get back from Australia. You're leaving tomorrow, right?"

"Come with me," he pleaded.

I looked away. "I can't. I'm going to the London Book Fair. It's my first time."

Matthew nodded, but it hurt me to see the sadness in his eyes. And I knew it would hurt even more when I built the courage to tell him unwanted news.

"All right, Becca. I'm still going to text you to make sure you're okay, and I expect you to text me back to let me know. Otherwise, I will worry and call everyone you know. Hell, I'd call the whole damn world just to know you're okay."

"Got it." I smiled.

"Well, Becca, like before, duty calls. I'll talk to you soon." Matthew stood up and planted a long, lingering kiss on my cheek and left.

Without turning to see him walk out the door, I looked down at my drink and let the tears that I'd held in stream down my face.

CHAPTER 19
MATTHEW

There was something strange about our conversation. I knew Becca wanted to be with me, so then what was it? Becca didn't know I looked through the window when I came out of Starbucks. She was wiping away tears. Wanting to comfort her, I almost went back in, but decided not to. Whatever was going on with her, she didn't want to share with me yet, and knowing Becca, I couldn't force her to tell me. She'd only close up even more.

Her pain was my pain. It hurt me to leave her, but I had no choice. All I could do was wait and give her space. Needing to get ready for Australia, I headed back to work with a stabbing ache in my heart.

Jenna

"Oh, Jenna, you look..." Ellen's eyes beamed with happiness, or were they tears? "So beautiful. Wait until Max sees you in your wedding dress."

Becky had already started tearing up. She turned her back on me to wipe them, then looked up at me again with a smile. "Gorgeous, Jenna."

"Thanks." I smiled shyly. "Becky, go try on your dress."

As Becky headed to the dressing room, I stared at myself in the mirror. I couldn't believe I was wearing an actual wedding dress. It was form fitted on top with spaghetti straps, and flared out from the waist. I felt like a princess.

"Here you go," Tina, the saleslady, said. She helped me put the tiara on, along with the veil that hung to my waist.

Something was different about the tiara. Although it looked like the one I'd picked out, it had tiny sparkling crystals from one end to the other. It glistened just the right amount against the light, but not too overbearing. "I really like this, but I don't think you gave me the right one. This might belong to someone else." I spoke as she walked toward the customer who had walked in. Since she didn't stop, I assumed she didn't hear me.

"Jenna," Ellen interrupted, "I actually brought that tiara from home. I told Tina to give it to you. I was hoping you might like it enough to wear it. I think you and I have the same taste. We like things simple yet elegant. And this tiara means a lot to me. It was my mother's. She's no longer with us."

Happiness filled my heart. I knew Ellen approved of me, but I never knew to what extent until today. I didn't mean to, but my eyes became glassy with tears. "Ellen," I gushed, and wrapped my arms around her, "it's beautiful. Thank you so much. This means a lot to me."

"I don't have a daughter," she said, as we let go of each other. "I wanted to have more children, but we were so busy. Rob and I hardly had any time for our sons. It wouldn't have been fair to the third child, the one I would have wished to be a girl. But we are so lucky. Max and Matthew turned out to be fine gentlemen. We're very proud of them both. Just like how your mom is proud of you."

"She is. She can't wait to meet you. They'll be here a week before the wedding." I paused to change the subject. "Ellen, you can think of this as gaining a daughter. You've been so kind to me since the moment we met. I was worried that you wouldn't approve of me, but you welcomed me with open arms. You have no idea how relieved I was. And you have no idea how much I'm grateful for all of your help."

Ellen chuckled lightly. "How ironic. I was worried you wouldn't like me. Because to tell you the truth, I didn't like my mother-in-law."

"Really?" I let out a snort.

"Don't tell Max that. He loved his grandmother. But as a mother-in-law, she wanted things her way. So I try not to say too much because I don't want to be like her." Ellen smiled. "Enough of my mother-in-law. Now, you have something old. Do you have anything new, blue, or borrowed?"

"I have a blue garter," I blurted, then became shy. I didn't know why, but any topic that related to sex was not something I wanted to talk to Ellen about, even if it was just a garter. After all, it was her son she would be referring to. "I just need something new and borrowed."

Just then Becky walked out in her lavender bridesmaid dress.

"You look beautiful," I said, smiling. Becky's dress was similar to mine, but it didn't flare out like a wedding dress.

"I love the dress on you," Ellen said to Becky.

"Thank you."

"When I was getting married many years ago, the bridesmaid dresses were horrendous. Thank God they improved over time."

"I have to agree with you there," Becky said.

Tina came back to make sure our dresses fit perfectly. Last week's alteration on my dress made the dress a little tight, but not unbearable. I had lost several pounds last week from not eating well, but I was glad to have gained it back. Having the morning sickness disappear as quickly as it came made me happy. I was finally starting to enjoy having a baby inside of me.

"Shall we have lunch before you both have to be back to work?" Ellen asked.

"Sure," Becky said. "I'm free, but I need to be back soon for the London trip. I'm taking the red eye."

"I'm starving," I seconded.

"Perfect. I'll call to make a reservation." Ellen took out her cell phone. "Why are you going to London, Becky?"

"I'm going to a book convention."

"That sounds fun."

Becky and I walked to the dressing room with our arms linked together. "I can't believe it's only two weeks away, Jenna."

"Me, too. And I can't believe I'm pregnant."

Becky leaned against her dressing room door and smiled. "I'm so happy for you."

"Thank you. And I'm glad you're working things out with Matthew."

"Even if Matthew and I weren't together, I still would be there at your wedding, you know that, right? I wouldn't miss it for anything."

"I know," I answered, but I wasn't sure. "Do you love Matthew?"

"I miss him. He asked me to go with him, but I have to go to London."

"I understand. Just remember what I said. If you love each other, then that's all that matters."

"But sometimes things happen you have no control over," Becky said quickly. She got into her dressing room so fast, I didn't have a chance to ask her what she meant by that.

Becky was hiding something. And I was determined to find out what.

CHAPTER 20
JENNA

Matthew and Becky in different countries made my heart feel uneasy. It was silly to think this way, but the distance between them seemed like it would create a barrier, and it would be harder for them to get back together. I had to stop thinking silly thoughts. Becky assured me everything was fine and they would talk things through, so why didn't I believe her?

Since our whole office staff had gone to Australia with Matthew, I was left alone. There wasn't much to do since May's issue had been formatted and was ready to go. We were holding back to include the pictures from the fashion show. Though I wanted to go with my department, Max insisted that I not fly. At the time we'd discussed it, I had bad morning sickness and just thinking of flying made me nauseous. I had agreed not to go without a fight.

I jumped when the phone trilled next to me. It seemed loud since there were no other noises besides me typing. I picked up the receiver while my heart pounded rapidly.

"Max," I heaved.

"Jenna. Did I scare you? You sound so surprised."

"You almost gave me a heart attack."

"I can give you a lot more than a heart attack."

I laughed lightly. Leave it to Max to flirt whenever he had the chance. That was one of the things I loved about him. His playfulness could soothe me anytime. "I'm going to take you up on that offer, Mr. Knight."

A soft chuckle rang in my ear. "It will be my pleasure. Are you sitting on your chair?"

I knew where he was going, but I pretended not to. "Yes, should I be sitting somewhere else?"

"Maybe you should be sprawled out on your desk ready for me. After all, there's just you in the office and everyone else is in another country."

"You're terrible for letting me stay here all by myself, Mr. Knight. A girl can get really lonely in this big office all by herself."

"That's the reason why I'm standing by the door."

I looked up and melted seeing the handsome hunk in front of me. His territorial gaze and the way he looked at me with a sexy grin made me quiver all over, especially when I saw him lock the door. "Jenna." My name rolled off his tongue with heat and passion. "I love it when you wear easy access clothes." The next thing I knew, I was in his arms.

"Max." I think that is what I said. Dizzy from his body heat, the way he nuzzled me made me weak at the knees. *Oh Max. Take me. Take me right now on my desk.* As if he could read my thoughts, his lips conquered mine.

"Max," I started to say as he laid me gently across my desk. My legs were bent so that my heels rested on the edge of the desk. With my legs spread apart, he had a clear view of my G-string. "Don't you have a meeting right now?" I whimpered.

"You know my schedule way better than my own secretary." Max lightly kissed down my leg, to my ankle, back up with his tongue, and slid inside of my panties to my clit. I gasped.

"Max." I heaved, arching my back. Wanting to touch him, I reached for him, but he wouldn't let me. My muscles had gone completely limp. I had no control over them.

Max continued to tease me, lick me, suck me until I felt like I was going to climax from his tongue alone. I needed more. I needed him. Finally managing to grip his arms, I pulled him up halfway. "Max. Please," I pleaded, knowing how he liked to hear me beg.

It didn't work. Max stood up suddenly and helped me up, too. "Jenna, we need to go."

Baffled, I looked at him for more explanation.

Max took my hand, kissed the back of it, and looked squarely in my eye. "My, Jenna. Do I make you forget? Do I make you feel so good that I could make you forget we have a doctor's appointment?"

My eyes shot wider. Oh my God! "Max," I squealed, straightening my skirt and my hair. "You're so bad." I rushed to grab my purse and leaned up against his strong chest. "I mean...you make me feel so good, Max. You make me forget everything. Let's go." I grabbed his hand and led him out the door, but then I stopped. Hearing a jovial chuckle meant only one thing. Max loved the compliment and his ego went up a notch.

"You think what you just did to me was funny?" I leaned up against his chest and gave him my serious face, but I busted out laughing when Max puffed his bottom lip out with droopy eyes. He was too freakin' adorable. I wanted to suck that bottom lip.

"No, but I made you laugh." His browed twitched playfully.

He was so right. "Oh yeah? Let's make a bet and see who gives in first. The week before our wedding, we're not allowed to see each other. We can text, but we can't spend the night at each other's place. Let's see who breaks the rule first."

"You think I'll break first, don't you?"

"Yup." I glared at him. "Deal or no deal?"

"What's my reward?"

"What?" I smacked him lightly. "Your reward? Maybe I'll win."

"Hmmm." Max rocked us back and forth, still holding onto me. "We'll see about that. I'll think about what I want from you. I can't wait to win."

"Bad, Max, really bad."

"I can't wait to do things to make you break."

Oh no! What had I gotten myself in to?

Max

I had to admit, I was excited to go to my first doctor's appointment with Jenna. It seemed surreal that I was going to be a father earlier than I expected, but I was okay with it. I had to be. Jenna needed me, and I needed to get a hold of myself for this life-changing event.

"Dr. Howard will see you now," a petite nurse said, smiling. Keeping the door open, she waited for us to enter to close the door behind her. She was shorter than Jenna, but older.

"This is my...my fiancé, Max," Jenna introduced as we walked down the hallway. She stumbled over her words for a moment. It's not a word you would use everyday.

"Nice to meet you, Max."

I shook her hand. "It's nice to meet you...Anne." I hesitated a little, trying to get a glimpse of her nametag.

With a quick glance, I looked up. Her nametag was right on her left breast. I didn't want her to think I was staring at it.

With a smile, Anne opened the door for us and entered behind us. After she asked a bunch of questions, measured Jenna, checked her blood pressure, and asked her to put on a gown, she left.

"Does she ask you this many questions every time you come?" I asked, sitting next to Jenna.

"This is my second appointment. I'm guessing she'll ask me tons more as we get closer."

"I see. I guess I understand why. Are you sure you're feeling better and not just saying so to appease me?" I was worried. I had seen Jenna eat better, but I did wonder if somehow she was faking it.

"Yes, Max. Don't worry." Jenna sounded a bit annoyed, so I decided to keep my mouth shut. Just then, the doctor walked in.

"Good afternoon, Jenna." The doctor turned to me. What the hell? He was a man. I was completely in shock. Knowing Jenna and the way she was, I assumed she would be too embarrassed to see a male doctor. This was her OB/GYN? That meant that he saw her practically naked. It shouldn't bother me, but it did. It was one thing to hear a name, it was another to see the man's face who would be poking at my Jenna. And being a young doctor didn't help either. He had hardly any years of experience behind him.

"This is my fiancé, Max."

"It's nice to meet you," Dr. Howard said and sat on the rolling chair. After he opened up Jenna's file, he started asking questions. "How are you feeling?"

"I'm much better. I'm starting to eat more."

"That's great. It looks like you've gained a couple of pounds." He paused. "Any signs of distress?"

"No. So far so good."

"Good. Would you like to hear the baby's heartbeat?" Dr. Howard looked at me.

That question came as a surprise. It took me longer than a second to answer. "Sure." I think the sound of my tone was uncertain.

"Lay back for me, Jenna."

Grrr! I didn't like that way he said those words. Now he was lifting her gown to expose her stomach. I had to calm down. After he put a splat of gel on this device that looked like a small, hand held back massager, he circulated it around Jenna's stomach until...Holy Jesus! The sound of a tiny heart beating rapidly was the most beautiful sound I'd ever heard, aside from Jenna's moans of pleasure. My heart expanded with bliss, and having a baby became more real to me.

My eyes locked on Jenna's with a warm smile. That warmth spread through my body, giving an indescribable feeling. I didn't know what to say or do except stare lovingly at my wife-to-be and think about the unexpected baby growing inside. Something happened to me as shivers of joy ran down my spine. Another level of excitement rushed through and I couldn't wait for our baby to be born.

"We should know the sex of the baby by next month," Dr. Howard said, helping Jenna up. I didn't mind his hands on her this time. In fact, I grew a new profound respect for him as soon as I heard the heartbeat. He was going to be the one helping Jenna through this pregnancy, and most importantly, he was going to be the one delivering our baby.

Jenna looked at me without a word. She was asking me if we wanted to know the sex of the baby. "Maybe we should keep it between us. Whatever you want, babe."

"Max and I will discuss this further at home." Jenna sat back into her chair.

"Sounds good," Dr. Howard said. "The baby sounds healthy. I'll see you next month."

I cleared my throat, feeling uneasy about asking a question that might sound selfish. "I was wondering...is it safe to...when should we stop? Will it hurt the baby?"

Dr. Howard's eyes sparkled with amusement and he let out a soft chuckle. "You can have sex as long as Jenna is comfortable. You are not hurting the baby in any way. That placenta in Jenna's uterus is thick and strong. Her hormones will be skyrocketing. Enjoy. See you both next month. Oh, by the way, I would strongly encourage you both to take a Lamaze class. It will help you prepare for the possibilities and answer questions you might have." With a smile, he left.

CHAPTER 21
MATTHEW

It had been less than a week, but I missed Becca like crazy. Feeling like there was something left unsaid, and like we weren't together, didn't give me any comfort either. Her messages, always short and to the point, didn't help me guess how she felt. Something was wrong. There was nothing I could do from so many miles away; I would have to wait until I got back.

It was strange to be in a country that had the opposite weather. The memo I'd read before packing said it would be cooler. Thank goodness I'd brought a thicker coat. Before I left Los Angeles, the weather was warm, seventy-five degrees, but it was freezing cold here. I had to admit, their accent amused me and I purposely asked a lot of questions just to hear them speak. My co-workers and I were heading to dinner, but just before I left I texted Becca.

What are you doing?
I'm in London now.
I feel like I've been gone a long time.
We'll see each other soon.
You're not running away, are you?
No.
You want to talk on the phone?
I have things to do.
Now?
Yes. We can talk when I get back.

Have a safe flight back home.

You too.

I miss you.

Becca didn't respond to my last message, and it hurt like hell. It felt like she was trying to end our relationship. If she didn't care for me anymore then I would have to let her go, but if it was because of the situation with Tessa, I would not let her. We'd just have to get through this.

One of my male co-workers knocked at the door. "Ready boss?"

"I'll be right there," I replied, staring at my phone, waiting for Becca's message. Fuck! Forget it. I was going to enjoy my friends, who I'd been turning down chances to go out with this week.

Everyone had gone to a nightclub after dinner except for me. Feeling like a ton of bricks rested on my shoulders, I didn't want to damper my co-workers' moods by sulking in front of them. Instead of going straight to my room, I swung my coat over my shoulder, loosened my tie, rolled up the sleeves of my dress shirt halfway, and took a detour to the bar near the lobby.

There were a few couples at the tables and some people sitting at the bar. It was dark and nearly empty, just the way I liked it.

"Give me any hard liquor," I said to the bartender.

"That bad?" The bartender poured the liquor into the glass.

"I guess it could be worse." I took the bill and signed it. "Please, charge it to my room."

"Thank you." He sounded grateful, seeing that I left a good tip for him.

With a drink in my hand, I sat in the corner booth alone, thinking of Becca. A pretty brunette startled me when she brushed up against me.

"I hope you don't mind. You looked so lonely. I thought you might want company." Her tone was sultry and definitely flirty, but I was turned on by her accent. Having a closer look, I noticed her beautiful hazel eyes with long eyelashes and full lips.

"Actually..." My eyes fell to her low-cut dress. Leaning forward, she practically threw her boobs at me. And man, could she expose them even more? She was an attractive woman. It was too bad she lacked self-esteem and felt like she had to dress like that to get a man to notice her. She was the type of woman I could have a one-night stand with, but I had to get that thought out of my head.

"My name is Christina." She licked her lips when she said her name. Then she tried to run her hands across my chest, but I stopped her. "Don't be like that. Let me make you feel better. You look so sad. A handsome guy like you shouldn't be all by himself." Her hand slid up my thigh so fast I jumped when her hand set on my crotch.

I don't know why, but anger struck me. Not at her, but at Becca. It came rolling so fast I had no idea how to process it. Maybe it was the way Becca shut me out, or maybe it was the lack of communication between us. Maybe it was that last text I sent her, and that she'd never replied back with, "I miss you, too." Maybe she was messing with me, trying to hold on to our friendship until after Jenna's wedding and then she'd let me go.

Fuck that.

I stood up, forcing Christina to do the same when I scooted out of my seat. "Come with me." She happily followed behind me.

What was I doing? Thoughts of Becca entered my mind: her smile, her smell, and her naked body on mine. If I did this, then for sure Becca and I would be over.

Just as we were about to get on the elevator, I turned to Christina. "I can't do this." I raked my hair back with a heavy sigh. "Sorry. You're an attractive woman, but I'm with someone."

"You don't look happy. I won't tell her."

I let out a chuckle. The woman was definitely a bimbo. "Of course you won't tell her. You don't know her. Sorry. Go find someone else that will be nice to you."

"I don't need nice. I like it rough and hard. You can fuck me anywhere. I just want one night with your delicious body. I'm lonely just like you."

Shit! Her words, her gorgeous body and face were hard to turn down, but I had to. "Sorry, doll. If circumstances were different we would be up in my room, but not today."

She looked pissed off. "Your loss." That was all she had to say before she stormed off.

What the hell was I thinking? I ran my hand down my face in frustration. I missed home. I missed Becca. Just a few more nights.

Becky

I was always short and to the point when messaging back to Matthew. It wasn't lack of words, but fear that I would break down. I missed him so much that it hurt like hell.

171

The London Book Fair was a huge distraction. I loved being lost in books and being surrounded by people who loved them. Excitement drifted in the air and sparkled in people's eyes. It never failed. Every time I went to a book convention, I always spotted the person who brought rolling luggage to purchase as many books as possible, and not have to carry them in their hands. Now that was love for books.

My job for the day was done. I'd met a lot of potential authors, passed out my cards to publisher reps, and made international contacts. Just as I was about to head back to the hotel, I got a message from Tanner.

Becky, stopping by to see you.
I'm about to go back to my hotel.
Have dinner with me.
Okay.
I'll text you the address of the restaurant.

I arrived at the restaurant to see Tanner waiting by the door. His dark hair was slicked back and he was smoking. His green eyes sparkled underneath the light when he saw me. He wore dark slacks and a buttoned long-sleeved shirt. Lean and nicely toned, he was about six feet tall.

"You smoke? You're a doctor and you smoke?" I teased, as if to scold him playfully.

"Hey, beautiful. Don't tell my clients." He flashed a nervous smile and crushed the cigarette with his foot. Then he gave me a warm hug and kissed my cheek. Sliding his hand behind my back, he opened the door and led me to our seats. He had arrived earlier than me and reserved them. There were two glasses of water on the table, and I graciously started drinking mine.

"Did you have a productive weekend?" Tanner asked, flagging the waitress.

"Yes, I did. Thank you for asking."

When the waitress came, we ordered, and Tanner started asking questions again. "How are things with Matthew?"

Tanner knew I was with Matthew, but he also knew things weren't going well between us at the time of Nicole's wedding. "Why do you ask?" I tried to sound as polite as possible. After all, he was only making friendly conversation.

"You look a little out of it, and your eyes tell me there's trouble in paradise."

I let out a soft laugh. "Not only are you a doctor, you're also a psychologist?"

"I can be whatever you want if I can bring back that pretty smile of yours."

"There is only one thing that will make me smile, but according to how it's looking, I don't think I'll ever be able to smile again."

"That bad?"

"From my perspective, yes, that bad."

Tanner took a sip of his water. "Why don't you tell me about it? I can give you a diagnosis. No charge. Free on me," he snorted.

"But you don't specialize. You're a family doctor."

"We had to learn the general aspects of all health situations and conditions. I may not specialize in a specific field, but I know enough. If I don't, I'll let you know." He winked.

"Okay." I nodded. After all, he was a doctor and I needed a second opinion.

"Before you tell me what it is, my place is a short train ride from here. Would you like to talk there? I promise this isn't a pick up line. And I promise I won't try anything." He lifted his hands to surrender. "I swear."

When I didn't answer fast enough, he continued, "My place is all yours. I have two bedrooms. You are welcome to stay. I told you before you could stay during the book fair, but you are so stubborn." He laughed. "Any friend of Nicole and Keith is a friend of mine."

"I would love to see Paris."

"Do you have to fly out soon?"

"Actually, I left the ticket open ended. After all, I was coming to London, and confession time...I thought about visiting you in Paris." A part of me felt guilty toward Matthew. I didn't tell him I might visit a friend. This would keep me from going home for several days, and he was expecting us to talk as soon as we both got back. I also didn't think he would be keen on my visit, especially since Tanner was a guy he'd never met.

"That's great. Let me take you back to your hotel so we can get your luggage."

"I can only stay for a few days. I need to go back and settle things with Matthew." Tanner started texting. "What are you doing?"

"I'm taking tomorrow off."

"Are you serious?"

"It's Monday. It's my busiest day. And yes, I would ditch work to hang out with a friend who I won't be able to see for another who knows how long."

"You can always fly to Los Angeles."

"Keith is a dear friend, but it will be a while before I visit him."

"Here you go," the waitress said, placing our plates in front of us, then left.

"Well...if you ever do come to Los Angeles, you can stay with me."

Tanner's eyes grew wider. "Really? How about Matthew?"

"He has his own place." My tone came out flat and uncaring.

"You make it sound like you're already broken up, and you haven't even spoken to him about whatever situation you're in. You should just tell me now because my curiosity is killing me."

With a deep intake of breath, I told him about my dilemma. Not just that, I told him about Amber and Tessa.

"Oh, Becky, Becky...you need to tell him, girl. That's not fair to him."

"Don't make me feel guilty, Tanner. You're supposed to be on my side."

"I think you're afraid. You're running away. I could've asked you to go to China and you would be willing to come with me. You're a runner."

"A what?" I laughed.

"When things go wrong, you try to pretend it didn't happen. You would say or do anything to block out the pain. And the further you go away from the situation, the easier it is for you to deal with." He rested his hand on mine. "Regardless, it will still be there, waiting for you."

Tanner was right, yet I didn't want to hear it. I pulled my hand away. "I just need a few more days."

"To do what? It's not going to go away."

Tears started to form in my eyes. I didn't want to cry in front of Tanner. I needed my friends. What the hell was I thinking? "I know it won't go away." My irritation level rose. "Do you want me to stick around or what?"

Tanner gave me a crooked smile and leaned back into his chair. "Sorry. I'm just worried about you."

"I'm fine," I sighed.

"Eat your pasta before it gets cold." He pointed to my plate with his fork.

I took a big gulp of water. "You eat yours," I sneered playfully.

Tanner was sweet and caring in his own way. I loved the way he listened and gave me advice like a good friend would. That only made me miss Jenna, Kate, and Nicole even more. However, sometimes I wished Tanner would keep his mouth closed and his opinions to himself.

CHAPTER 22
BECKY

It took one hour on the train to get to Paris, then we took a cab to his apartment. I felt a rush of excitement flow through me for being at a place I'd always dreamt of being. It was so surreal that it felt like a dream.

Tanner's place was cozy and neatly in order. The furniture was elegant and modern with a few paintings on the wall and a great view of the city. It reminded me of Matthew's place, so I walked away from the window.

"This room is all yours, Becky." Tanner pushed the door wider. "If you're not sleepy, we can talk more if you like."

"I'm really exhausted. I'll see you in the morning." I smiled. "Thanks for letting me stay here."

"Sleep in as long as you like. I'll give you a tour of the city when you feel up to it."

"Thanks."

With that, he closed the door behind him. After I took a shower and got ready for bed, I opened up my laptop and checked my email and texts. Not wanting to be rude, I had turned it off during dinner since it was beeping like crazy. I had forgotten to turn it back on.

Jenna texted me asking how I was doing and when I was coming home. I hadn't told her the exact date of my return. Matthew was asking me the same questions.

Becca, I'm home. I'll be waiting for your return.

I'm staying a couple more days with a friend.
I'm not happy.
I'll be home soon. We need to talk.
Yes, we do. You should be here right now.
Sorry. Just need to clear my head.
Okay. I'll be waiting. I love you.

I turned off the phone and went to bed.

Matthew

Three simple words. Three words she could not text back. I had a bad feeling she wasn't coming home, and that thought turned my stomach inside out. There were many scenarios I could have taken. One, beg her to come with me to Australia. Two, surprise her in London by showing up. Neither one of them seemed like a good idea at the time. Feeling utterly lost, confused, and not knowing what to do, I decided to head to my best source once again.

"Hello, Jenna. My beautiful sister-in-law." I sat on her desk.

"Matthew." She looked surprised. Her cheeks flashed some color when she gave me a shy smile. She hadn't seen me walk into the room. Frankly, I was surprised to see her there at that hour. Everyone had gone home.

"How are you feeling?"

"Much better. I can eat well now."

"Do you know if I'm going to have a nephew or a niece?"

"We'll know next appointment."

"That's great." I paused a bit. "So what's going on with Becky? Have you heard from her?"

Jenna squinted her eyes and bit her bottom lip. This was a sure sign she was hiding something.

"Haven't you heard from her?" She looked worried.

"Yes, but I don't think she's planning to come home in a couple of days like she said she would. I think there is something else going on that you're both not telling me."

"Matthew, I have no idea what you're talking about. I wish I knew what was going on with Becky. I've been so sick lately that I hardly had time for her. I feel so bad. And now she's beyond my reach and all I get is 'I'll talk to you about it when I get home.' The time difference doesn't help either. And I need to pack up. Max is coming to take me out to dinner. I was waiting for him."

"Hmm...you, too? She told me the same thing." I stood up and walked across the room. "Maybe I should go visit her."

"I don't think that's a good idea." Jenna said that way too fast. She grabbed her bag and started to head to the door.

Jenna wasn't telling me everything. I had to find out what it was. "Does Becky go by a different name?"

Jenna stopped moving and turned to me. "What do you mean? Why would you say that?"

"I called the hotel Becky told me she was staying at." I took a step toward her. "There is no Becky Miller or Becca Miller or Rebecca Miller. There is no Miller. I thought the receptionist was an idiot, so I called again and spoke to the manager."

Jenna's face turned white and it looked like she'd stopped breathing. "Oh." That is all she said.

"Jenna. Where is she?" I stood in front of her, blocking her way. "Please. I'm in love with her and I know she loves me...or at least I thought she did."

"She does," Jenna murmured under her breath. Her eyes stared ahead blankly as she thought. "I think I know where she is, but you're not going to like it."

"Where?" I snapped her out of her daze.

"With Tanner."

"With whom?" My tone raised a bit and Jenna twitched. I didn't mean to scare her.

"Tanner was one of Keith's groomsmen. He lives in Paris."

My eyes grew wide and my jaw muscles became tight. "That's not too far from London." I gave Jenna a quick hug and a kiss on her cheek. Then I started heading out the door.

"Matthew, where are you going?"

"To get Becca back and to kick someone's ass."

"Matthew!" The tone of Jenna's voice stopped me in my tracks. Whoa. This was the first time I'd ever heard her pissed off like that.

I swung back around, and answered her in my sweetest tone to calm her down, "Yes, my sister-in-law?"

She blushed a little, probably not believing she practically yelled my name in anger. "You don't know where Tanner lives. And please don't do anything foolish."

"I have Keith's contact information, and don't worry, I'm only going to scare the shit out of Banner for stepping in my territory."

"I don't recall saying his name is Banner. It's Tanner."

I curled my lips and twitched my brows to show Jenna that I was being playful. "Banner, Manner, Fanner...whatever. I don't care what his name is."

"Oh my God! You're just like Max," she squealed, laughing.

"Who's like Max?" Max entered and slapped my back lightly as a show of his affection. "Of course he's like me. He learned from the best."

"Of course," I said, humoring them both. I walked away when I saw Max hugging Jenna. God, I missed my Becca.

Jenna

I debated whether to call Becky and let her know Matthew might be on his way. Shoot...who was I kidding? Matthew was on his parents' plane to Paris; there was no doubt about that. About time.

Dr. Howard saw patients every other Saturday. Max and I were happy to make an appointment on one of them. It was difficult to arrange an appointment with his tight schedule.

"The baby's heart is strong," Dr. Howard said, smiling. "Everything looks great. Would you like to know the sex of the baby?"

I turned to Max for an answer. He gave me that sexy smile, but he seemed uncertain. "Why not? This way we can prepare the nursery. We'll just keep our family in the dark." He released a short, wicked laugh. That sound was too adorable, too hot, and my mind reeled with naughty thoughts.

Dr. Howard laughed with us. Pulling out a gadget, he poured some type of gel on it while I glanced at Max and gave him a smile. His hand tightened on mine when Dr. Howard lifted my gown. I thought Max was going to punch him.

Dr. Howard said with a chuckle, "I always get the same expressions from the husbands."

"It's fine, Dr. Howard. I have no problem with it as long as you keep your mind to yourself. I'm just joking." Max chuckled, but I knew he wasn't.

Dr. Howard laughed, too. "Just keep your eyes on the screen."

My heart skipped a beat and my stomach fluttered from the sight of seeing our baby on the screen. Max's facial expression softened and he released a soft coo. His fingers slipped through to make a fist with mine. I felt his love for the baby and for me.

"Baby, open up. Your mommy and daddy need to see if you're a boy or a girl," Dr. Howard sang. He moved the gadget to the left. "Jenna, move to your right a bit."

I did as instructed. Max helped me turn.

"There...right there," Dr. Howard muttered. "Can you see?" He pointed to the screen.

Max and I leaned in. Wow!

After we said our good-byes to Dr. Howard, I got dressed. We set up the next appointment and left, feeling giddy and fulfilled, for our Lamaze class.

CHAPTER 23
MATTHEW

I re-checked the address Keith had texted me and got out of the taxi. I'd anticipated the long speech I would have to give to Keith to get Tanner's address, but he'd just sent it through text, no questions asked.

I was tired as hell from the time change, but I didn't care. It was late night in Paris. I hoped they were home. As I frantically looked for the apartment number, a bunch of thoughts ran through my mind. My heart couldn't keep up with my anxiety attack, and I was sure my blood pressure had soared over the normal limit.

Here we go. I took a deep breath and rang the doorbell. It was like déjà vu. This was the second time I had flown somewhere to bring her back home.

The door swung wide open and I sucked in air. Seeing Becca in front of me did funny things to my emotions. I was all tongue twisted and I was sure my heart was dancing from happiness...until I had a clear vision of him. Banner wore shorts and was shirtless, and Becca was in a white robe.

"Matthew?" Becca was very surprised. "What are you doing here?" Her eyes shot wide open and her line of vision followed mine, which went straight to the asshole who'd taken my Becca. "I can explain." Yeah, right. I knew the meaning behind those words.

Becky

Holy shit! Matthew was in full rage. He didn't answer me. In fact, I didn't think he heard me at all. He stared at Tanner with a look to kill. I knew Tanner was in deep shit when Matthew's body tightened and he rushed past me.

"Matthew," I shouted, but he didn't stop. He went full force. Oh my God, Matthew was going to kill Tanner.

"Hey, Matthew. It's nice to—" Tanner finally caught on that Matthew was about to take a swing at him, but he didn't move. He just stood there, most likely hoping Matthew would come to his senses, but he didn't.

Matthew's arm swung back with his elbow bent. His shoulders tensed to throw the punch when I yelled at the top of my lungs as fast as I could, "He's gay! Tanner's gay!"

Matthew dropped his arms. He looked at me, and then to Tanner. "Hello, Tanner." He gave him his hand to shake and Tanner took it. "It's nice to meet you. Sorry about the late visit."

Tanner exhaled a breath while he took a step back. His eyes scanned Matthew from head to toe. I could tell he liked what he saw from his grin. "You can come over any time. Becky didn't tell me you were this deliciously good looking. I'm so jealous."

Matthew raked his hair back in discomfort. "Um...thanks." His tone was uncertain.

I wondered if he'd ever had a guy talk to him like that before. I'd never seen him flustered, and it made me laugh.

Tanner placed his hand over his heart and released a deep "I'm in love" sigh. "You were going to punch me for her. Oh...my...God! That is so romantic. You're not only a knight in shining armor, you're every man's dream. Plus, you're so freakin' hot."

Matthew's eyes grew even wider. He took a side step toward me, as if asking me to save him. I covered my mouth with my hand to keep from bursting out laughing.

Tanner must have sensed Matthew's uneasiness. "Well, I'm sure you two have a lot to talk about. But if she decides to dump you, my bed is available." Tanner winked and left.

I was dying of laughter inside, but I was also mad as hell with Matthew. He finally turned to me with his head down. "Becca," he heaved softly, most likely from embarrassment.

"My room, now," I commanded.

Matthew

"What are you doing here, Matthew?" That was the first thing she said to me. Didn't she know I'd flown all those miles to be with her, to bring her home because I missed her like crazy? Did that even matter?

I plopped on the bed and put my face into the palms of my hands for a second before I looked back up at her. "This is your fault. You left me hanging. You said we would talk when you came back, but you delayed your trip home. Then I found out that you were with a guy. How do you think I felt? What do you expect from me? I would fight for you, don't you know that?"

Becca leaned against the dresser and looked down. "You're right. This is my fault. I haven't been straight with you and you need answers, just like I needed mine."

My head turned sideways and I glanced at her in confusion. "What answers do you need? I think I was very clear when I told you how sorry I was and how much you mean to me. I told you I loved you, but you never said those words back to me."

The physical and emotional distance I felt from her was breaking my heart. I'd lost her. Blood rushed down my body and my muscles began to feel weak. The stabbing, painful twist in my heart was making my eyes sting. My breath quickened when the room started to become small. There wasn't enough air.

"Becca, if you don't want to be with me anymore, just say it. I want you to be happy. If I don't make you happy, I'll let you go. I'll walk out that door and never bother you again."

Becca looked at me like she couldn't believe I had just said that and her posture straightened. "Matthew, I don't want you to leave me, but I'm so afraid you are going to." Her eyes began to tear.

Becca wiped her tears and held her hand out to stop me from going to her. "Just hear me out first." She inhaled a deep breath. "I'm a runner. I've always run away from my problems. I'd rather block them out and pretend they never happened than to face them. I'm trying not to do that. Unfortunately, old habits are hard to break. I've wanted to tell you, but I'm so afraid of losing you. It's the reason why I've been avoiding talking to you."

"Becca? I don't understand."

There was a long pause. Becca fidgeted with her nails as she spoke. "I'm sick."

"What do you mean? Are you going to get better? Is it cancer? What is it?" I stopped asking questions when I realized I wasn't giving her a chance to speak.

"I have a chronic kidney infection. I've had it since I was a child. I missed many days of school because I was in and out of the hospital. Finally, doctors contained the infection. My kidneys have been scarred and damaged, the reason I have less kidney function."

My chest began to relax and my lungs released the air I was holding in. I clasped my hands together and lowered my elbows on my thigh to think. "It came back?"

"Yes." Becky nodded.

"I'll find the best doctors for you. We'll do whatever it takes to make you better."

"I haven't finished, Matthew." She paused. "It gets worse."

I inhaled a deep breath again. What else could there be?

"I won't be able to give you children. The extra fluid needed to carry a child will cause more stress. When a woman gets pregnant, all of her organs have to work harder. This is fine for healthy women, but not for someone like me. The percentage of babies making it to full term is very low. And there is the possibility of the mother not surviving the pregnancy."

For me, this was all too simple — easy to fix — but I guess it didn't seem like it to Becca. I was trying to understand the reasoning behind her running away. Wanting to comfort her, I stood up and took a small step. I didn't want to make her feel uncomfortable. "We'll adopt. Your health is more important. I love you, not the idea of having a baby."

Becca pulled out her hand again. "Don't. Your parents want lots of grandchildren."

"And they'll get them, but they'll also love any grandchildren. My parents aren't like that."

"I know, Matthew."

"Then what is it, Becca? You're driving me crazy. Please, talk to me." I stopped halfway to her. I wanted to hold her so bad and make her pain go away, but I couldn't, and it was killing me. I took more steps to her as Becca wiped her tears. Then I halted in shock at her next words.

"I'm pregnant," she blurted. The river of tears started to flow down her face and she started to fall to the floor, but I reached her just in time. I sat on the very spot she would have fallen and held her tightly in my arms. "I almost had an abortion because I was too scared of what could happen," she gasped between breaths into my shirt. "I feel horrible, because how could I even think those thoughts? I love you too much. I want to give you our child. I don't want anything to happen to our baby."

As I held her, pain seared my heart and the tears formed in my eyes. I tried to grasp the reality of the situation and understand what Becca had been going through the past couple of weeks alone. Becca continued to sob in my arms, and I let her. Cradling and comforting her as best as I could, I kissed her and told her everything was going to work out...but those were the only words I said. I wasn't sure of anything. Recalling our fight regarding Tessa and Amber, I was relieved that I hadn't mentioned to Becca that Tessa had been pregnant. In fact, I hadn't told anyone, not even Max. Becca would never know. That information would devastate her.

Fate did funny things in life and sometimes in twisted ways. I had a second chance at having a child, but I could lose the child, or Becca...or both. What the fuck was I supposed to do? There was no decision to make. Becca's life came first.

"I'm taking you home, Becca. We'll get through this."

CHAPTER 24
BECKY

After breakfast, Matthew gathered my suitcases and opened the front door. "It was nice to meet you. Thank you for taking care of Becca for me." Matthew shook Tanner's hand.

Tanner let out a small sigh and his eyes twinkled. "Becca is so lucky. And it was my pleasure. She's a special friend."

"Yes she is," Matthew agreed and rubbed my back.

"Even wearing your clothes from yesterday, you still smell delicious," Tanner added, making Matthew's eyes widen a bit.

"Yeah...umm...I was only thinking of bringing Becca home. I didn't bring anything with me."

Tanner sighed again. "What a man." His body shook a little. "I'm so glad you worked things out, but I'm going to miss my girl." Tanner gave me a tight squeeze and kissed me on my cheek. "My place is always available. And if things don't work out, you know where to find me."

"I will, but you don't have to worry. Things will work out." I smiled at Matthew, who looked back at me with loving eyes.

"Oh, honey, I wasn't talking to you. I meant the hunk I can't keep my eyes away from."

Matthew and I couldn't help but laugh. I was glad Matthew found humor in the situation.

"You need to put some cucumber on your eyes to get rid of the puffiness from all of that crying," Tanner suggested.

"I will. And you stay well. Call me if you want to come visit Los Angeles."

"Not any time soon, but I will someday."

With one last hug from me, and even a hug from Matthew, Tanner's door closed behind us. I couldn't wait to see Jenna. We had a lot of catching up to do.

Becky

"I don't think this is the way to the airport." I gazed out the taxi window, admiring the city for the last time.

Matthew kissed my fingers and placed both our hands on his thigh. "We're taking a detour."

"Where are we going?"

Matthew curled his lips into a wicked grin. "Like the readers who love book boyfriends would say...to show you something that is swoon worthy."

I smiled from ear to ear. He was so freakin' adorable, and he said the most panty-dropping things. "Really? I can't wait."

The taxi driver pulled over and we got out. I didn't see much except the bridge. Matthew took my hand and led us there, where I saw locks of various sizes and colors taking up every inch of the bridge. We were standing at Pont des Arts near the Louvre.

"What are we doing here?" I asked. Overwhelmed with what I was seeing, I didn't notice the lock and key in front of me until Matthew snapped me out of it.

"Becca, look." The lock and key was plain and silver. It was one of the biggest locks I had ever seen. To my surprise, Matthew was down on one knee.

"Matthew, get up. What are you doing?" I glanced around to see if anyone was watching, and sure enough there were a few, but they turned away when we met eye to eye.

"When I decided to come here and take you home, knowing I was going to Paris, I bought this lock and key. I wanted to bring you here and show you how much you mean to me. How much I am committed to us. But now the situation has changed. I'm going to be a father. We are going to be parents."

"I don't know, Matthew. The baby might not survive." It pained me greatly to say this.

"I have faith, Becca, but no matter what, you come first. Fate has given us a second chance and we'll both face whatever obstacles await us. We are both fighters. We are both stubborn. We were meant for each other. I love you, Becca. This isn't how I imagined I would do this, but since we are in Paris, this is my chance. Becky Miller, would you do me the honor of being my wife? I want to spend the rest of my life with you...children or no children. I want to have something forever with you. Will you marry me?"

Tears streamed down my face while my body quivered from words that escaped Matthew's mouth so fast, I wasn't sure if what I heard was real. I dropped my hand that was covering my mouth from shock. Though I had imagined Matthew proposing to me many times before, I never could have imagined it would feel so good. I was high. My heart expanded to its fullest and I felt a rush of indescribable joy.

"Becca, say something." Matthew looked worried.

"Yes," I whispered. I cleared my throat because I wasn't sure I'd answered out loud. "Yes!" I said, a little bit louder.

Matthew jumped up. "She said yes," he bellowed, and swung me around. There was so much happiness in Matthew's tone and in his kisses.

"But we can't get married. I mean...let's wait. I mean..." Oh God! I was messing this up. I didn't want him to get the wrong idea. "I want to marry you, but I don't want to rush this."

"Whatever you want. We can get married before or after the baby is born. Even if something happens, I still want to marry you, Becca. I've known I wanted to marry you from the moment you told me you wouldn't date me if I was the last man in the universe."

I let out a laugh. "I knew I couldn't live without you when you asked me if I was going to stand there and undress the rest of you with my eyes, or if I was going to help you wash the Chinese food off your sweater." I paused to let him recall. "I had already undressed you in my mind and we had already fucked."

"Holy Jesus, Becca. Be careful what you say. I might rip off your clothes right on this bridge and let everyone watch us." Matthew shook his head as if to get rid of the thought. "Here. Let's do this together." He showed me the lock again, but this time he pointed out to me the part that had the writing on it.

The lock read:

Becky & Matthew
Forever

After I signed the back, Matthew did the same. "I want ours to be the first one." Matthew placed it on the gate and locked it. No one could miss the extra-large lock among the surrounding ones. "Toss the keys into the river."

"What? Why? We'll never be able to open it." I glanced at the key in confusion.

"Exactly. I never want us to unlock or break this lock. Throwing the key into the river is symbolic of our love for each other. That whatever we will have to face in the future, we are unbreakable. I picked out the silver because silver stands for forever," Matthew explained.

"Matthew, it's perfect." I wrapped my arms around him and embraced him with all of me. What I really meant to say was that he was perfect. "Seal it with a kiss," I said. I held out my hand with the key on my palm. After Matthew kissed it, I did the same. With one last look, I tossed it as far as I could.

The old Becca would've said no to the proposal, because I would have been insecure and thought he had only done it because I was pregnant, but I knew better. Matthew had shown me time and time again that he loved me. And with all my insecurities and mistakes, he was in it forever.

Jenna was so relieved to see me home that she decided to spend the night at our place instead of with Max.

"I can't believe you didn't tell me you were pregnant. Is that why you happened to have the home pregnancy test?" Jenna shifted on the sofa to face me.

"Yes, but you were going through so much that I didn't want to add to your stress. Actually, the test came out negative. I took it again after two weeks." I sighed and handed her a cup of tea.

"Thanks." She paused. "What's going to happen?"

"Matthew and I saw my doctor and he explained all of the possibilities to us. We're going to pray that the baby will survive in my uterus." I gazed at my stomach.

"Your health comes first, Becky," Jenna said, looking concerned.

"I know. Matthew reminds me of that every day. I want this so bad, Jenna. I want to give Matthew a child. A child created by us. If I could just have this one baby, then we can talk about adopting if we want more."

"When will you know if you're out of danger?" Jenna asked. She hadn't taken a sip yet. She might've forgotten to breathe, she was so focused on me.

"I won't be in the clear until the baby is born."

"Whaaat?"

"I know, I know, but I've been okay so far. My kidney function is under control. Things are looking great."

"Okay, but just make sure to tell your doctor everything."

"Don't worry. Matthew is on me twenty-four, seven. He's going to make an appointment with another doctor to ensure that we have the best care."

"I'm sure he will." Jenna finally took a sip. "You're so lucky. I mean...you never had morning sickness, did you?"

"No, I didn't. I was lucky in that department, but I'd rather have morning sickness than a high risk pregnancy." Jenna became still. I regretted the comment. "Jenna, I didn't mean anything by that. I'm so sorry."

"Becky. No. You're right."

She looked so guilty and it was my fault. My stupid mouth. I tried to lighten the mood. "Are you ready for your wedding next week?"

Jenna inhaled deeply. "Ellen has been wonderful. I don't think I could have planned everything so fast." The smile came back on Jenna's face. "My parents are flying in tomorrow. My mom will be here just in time for the bridal shower. Thanks for arranging it around her schedule."

"Of course. We can't leave your mom out. I just feel really bad that we didn't get to have a bachelorette party for you."

"First of all, I don't want to do the Las Vegas thing. I don't think Max would approve. Second, the wedding came up suddenly. We didn't have time to plan. I'm just glad you agreed to be my maid of honor and your relationship with Matthew is back on track."

"Of course, anything for you. How are you feeling?"

"I'm pretty calm right now, but I don't know how I'll be the day of the wedding."

"Jenna, I'm so happy for you."

Jenna took another sip and changed the subject. "How about you?"

I swallowed my drink. I gave her one huge, dorky smile. "Matthew proposed to me."

"He did?" Jenna's eyes shifted to my hand, which held no ring, but she still looked excited. "When? How? Oh my God!" Jenna embraced me tightly. When she let go, her eyes were glistening with tears. "I'm so happy for you."

"I told him I wanted to wait. I'm already almost at the end of the first trimester, just like you. I have no time to arrange a wedding. And there is no guarantee on my health situation, so I told him I wanted to wait until after the baby was born."

"Okay." Jenna nodded. I knew she would agree. It was best to wait. "When are you due?"

"Actually...we're due around the same time."

Jenna squealed. "You're going to tell Nicole and Kate, right?"

"I'll tell them at your wedding."

"We can have a baby shower together." Jenna bounced in her seat. Her smile was big and her eyes twinkled under the light of the lamp. "I never imagined that we would have a child at the same time and marry into the same family. What are the chances?"

"I know, right?"

"Did you tell your parents?"

"They don't know yet. We will be visiting my parents the day after your wedding. I'll tell them then."

"How about Matthew's parents?"

"We'll tell them after your wedding, but before we leave for San Francisco."

"Okay." Jenna smiled. "Our lives have changed so much in such a short amount of time."

"Yup," I agreed. "Did you start packing for San Diego?"

"You know me so well. I did. I think I'm packing too much," Jenna laughed. "Did you?"

"I sure did. One can never pack enough."

CHAPTER 25
JENNA

After I helped my parents settle into their hotel, my mom came with me to the bridal shower dinner and my dad waited to be picked up by Max. Max and the men had dinner plans. Though Max and I had agreed to stay away from each other this week and finally be face to face on the wedding day, it was extremely difficult to do so. We even avoided each other during work hours as well. I missed him so much, especially when he would send me texts.

I'm thinking of you.

I'm thinking of you, too.

I hope they are naughty thoughts.

I laughed out loud.

"What's so funny?" Becky nudged me during dinner.

Everyone was in their own conversations when I took the moment to read Max's text. "It's Max. He's making me laugh."

"I think he also made you blush."

"Shhh." I laughed again. Although Ellen and my mom were chatting and couldn't hear us, I felt awkward flirting with Max in front of his mom.

Nicole and Kate were in charge of the games. We played a game where one person wrapped their teammate with toilet paper and created the most creative wedding dress. It was hilarious. The second game we played was unscrambling a list of words. That was difficult since most of us had no clue. Ellen won that game. For the last game, they had to hold a paper plate on top of their head and blindly draw me in a wedding dress. It had simple instructions, but was difficult to do. We all laughed like crazy. Unexpectedly, my mom won a prize for that game.

Due to the small wedding, I had asked Becky not to invite a bunch of our friends. I only wanted a few good friends to join me tonight. Now, it was cake and present time.

"I'll write down who brought what," Nicole said. "Kate will take the pictures, and Becky will help you."

"Thank you," I said, since all of the attention turned on me. "First of all. I want to thank all of you for coming out tonight. A few of my cousins flew all the way from New York. A few of my college friends came from Texas. And I'm so happy my mom was able to join us for the bridal shower." I turned to my mom with a smile. "And I would like to thank Ellen, my soon to be mother-in-law, for all her help and for suggesting this wonderful restaurant."

Becky stood up and handed me my first present. I unwrapped it and gave Becky the wrapper, which she shoved into the trash bag.

It was a crystal vase from Tiffany's. "Thank you, Tanya," I said to my cousin. Kate took our picture and Becky gave me the next one.

"Thank you, Mom." Mom brought me some kitchen utensils that Max and I had registered for at Bloomingdales. That wasn't all. My eyes started tearing when I saw an engraved bracelet from Tiffany's. It read:

Max and Jenna
Forever

"Oh, Mom," I gushed and hugged her. "This is beautiful."

"Now you have something new to wear." Mom started getting teary-eyed, too. "I can't believe my little girl is all grown up and getting married."

"I can't believe it, either," I said softly.

Mom gave me big smile and sat back down in her seat after Becky took our picture.

"This is from your mother-in-law," Becky said, handing me a huge box.

When I took it from her, it was so light I wondered what was inside it. After I unwrapped it, I opened the lid and pulled out an envelope.

"Max already knows about it," Ellen started to say. "Robert and I are paying all expenses for your honeymoon. Inside is the information for the hotel that is paid for. That's not all. Max doesn't know this yet, but I've transferred money to your joint account to help pay for your future house. Max told me you were both thinking of moving to a house close to us."

"Yes." I nodded. My jaw dropped...I was in shock for sure. I knew Mr. and Mrs. Knight were generous people, but a house was way too much. "I don't know what to say, Ellen."

I stood up when Ellen approached me. "No need to thank me, Jenna. Max is a lucky man." She leaned into my ear with a hug. "I can't wait for my grandchild to be born. There is something else inside the box." Ellen sat back down next to my mom.

I reached in and took out another box like she said there would be, and I blushed big time when I opened it.

My guests started to laugh when I pulled it out. It was black, skimpy, lacy lingerie.

"I just wanted to make sure you had one. After all, I want you to seduce my son more often and make him a happy man. And also, I want more grandchildren."

"Okay," I laughed, feeling my cheeks burn. The idea of my mom knowing I was going to wear one made me die of embarrassment.

"Don't be so embarrassed, Jenna. Embrace your youth and your sexy body," Ellen continued. "I have the same one except mine is in red."

Everybody laughed and whistled. I probably looked like I was on fire, but that was nothing compared to what Becky, Kate, and Nicole had in store for me. Inside their gift box was a vibrator, a rubber dick, lubricant, a whip, handcuffs, and a sex game. I had never seen one before. I had to hold the items up one by one to show everyone. Oh my God! I wanted to hide...no, I wanted to faint.

I was supposed to take the day off and get pampered with Becky at the spa of my choice at Max's order. However, Matthew asked me to come in for a couple of hours, so the spa would have to wait until after lunch. Matthew texted me and informed me he was in the meeting room and asked me to go there.

"Surprise!" I heard when I opened the door.

It took me some time to process as I glanced around to see so many smiling faces, but my heart skipped a beat when I saw my fiancé leaning against the table with his hand behind him to support his weight. He looked so delicious and edible that my mind ran with naughty thoughts...even in a room crowded with my co-workers. His sexy grin was enough to melt me to the floor. When he winked at me, it took every ounce of my will power to keep from straddling him on that table and taking him, especially since we were trying to stay away from each other.

"Jenna, congrats." Lisa from my old department wrapped her arms around me, interrupting my thoughts.

"Thank you!" I smiled. Countless "congrats" later, Max and I were asked to stand at the center of the room. After a quick speech from Matthew, everyone grabbed a plate for the buffet that was set up at the back of the room. The room was decorated with silver and white balloons, paper decorations of wedding bells, and a banner that read "Congratulations to Jenna and Max." I hadn't noticed them until then. I was too busy being shocked.

"Good afternoon, babe." Max kissed my cheek. His soft lips made me want more. I inhaled a deep breath and tried to contain my sex drive, but it only revved up. Max's hand caressed my back. And when no one was watching us, he would slip it down to my ass.

"Max." I jerked a little, leading his hand to the front.

Max nipped my ear, and then he huffed a low growl against my ear. "I can't help it. I don't like our agreement. I haven't been able to touch you in five days. That's a long time."

"A deal is a deal. It's killing me, too." I licked the side of his ear to tease him back.

After we ate, Max and I opened our gifts together. Many of the items were from our registry, even though we didn't register for much since I was moving into Max's place.

"I have something to show you," Max said after most of our co-workers had left the party.

"What do you need to show me, Mr. Knight?"

"It requires you to go to my office."

I narrowed my eyes at him. "Does it now? Are you sure it's not a trick to get me to break our deal?"

"I wouldn't dare, but I bet you would break it if you had the chance. Seriously, Jenna, I do need to show you something." Max stood up and offered me his hand.

"Okay. I'll walk beside you. No touching."

"Agreed."

Max opened his desk drawer and placed a picture in my hand. "What is this a picture of? I don't understand, Max. It's nice, but the bedroom is empty."

"It's ours if you want it." He beamed a smile. "I wanted it to be a surprise. I had a realtor search for the perfect house for us. We can't raise a family in a penthouse apartment. Our baby needs a big backyard. We can take a look today. It's brand new and it's close to my parents' house. That way, we can have reliable babysitters nearby."

I didn't know what to say. "Max. Thank you. Your mom told me she deposited money for our wedding gift into our joint account. Is that why you searched for the house?"

"No, babe. I started looking when I found out that you were pregnant. We don't need financial help from my parents, but I accepted it because it made them happy. We can always return the favor in different ways."

I didn't say a word. I threw myself at Max for a tight squeeze. I loved this man with all of my heart and soul. I couldn't wait to be his wife. "Thank you," was all I could say as I continued to press my body to his. I wanted his touch, which I'd missed for the past five days. His touch was my source of life. It gave me happiness. It gave me strength.

Max's body on mine was intoxicating. It got worse when his lips turned toward my lips and he looked at me with dreamy eyes. Damn him. I needed him. I craved him. My will power faltered when his hand caressed my hair, my cheeks, and ran seductively on my bottom lip.

"Jenna," Max called in the most hypnotic voice. His hand trailed the front of my blouse. All kinds of pleasurable tremors shivered through my body, but I would not give in. My heart felt no mercy as it beat in fast tiny rhythms. Heat flushed through every inch of me. And my sex burned for him so much that I could already feel the twitch of my clit.

"I'm just going to have a little taste. I'm not asking for permission. I'm letting you know what I'm doing."

Before I registered what he'd said, Max's tongue and lips devoured my neck, bathing me down to my breast. How in the world? When did he unbutton my blouse?

"Max," I whimpered. "I'm...I'm not...giving in. I'm not going to lose the—"

Too late. Max's lips crushed mine. His kisses were intense and hungry. It felt like the first time we'd ever kissed. All the effort of trying to stay away from each other intensified the need and want. Pure lust and love was a deadly combination when they were released. Max pushed up my skirt and his hands were all over my ass. Pushing away my panties, his hand was rubbing my clit. I wanted more.

Max anchored my legs around his waist and started to walk. We were so lost in sucking each other's tongue and lips that Max banged against the wall cabinet. Then we banged against a few chairs, knocking them over when I tried to loosen his tie. We were on fire.

Max placed me down on his desk and raked his hair back. His chest rapidly moved up and down from being out of breath, and so did mine. I didn't care if I lost the bet any more. I wanted Max inside me.

"Jenna, I don't want to win the bet," Max said breathlessly.

I tried to come out of the daze. What did he just say? "Max. I don't want to win." I was tortured inside from needing him and he wasn't going to give me release. I couldn't help myself. I started to laugh. I tried to turn the tables and seduce him with my words. "If I did win, I was going to make you my slave and have my way with you in your office. This place reminds me of when I fell in love with you." I placed my finger inside my mouth and sucked it.

Max lifted my chin with the tip of his finger and gave me his signature grin. "You can have me anywhere, babe," Max growled softly. After he pulled out my finger, he placed it into his mouth. His eyes bored into mine. He was killing me.

Oh God! This wasn't working.

I let out a moan and a whimper from being turned on again. The sound continued until Max stopped sucking my finger.

"We need to go. I need to show you the house. And if you like it, we can sign the papers today."

"Really?" I slid off his desk and fixed myself to look more presentable. "Why didn't you tell me in the first place? You did this to me again. Made me all excited and ready for you, then we have to leave."

Max chuckled out loud. "I love to tease you, babe. I love to see your expression when I make you feel good."

Max moved in for a slow kiss, pulling out my bottom lip with his teeth.

"Not fair," I pouted, but I let it go since I also had to meet Becky before dinner.

"It's always a pleasure, Mrs. Knight."

"I'm not Mrs. Knight yet," I warned.

"In four days you will be. I can't wait."

"You already have me, Max," I said sincerely, softening my tone.

"And you already have me." He kissed my forehead tenderly, then pulled back with a wicked grin. "I think we need to break in the house. Any way you want it, I'm all yours."

It was my turn for payback. "I think I like winning. We can...Max!"

Max lifted me over his shoulder and gave me a smack on my ass. "I'm going to let you win. I'm going to strip you naked and take you in every section of the house, but it will be under my rules, my terms."

CHAPTER 26
JENNA

Max pushed a remote and we entered through the gate. At first, all I saw were the trees, then the road curved into a long driveway. The garage was to the right, but Max parked right in front of the entrance, as did the realtor. Immediately, I fell in love with the exterior of the house. The layout reminded me of his parents' home.

"Shall we?" Max asked, placing his hand behind my back. "Justin. This is my fiancée, Jenna."

"It's nice to meet you, Jenna." Justin shook my hand.

"Likewise," I said, releasing his hand.

Justin fidgeted with the lock box, opened the door, and we walked in. Wow. A beautiful, crystal chandelier hung above and sparkled against the natural light. There were two stairways, one on each side, and the tan marble in the foyer was polished to shine. It definitely reminded me of Max's parents' place, but further in, it was a different layout.

After we saw the grand family room and the huge kitchen with the finest appliances, we went upstairs. There were six bedrooms, each with its own full bathroom. Then the realtor took us to the last bedroom. My eyes grew bigger when the door swung wider. There was no furniture there, but I saw the potential. The added bonus was the massive bathroom. It was bigger than the one in Max's place. And the closet was to die for, a walk-in his and her closet. It was bigger than my own bedroom.

"It's beautiful, Max."

Max had a huge, satisfied grin spread across his face. "Wait till you see the backyard." He took my hand and led us to the balcony. There was a swimming pool, a jacuzzi, a basketball court, a tennis court, and a perfect sitting area where we could enjoy ourselves with our friends. It was amazing.

"So...what do you think?"

I looked up at him. "I love it, Max, but it costs too much."

"Don't worry about the price, babe. If you love it, this will be our home. We're also a couple of blocks away from my parents' place. They would make great babysitters."

What could I say to that? "I love it. Let's do it. Let's make this our home."

Max wore a huge smile on his face and spun me around. After he made sure my feet were planted on the ground, he turned to Justin. "You heard my fiancée. Let's do it."

We went back down to the kitchen area and signed a stack of documents. Justin left after giving Max the key to our new home. "I want to show you a special room."

I chuckled to myself from his words. "What kind of special room, Max?"

"I like where your mind is headed, but that room will come later." Max took several steps up the stairs, and I followed him.

"I thought this room could be the nursery. It's the closest to our room. What do you think?"

"I think it's perfect." In my mind I saw the most beautiful crib, a white dresser, with some stuffed animals on top for decoration, and lots of books on the bookshelf next to the rocking chair.

"I'm glad you approve." Max's brow lifted in a naughty way. "Now, time for the other special room."

"What?" I laughed. "I was only joking."

"I wasn't." Max's eyes became dark and greedy. "Come here." His demand rang hot in my ears. I had already surrendered to his expression, but then I crumbled completely. My body became limp. I couldn't move. All I could do was stare at him and feel my hammering heart race for him...wanting his touch...needing his love...waiting for him.

Max lifted me up in a cradling position, walked out of the nursery, kicked the door that was slightly ajar to enter our bedroom, and placed me down on the floor. He stepped back to create a wide space between us. What was he doing?

"I'm sorry you didn't have a bachelorette party."

"I don't care about that. I'm sorry that you didn't have a bachelor party."

"I didn't want one. It wouldn't have been fair if I had one. Regardless, you're the only one I want to see undressed...the only one touching me. I'd better be the only one." He said this with a slight attitude.

What he did next came as a complete surprise. He pulled out his phone and started to play a tune. Max bored into me with his eyes as if I were his prey. With a sexy grin, he peeled off his suit jacket and flung it over his shoulder to the beat of the jazzy music. It was a perfect song for strip dancing. I thought I'd even heard this song at Chippendales. Oh my!

Max licked his bottom lip and with one graceful, slow movement, loosened his tie at the same time. Then he swayed his hips from side to side as he unbuttoned the first, then the second button of his dress shirt. He slowly rolled up his sleeves while he bumped and grinded in the air. Could he have made that any hotter? Holy Jesus, I was having my own party with a stripper.

Max unbuttoned the rest of his shirt to reveal his tight, six pack abs. I'd seen it many times before, but presenting himself this way gave off a whole lot of hotness. With one sleeve out at a time, he stripped off his shirt, then with a sway of his hips, he glided to me and unzipped his pants in perfect beat with the music. When his pants dropped, I gasped. I wanted to touch him, but he put out his hand in front to stop me.

"I told you I can dance," he said in that low, husky tone. He held my hand and helped me up. After the show he'd just given me, I was utterly weak at the knees. Max had on only his briefs and socks, but he was swoon worthy to the max. "I've changed my mind. I think I want to win." Max's lips dove for mine. I didn't see that coming.

"You're bad," I mumbled into his lips and pulled away, panting. "You —"

Max was getting dressed. "Time to go, babe. You're late for your appointment with Becky."

I looked at my watch. "Oh crap," I whispered to myself. I gazed back to Max. "You're so bad. This is the third time you made me forget. Ahhh!" I yelped, and jerked forward. Max had smacked my butt.

"I love your ass, babe," he murmured into my ear. Then he headed out of the room.

Bad Max! Very bad Max!

Very sexy Max.

"Becky, I'm so sorry. Did you get my text?" I asked, finding my seat next to her in the waiting room. She was engulfed in a magazine article.

"Jenna." Becky jerked a little in surprise. "Umm...text. Oh. What time is it?" She looked at her watch. "You're only ten minutes late. You're fine. I didn't know you texted." Becky shrugged innocently, showing me the magazine. "Sorry. I can't believe I'm reading about pregnancy and what to eat and what to expect."

I smiled to agree. "Did you check us in?"

"Yup. Just waiting for you. Let's get pampered up."

After we got a facial, we had a manicure and pedicure. Then we went out to early dinner and headed home. Since Matthew had dropped Becky off at the spa, I drove both of us home.

"Tonight is your last night here," Becky said when we walked in. Her tone was somber, producing an ache and emptiness in my heart. "I can't believe this day has come."

Becky tossed her purse on the dining table and I did the same, and we both plopped on the sofa. Then she extended her hand to show me a pair of pearl earrings.

"They're beautiful. Did you buy it?"

"My sister gave them to me. I thought they would be perfect with your wedding dress. I overheard you saying you needed something borrowed."

"Oh, Becky. I would be honored to borrow them. Thank you so much." I closed them in my hand.

"You know you can borrow anything of mine. We practically share everything anyway."

"I know." I didn't want to admit it, but my heart was breaking. Becky had been the sister I always wanted, and I was leaving her. "Do you remember the first time we met?"

"How could I forget? I knew the minute you walked into my life that we would be best friends."

I leaned back and rested my feet on the coffee table. "I had that feeling, too, but I have to admit I was sort of worried."

"Why?" Becky leaned back, too.

"I figured you would either be a good or a bad influence on me."

Becky laughed. "Well...you were right. Lucky for me, you were a good influence on me so I felt like I had to act proper. Which got me out of many troubles. So, thank you."

"Proper?" I squealed and moved my legs to face her. "Ugh. I sound so boring."

"Boring is not what you are, or you wouldn't have attracted the boss's son, one of the most eligible bachelors. You stole his heart. You'll have your forever with him and a baby coming soon."

I rubbed my belly, which seemed to have pooched out somewhat. Though people couldn't tell by looking, I felt it. I saw the growth. I changed the attention to Becky. "Look at you. You're changing into a responsible adult with the man of your dreams. We are going to have what we've always wanted, but never imagined that we could."

"Sometimes I think this is all a dream," Becky sighed. "And if it is, I don't ever want to wake up from it, Jenna. I'm afraid that everything good will disappear. I'm sorry, but I'm so sad that you're leaving me."

Tears blinded my vision. I felt the same way, but I didn't have the courage to tell her out loud. It would only make it too real, too painful. "I'm not leaving you, okay?"

My lips trembled. Oh God! I was going to lose it. "But I'm going to miss you like crazy." I wiped my tears, but they fell so fast I couldn't hide them.

"We've been through so much together," Becky sobbed. "I know you're not that far away, but this place will never be the same without you. Every time I step inside this apartment and glance toward your room, I'm going to be really sad. I'm sorry to make you feel bad, but I can't help the way I feel. You've been my mentor, my strength, and my hope. I just want you to know that."

I embraced Becky, but words wouldn't come. I needed to comfort her and me. "Oh, Becky," I said, holding her as I rubbed her back. "Don't be sorry. I feel the same way. I just couldn't say it. You were always the one that could express your feelings better than I ever could. You made me see the goodness in me. And you've always helped me through all of my problems as if they were yours. You are my forever sister, Becky. No one could ever replace you, and no one could ever take away what we had, and will still have. Our babies will be friends. They are going to be cousins. We are going to be married into the same family. We're going to see each other a lot."

We both pulled away to wipe our tears. "You're right. There is so much to look forward to."

"Let's not make this a sad occasion, but a happy one instead. When one door closes, another one opens, right?"

Becky nodded to agree. "To new beginnings."

I hugged Becky again and released her when her cell phone rang.

"Shoot. What time is it?" Becky stood up and pulled her phone out of her purse. "Matthew asked me to meet him at Long Beach pier." Her fingers moved speedily as she texted. "I'm letting him know I'm on my way."

"It's so late. Don't forget we're picking up my parents at their hotel first before we head to San Diego."

"Don't worry. I'll make this quick. I'm not sure why he wants me there. He wouldn't say, only that it's important." Becky grabbed her sweater and her purse, and turned the doorknob.

"Don't worry about anything. Drive carefully. If you need to stay late, then it's fine. You can always sleep in the car since I'll be driving us there."

"Okay. Love ya. Bye." The doorknob jiggled from the other side as Becky made sure she locked the door. I smiled thinking of the huge surprise that waited for her.

CHAPTER 27
BECKY

Why Matthew needed me at such a late hour was beyond me. He knew I had a long day tomorrow, and so did he. *What is so urgent?* I texted. I walked down the familiar boardwalk to his parent's yacht. I had only walked several feet when I spotted a man leaning on the lamppost. He was tall with a muscular build. When he turned around, he stole my breath away, and at the same time I realized it was Matthew. He was sucking on a lollipop, gazing at me with a wicked grin.

"Want a taste, Becca?" he mumbled with the lollipop in his mouth.

"I want to taste something else," I teased, placing my hand inside his jeans pocket. I angled my index finger just right to where I could almost touch his balls.

Matthew jerked back and wrapped his arms around me. "If you're good, I might even let you taste what you're trying to touch."

"Sweet." I twitched my brows.

"It'll be more than sweet."

I laughed lightly, loving his playfulness. "Why am I here? I'll see you tomorrow in San Diego."

Matthew placed his arms around my shoulders and started walking down the boardwalk. "We'll be surrounded by people when we're in San Diego. I wanted you by yourself. I actually have a question to ask you."

"You could've texted me or called me. You made me drive all the way to Long Beach just to ask a question? Where is the common sense in that?" I scolded. "You...Matthew!" Matthew dropped his hands and something soft covered my eyes. "What are you doing? I can't see." Then I realized it was a blindfold.

Matthew pressed his body next to mine and led me to our destination. "I've got you. Don't be stubborn."

Even though I knew there was nothing in the way in front of me and Matthew guided me, I stepped hesitantly. Walking in the complete darkness at night was not my idea of fun, but I played along. Whatever it was, it was important to him. When the blindfold came off, I saw many blurry, bright spots. I blinked rapidly and rubbed my eyes. When my vision cleared, I was blown away.

"Matthew." His name flowed out of my mouth in a whisper as I slipped my hand into his. Countless electric candles covered the top and second level deck of the yacht, where we were standing. "It's amazing, Matthew. You did this all by yourself?"

"Surprise, Becca. Well...I had a little help." He kissed my forehead tenderly and brought me up to the third level deck. He took my purse and placed it down. "You don't need this right now." Then he pulled the finished lollipop from his mouth and put the stick in his front pocket. Matthew shrugged sheepishly. "I don't want to litter, even on my own boat."

I laughed at his words because that was exactly what I would have done. "Is Carlos around?" I asked, thinking about the things we had done on our last boat ride.

"No. It's just you, me, and the universe." When he looked up at the sky, I did the same. The full moon glistened and splashed the color of yellow against the ocean. The tiny countless stars were much more apparent tonight. Matthew and I were in our own universe. It was so beautiful up here that my whole body shivered with happiness and the soft, cool breeze that brushed against my face.

"You're amazing," I said, gazing into his eyes, which sparkled against the candlelight that completely surrounded us.

"I know." He gave me a mischievous smirk, and then placed his hands inside the back of my jeans pocket.

"You're also arrogant."

"I know, but you're worse. You're very stubborn." Matthew pressed his cheek on mine.

"That I am. However, you can also be very sweet and romantic."

"Very true. And you are a big tease, but I love that you are."

I gave him a kiss on the lips. "You make it easy for me to be that way. And yes, I do love to tease you."

"Don't ever stop." He leaned his forehead on mine.

"I won't."

"I need you to promise me that if you think your life is in danger, you come first. I can't lose you, Becca." Matthew tangled his fingers through mine. "Promise me," he asked when I didn't answer.

"I promise."

"You can be stubborn about anything, but not this. You are my firecracker. I wouldn't change anything about you, but this is one thing I'm asking from you. I want to be with you for the rest of my life, and if there is eternity, I want you right next to me."

Tears rose to the surface, and I tried to keep them at bay. I was already an emotional wreck from the conversation with Jenna and my pregnancy hormones acting up.

"I feel the same, Matthew." I hadn't realized we were inside the circle of candles until I pressed my head against Matthew's chest. "You're not a witch or a demon, are you?" I laughed.

"You read too many paranormal books. They are corrupting your mind."

"No, they're not." I took offense to that. With a light slap across his arms, I turned to walk away.

Matthew flung his arms around my waist pulled me back to him. "Not so fast. Okay. Okay. I'm sorry. I can be whatever you want me to be. I want to be the hot, naughty demon that gets to do all sort of wicked things to you. But before we play make believe with your fictional characters, I need to ask you a very important question, the reason why I asked you to come here in the first place."

Matthew sank to his knees. He'd already asked me to marry him, so what the heck was he doing?

"Becky Miller. You are the stars that shine upon my darkness. You are the moon that glowed into my heart to show me I could love again. Whatever the universe has in store for us, I know we can get through it together because our love is strong. I want forever with you. I've already asked you this question, but I wanted to do it the right way. The way you deserved to be asked. Will you be my wife, Becky, and marry me when you are ready? But don't wait too long."

Tears had started streaming down my face the moment Matthew began speaking. I couldn't believe the beautiful words pouring out of his mouth. It wasn't that I didn't think he could say something like that, it was that the words he was saying were meant for me. "Yes." I nodded.

Matthew swooped in and gave me a long, passionate kiss, then he ran to the edge of the deck and yelled, "She said yes!" He came back to me.

"What was that for?" I laughed.

Matthew didn't answer. He went to the side of the deck, opened a storage compartment, and placed a box in front of me. When he opened a box that read Cartier, the ring sparkled brilliantly against the candlelight. That thing looked so big. I knew he would get me one someday, but I hadn't expected today. It was an overwhelming surprise. I gasped lightly with my hands covering my mouth. "It's beautiful, Matthew." He slipped it on my finger, and it fit perfectly. "How did you know my size?"

"Jenna, of course. It's a princess cut. Three karats. I wanted you to have this before Max and Jenna's wedding. My parents already know I'm proposing tonight, and so do Max and Jenna. The only important people that don't know are your parents and your sister, Rachel."

"Jenna knew?" I laughed. "They'll know when we visit them. They already love you. I've told them so much about you, and they can't wait to meet you."

"How could anyone not?" Matthew winked.

"Arrogant," I laughed lightly, enjoying the humor between us.

"Stubborn."

"Jerk."

"Crazy."

"Ass."

Matthew puffed his bottom lip out into a frown. "Not liking where this is headed."

I curled my lips into a huge smile. He cracked me up. "Adorable. Absolutely amazing. Hot. Sexy. Gorgeous. Edible. Juicy."

Matthew's eyes grew with lust and want while his body pressed to mine. "Don't forget...drool worthy and deliciously fuckable."

Holy fuck. "Yes!" I said out loud.

"Shit! I almost forgot."

"What are you doing?" I asked. He went back to the edge of the deck. "Carlos, she said yes!"

"What? You said we were alone." Matthew ran back to the storage compartment. He pulled out a gadget and spoke into it.

"Now, Carlos."

The second Matthew came back to me, the sky lit up with fireworks. They weren't massive like the kind you would see at Disneyland, but they were grand enough. Assorted colors splashed against the dark sky. No matter how many times I had seen them, it always seemed to take me away from reality and into their beauty.

"This is how you make me feel, Becca. You bring color and excitement into my life." We turned face to face when the show was over.

"I can't believe you did this for me," I sobbed, and tried to wipe my tears. "No man has ever made me cry so many happy tears. How?"

"My parents have connections, which are my connections, too. I had to ask Carlos to come with me. Who was going to push the buttons?"

I snorted. Oh God! I thought some snot flew out. "Oh, Matthew. You're too much."

Matthew rewarded me with a loving, warm smile. He slipped down to his knees again with his arms wrapped around my waist and unexpectedly kissed my stomach. "My little one, you make me feel this way, too. Please be strong for Mommy and Daddy. Don't let anything happen to you or your mommy, okay?" Matthew caressed my stomach, as if he was touching the baby. "I promise to do whatever I can to make sure you are healthy and make sure nothing bad happens to you, but I need your help. I can't do this alone. You need to fight and grow big and strong. We don't even have a name for you, and I haven't even held you in my arms, but know that I love you with all of my heart, and my love will grow as you grow. You have a family waiting for you. You even have a cousin that will be born around the same time, so please don't let anything bad happen."

I inhaled a deep breath. I felt the depth of Matthew's love and his worries for our unborn child for the first time. It meant the world to me to know how much he already loved our baby. He'd never expressed how he felt, so a part of me had doubts. Whatever the reasons before, it was clear now. I felt it at that very moment. Matthew was as scared as I was, but he wanted our child as much as I did.

There was a big possibility that there would be dangers ahead, but Mathew and I would get through this. We'd be each other's strength. We'd hold on to hope. We'd ride out the storm. As long as we had each other, come what may. Matthew and I would make it. We had to.

CHAPTER 28
JENNA

We walked inside Grand Del Mar after depositing our luggage with the bellman. The first thing I saw was a wooden table in the center of the lobby with a huge bouquet of colorful flowers. Past the lobby, the sun shone through glass doors. A black grand piano and elegant yet modern furniture filled the room. The decor all around was exquisite and very much to my taste. I knew I would love it there.

"This place is amazing," Mom exclaimed.

"We should check in," I said, clicking my heels across the marble floor to the smiling receptionist.

After we checked in, a nice gentleman walked us to our villas. Max had told me that he had reserved all of them; not just for us, but for our guests as well. Though we didn't need to rent all of them, he didn't want strangers near us.

"This is our room," I said to my parents. Max and I agreed that we wouldn't spend the night together until after we got married. "Becky, you're right next door. Let's get unpacked. Either I'll stop by or you stop by in half an hour. Sound good? I also need to check in with the wedding coordinator."

"Sounds good to me. We can do our own thing before we meet up with the rest of the party. Dinner is at six, right?"

"Yes," I replied. "Max will fly in since we need the plane to get to Paris."

"And Matthew will be driving with his parents," Becky added.

"Perfect. See you in a bit."

The bellman placed our luggage in our rooms. After I tipped him, he left.

"This place is too big for the three of us. It must cost a fortune," my dad commented. "I can't believe the Knight family reserved all of the villas."

"It's for a wedding, after all," my mom said, smiling at me. "They're very generous."

I nodded and smiled to agree.

The Brisa Villas were about 4,500 square feet with three bedrooms. It felt like a home, yet it provided the conveniences and amenities of a world-class hotel. These charming Mediterranean-inspired estates were adorned with European antiques. It even had an expansive gourmet kitchen, media room, and state-of-the-art audio systems.

I walked to the dining table and picked up a pamphlet to read through the list of amenities: unlimited golfing on a private, secluded area, passes to San Diego parks, complimentary wireless Internet, and wine, soft drinks, waters, and organic iced teas refreshed daily. This was fantastic, though I wouldn't need most of their services. Since we were getting married here, Max and I had special bride and groom amenities, the room Max would stay in until I joined him after we got married.

After we unpacked, Dad went to play golf. Mom, Becky, and I walked around to explore. While passing through the bakery, Becky and I bought chocolate chip cookies. I didn't know if they used a special ingredient or if it was due to me being pregnant, but whatever the reason, it sure tasted mouth scrunching delicious.

When we entered the small shop, Becky's engagement ring caught my eye. It sparkled against the bright light. I'd caught her staring at and admiring it several times in the store. Her attention was more focused on the ring than the beautiful items the shop had displayed. I understood her. I had done that many times when I first got engaged. In fact, I still did it to that day. I couldn't believe Becky and I had gotten engaged in the same year.

"It's so peaceful and secluded here," Becky said when we exited out to the pool. It led us right to a path. "Now I understand why Max wanted to get married here."

"Maybe Dad and I will stay here a bit longer. I'm really loving this place," Mom said, linking her arms with mine.

"You should. You don't get to travel often." We walked in silence as we observed the nature around us. The endless path took us past the garden, the fountain, and the sandbox where the children were playing. It made me smile watching them play. A little boy's parents helped their son build a fort. Someday, Max and I would be doing the same. When I caught Becky smiling, I wondered if she was thinking the same thought.

"I can't believe my baby girl is getting married," Mom said with teary eyes, gazing in the same direction. "You used to be that little. It went by so fast."

I nodded with a smile because that was all I could do. Tears were already threatening to fall. A part of me felt so sad that I wanted to cry. It hit me hard that tomorrow would be the last day anyone would call me Jenna Mefferd. It felt like a part of me would disappear, but I couldn't think of it that way.

"When we were getting married back then, our generation would say we were losing our daughter, but I would like to think that I'm gaining a son. Max is lucky to have you, and you're lucky to have him. I know that I'm not losing you. Don't forget that your dad and I are always here for you."

Mom's hug and tears made me lose it. As tears ran down my face and I felt my mother's love, I was a little girl all over again. I was no longer a child, nor a teenager, nor a young adult—though I might have acted like one or the other many times before—I was going to be a wife and a mother. I would not only have one set of parents, but two. I would also have gained a brother-in-law, and hopefully a sister-in-law, soon.

When Mom released me, she wiped my tears like she had many times before when I was a child. "Live your life to the fullest and be happy. I know I sound like a broken record when I say this, but I'm so happy that you were able to get pregnant quickly. I almost gave up. I'm so glad I didn't. There is no greater joy than raising a child. They give us one of the few precious moments in life. And your dad and I can't wait to be grandparents."

"Thanks, Mom," I sniffed. Soaking in her words, we started walking again. Becky turned to us with a smile. She had walked away to give us space. Her eyes were teary, too.

I looked at my watch. I couldn't believe it had been a couple of hours. "We need to meet up with our wedding coordinator. She's going to give us the details of what we need to do tomorrow. Then we can go get ready for dinner."

"Why are you doing this without Max?" Mom asked worriedly.

"It's because of our schedule and when Max is able to fly in. It's really simple. She needs to show Becky and me the room we'll be coming out from and where we will be standing. Also, where I will meet up with Dad so he can walk me down. It won't take long."

"I see." Mom nodded. "We'd better go get your father."

"Can't wait to see everyone," Becky said. "I just got a text from Nicole and Kate. They're here, checking in."

My phone buzzed inside of my back pocket, and I pulled it out. "Max just landed," I said aloud. Relief washed over me. He had arrived safely, but he still had to drive to the hotel.

We were about to go to dinner when there was a knock on the door.

"Must be the housekeeper." Dad opened the door. "Max." I heard a pause for a second. My dad must have given him a hug. "You're going to be my son-in-law. Call me Jonathan."

My heart thumped faster from the sound of his name. Instead of going to him, I hid behind the bedroom door. My mom rushed to the door. "Max, my son-in-law." She was going to give him a hug for sure. "You can call me Mom or Paige. I don't care which one. How was the flight?" Mom asked. When their footsteps got closer, my heart hammered even faster.

"It's always the same. I'd rather be on land."

My dad chuckled. "I have to agree, but we would fly for days for our daughter's wedding."

"I would fly anywhere for her, too," Max said, slipping his hands inside his dress pants and glancing around. Max was looking for me. "Are you comfortable here? Do you need anything else?" Max asked like a perfect son-in-law.

"Everything is great. Thank you so much. Have a seat."

"Don't keep him hostage," Mom laughed softly. "Jenna is in her room."

"Thank you." When Max took a step toward my door, I scurried away and hid behind the bathroom door. I was acting childish, but I was having fun.

"Come out, come out, wherever you are," Max sang. "You're not thinking of backing out, are you?" His voice and footsteps were closer. I was about to jump out in front of him, but I decided to wait.

"If I could have this view when you're not around then I wouldn't miss you as much."

What the heck was he talking about? What view? I turned to see Max staring at my ass through the space between the door and the door hinge.

"Max." I walked out, laughing.

"I found you," Max said excitedly, embracing me in his arms. He placed a tender kiss on my forehead. "I'm never going to let you go."

I snuggled into his warmth and his love. "You better not," I murmured against his chest.

Max pulled back. "How are you feeling?

"A lot better for sure."

"Are you comfortable here? Is it spacious enough?"

I snorted at his words. "Nope. It's not big enough." I lightly smacked his arm. "Are you seriously asking me that question?"

Max's eyes opened wide with a grin. "I thought it was a good question to ask. Maybe I should ask another. Did you miss me?"

"Yes," I said, unbuttoning the button at the top of his dress shirt, then the second, and the third. I felt Max's chest shudder lightly when I slipped my hand inside his shirt.

"Good." Max's hand slid up the back of my legs and he started kissing softly on my neck. "You look beautiful in this lavender dress." His hot breath against my neck caused a tingle in my clit. "I love how I can feel your ass." He lightly squeezed it. Then his finger slid further down, making me gasp with air. "I love your easy access dress."

"My parents, Max," I warned.

It was as if he had forgotten they were right outside the door. With one hand still on my ass, he rubbed the other over my stomach. "How is baby doing?"

"We are both good and we are very hungry."

"Then we better get going." Max raised my leg and anchored it on his hip. "There, much better."

"Okay." I nodded, but I had no idea what I was saying. Max was playing with my clit. His touches were slow and tender, but oh God, I wanted to take off his clothes. I started to unbutton his shirt, not caring about my parents.

"What are you doing, babe?" Max chuckled. He loved that I was losing control. "Remember our deal?"

I didn't get a chance to answer. Max tilted my body to the side and kissed me, devouring me like he couldn't get enough. "It's time to go. We're already a little late," Max said, pulling back.

My breaths were so heavy I had a difficult time answering. Max helped me to stand and make sure my feet were planted on the ground. "You're bad, Max." I straightened my dress.

Max fixed a few strands of my hair to their places. "I can't help it. Every time I'm near you, a switch turns on inside of me. I'm at your mercy."

I bore my eyes deeply into his. "Are you going to feel that way when I'm fat?"

Max laughed out loud. "Of course I will. You're not going to get fat. You're going to be very pregnant."

"Are you ready to be my husband and the father of our child?" I didn't know why I asked that question. I knew he was, but I needed to hear it one last time.

"Babe, I've been ready since the first moment I saw you. I'm going to be honest. You already know I didn't want to start a family right away, but that's okay. That's what life is all about. I can't wait for you to officially be my wife. And I can't wait to take you to my bed." He growled underneath his breath. "I'm going to make sure you remember our wedding night. You're not getting any sleep."

Max's words shot pleasurable shivers through me. Satisfied with his answer, I gave him a big smile. Max held my hand and led me out the bedroom door. Thank goodness my parents were in their room. Did they wonder what was taking Max and me so long?

CHAPTER 29
BECKY

"I'm coming," I said out loud, hearing the doorbell ring. It was funny to hear that sound. It sounded like I was home.

"Hello, beautiful," Matthew said all flirty, leaning against the door hinge with his hands in his pants pocket. I was short of breath, admiring this beauty in front of me. He wore a striped blue and white dress shirt and dark navy pants. He scanned my body, making his appreciation obvious. "Maybe we should be late to dinner. It's not like we're the reason why people are here." Matthew imprisoned me with his arms, walking backwards, away from the door.

"Yes. But we are in the wedding party. I'm sure someone will miss us," I replied between Matthew's soft kisses on my face. "Why didn't you just use your keys to come in? I saw that you had unpacked already while I was out and about with Jenna and her mom."

"What would be the fun in that?" he murmured against my lips. "We had an appointment with the wedding coordinator. The reason why I didn't let you know. We just finished."

"We really should get going."

"I guess you're right." Matthew pouted, then he became serious. "How are you feeling?"

"You don't have to ask me that every time you see me. Don't worry. I'll let you know," I said cautiously. I didn't want him to think that I was ungrateful.

"Okay," he replied, sounding defeated.

I felt terrible, so I tried to lighten the mood. "So, are we going to have a big wedding?"

"Babe, you can have whatever wedding you want."

"We better get going. Nicole and Kate already texted me twice. I was just about to get Jenna and her parents."

"No need. Max is their escort."

"And you are mine?"

"I'm always yours." Matthew winked.

Matthew had a way of saying the sweetest things. "That you are. Come hither." Hooking my index finger through the loop of his pants, I reeled him out of our villa.

"Here we are." I traced the 3D white wooden letters with my eyes. Addison, it read. "Pretty name for a restaurant."

"I like it," Matthew agreed. "My grandmother's maiden name was Addison. They named this restaurant after her."

"Really?" I squealed excitedly. How amazing it was to have a restaurant named after you.

"Just kidding."

"Matthew!" I lightly pushed his chest. He didn't even budge.

"No, but seriously. My grandmother's name was Addison."

Our friends cut off our conversation and stopped us in place. "Becky!" Kate bellowed, followed by Craig.

"Matthew!" Nicole said out loud. She shook Matthew's hand and gave me a hug.

"Have you been here before?" Craig asked.

"When we get a chance to get away," Matthew answered. "Is this your first time here?"

"Yes, but it won't be our last."

"So...what do you need to tell us?" Kate asked, changing our conversation.

I swung my arm out, making sure they had a clear vision of the diamond ring. I didn't know why I felt shy about flashing it.

"Awww," Nicole said smiling. "Congratulations."

"It's beautiful," Kate gushed.

"We should get going. We're already late. I'll tell you all about it during dinner...or maybe after." Mathew and I headed inside hand in hand, where a room full of people greeted us.

I met Matthew's cousins, aunts, and uncles. Their gestures showed how much they loved and cared for one another. Jenna caught my eyes from across the room. She had the brightest, happiest smile. As I continued to smile and gaze at her, sadness lingered in my heart. No matter how genuinely happy I was for her, even knowing I would see her soon, she was no longer my roommate. I'd miss her terribly.

After dinner, most of the elder couples headed to bed while the young ones ordered drinks and went to a hangout close to the bar.

"Did you set your wedding date yet?" Nicole asked. With her legs crossed, she snuggled to Keith on the sofa.

When I turned to Matthew, I almost kissed him, he was pressed so closely against me. It's like he needed to touch all of me. If he could, he would be on top of me. I had to laugh at that. "We're going to wait until next year." Nicole and Kate had no idea that I was pregnant. I planned to tell them when we got home. I wouldn't be able to hide it much longer.

Max and Jenna stood up. "We're going to bed."

"So soon? The wedding isn't until late afternoon," Kate said, giving Jenna and Max a hug.

"I don't know if I can sleep, so I'm going to try to get as much rest as possible."

"Oh...I understand. I didn't sleep at all on the night of my wedding."

"Really, hun? I slept like a baby," Keith snorted.

"Guys don't understand. All that work you do, you want everything to be perfect. We understand, Jenna. You want to be refreshed and look your best on the most important day of your life."

After their good-byes, they left.

"Let's go to bed, too," Matthew whispered in my ears so that only I could hear. Everyone else was in a heated conversation about the time shares one could purchase there.

"I'm not tired." I wanted to toy with him.

"I have lollipops in my room. All kinds of flavors." Matthew licked the tip of my earlobes, causing me to tingle between my legs.

"Do you have my favorite flavor?"

"My firecracker, I'm going to rub your favorite flavor on your cherry and suck it hard," he stated under his breath.

Holy Jesus, take me now.

CHAPTER 30
MAX

"You ready?" Matthew asked, standing by the door. Dressed in a Gucci black tuxedo, purple vest, and purple bow, he looked all grown up.

"I am," I replied, looking at the mirror in front of me to adjust my shirt.

"Have Mom and Dad come by yet?"

"Yes. A few minutes ago."

"I'm here to let you know it's almost time."

"I can't believe this day is finally here. It doesn't feel real."

Matthew patted me gently on my back. "It's because you never thought you would find the right woman to have forever with."

"I found love when least expected. Same goes for you. And I can't believe we're both going to be fathers soon."

"I can't either, but it's all good. It has to be."

I knew my brother best, especially when he tried to hide his worried expression...forehead creased and his brows angled. However, I understood why. I would feel the same way if Jenna was in Becky's situation. Matthew had visited me the day after he brought Becky back from Paris and told me everything. "Don't worry. Think positive thoughts. Make sure Becky goes to her appointments. She will have them more frequently than a normal pregnant mom. Rest assured that you have found her the best doctor.

And don't worry. I haven't told Mom and Dad. That's your job. But they will be thrilled. I got first dibs on babysitting."

"We'll see about that," Matthew challenged. "We plan to tell our parents after we visit her parents. I've never met them, but they know who I am."

"Good. Don't wait too long."

"Well...that's the music. It's time to go."

"Thanks for being my best man," I said, smiling at my little brother. No matter how old he was, he would always be the little brother I would protect.

"Thanks for agreeing to be my best man," Matthew said. "I don't know when that date will be."

"It's okay. I'm here. I'll always be here for you."

"I know." Matthew paused and his facial expression changed to a playful one. "Race you to the front?" Matthew dashed to the door.

"Not today. I'm taking my time. I'm going to savor every moment of today."

Jenna

Professional makeup artists did mine and Becky's hair and makeup, and they did a fabulous job. She tied my hair up elegantly and let a few loose strands down the side of my cheek. The makeup was natural, just the way I liked it, but it was definitely professional looking. I felt like a fashion model. My wedding dress hid my little belly, the reason why I had made sure my dress would flow out just enough from the waist. It was flattering to my shape, but hid what I wanted.

Becky looked gorgeous. Her hair was down and her makeup complemented her dress. Luckily we had picked out the dress in a similar style to mine, so no one could tell she had a little belly, too. Becky and I had compared our belly size the other day and debated the sex of her baby and who would have the biggest child.

Max and I had bought Matthew and Becky matching sterling silver bracelets from Tiffany's as a way to thank them for being our best man and maid of honor. It made me smile that she had it on.

"Jenna. You look amazing," Becky said. "I can't even tell you didn't get any sleep last night."

"Thanks. You do, too. I love that lavender on you."

"Thanks."

"Adrenaline is pumping through me so fast right now. I should be exhausted, but I'm not. I feel like I drank five cups of coffee. I feel like I forgot something."

"I'm sure everything is in order. You shouldn't have to worry about a thing. The list of things to do has been completed."

Becky helped me put the veil on. I had something old, the veil from my mother-in-law. Something new was the bracelet my mom gave me during my bridal shower. Something blue was the garter I wore underneath the dress. And Becky's pearl earrings were something borrowed.

"There. Now you're all set."

I jumped and my heart rate kicked up a notch when there was a soft knock. My mom walked in when Becky opened the door.

After she gave Becky a hug and a kiss, she just stood there and stared at me. "Oh, Jenna." Her lips trembled and tears wet her cheeks. "You look beautiful. Max won't be able to keep his eyes off you. Not that he does anyway. I have to admit, at first, I thought he would be overbearing, but he turned out to be better than I had expected. Max loves you so much. You know how I can tell?"

"How?"

"It's the way he looks at you. It's full of genuine love, honor, and respect."

"Yes, I know. I'm very lucky."

"That you are." Mom paused with an intake of breath. "Dad told me to hurry. He's waiting where they told him to. Well, I'd better get going." After a kiss on my cheek, Mom left.

The sound of music made my heart thump faster. That song was Max's cue to stand in front with Matthew. Almost time. My muscles tightened, and blood pumped through me so fast I could hardly breathe. All of those people out there were going to stare at me. What if I fell? What if I started crying? I was an emotional wreck.

"Deep breaths, Jenna," Becky reminded. "Inhale...exhale. There you go."

When the wedding coordinator appeared at the door with my dad and the photographer, I knew it was time. "Max and Matthew are at their positions," she said. "When you hear the harp, that will be Becky's cue. Then it will be your turn. But don't worry. I'm here to guide you."

"Okay." I nodded. "Thanks."

"You girls look beautiful," Dad said proudly, giving Becky and me awkward hugs. The veil was in the way. "I can't believe my little girl is getting married today. Just look at you."

I blushed and smiled. "And look at you, Dad. You're so handsome in that tuxedo."

My dad's cheeks turned red. "You think so? Mom liked it, too." He gave me a nervous laugh. He was too cute acting all shy around me.

The first harp rang.

"Becky," I squealed as my stomach dropped to the floor.

Becky gave me one last hug. After picking up both of our bouquets from the table, she handed me mine. Hers was a mixture of white orchids with purple roses, and mine was plain white orchids.

"You've got this," Becky reminded me. "I need to walk down first. Keep your head up and smile. Don't look at the audience. Keep your eyes on Max. I know what you're thinking. Hold onto your dad tightly. Take baby steps so you won't fall flat on your face." Then she turned and wedding-marched out of my sight. Becky made me laugh. She'd known exactly what I was thinking.

I snuck a peek to see Becky walk down the white runway. Rows and rows of white chairs filled with our family and friends were an overwhelming sight. My heart started hammering faster again...I was almost certain I was having an anxiety attack. Since I had a limited view from the back, I couldn't see Max, but I noticed the clear and beautiful sky, scattered with white puffy clouds. Since it was late in the afternoon, the position of the sun cast a nice shade over us. The weather was perfect, not too cold and not too hot.

"Time to go, Jenna," my dad said, linking his arm around mine. "I've got you, kiddo."

Max

When the harpist played the "Wedding March", my heart filled with powerful bliss, pounding against my chest. It wasn't that I was nervous about getting married, it was the anticipation of seeing Jenna in her wedding dress and finally making her Mrs. Knight. At any minute, I would see my Jenna walking to me. And...there she was with her dad. Like a thief, she stole my heart and breath. At that moment, I inhaled the most delicious air, so refreshing and refined. She looked like the perfect angel sent from above in all white. I knew she would look beautiful, but she'd exceeded my expectations. Taking tiny steps, ensuring she wouldn't trip—because that was my Jenna—she looked like a vision of splendor.

Jenna stared straight ahead and caught my eyes. Her smile was sweet and somewhat shy. She also seemed a bit scared. I didn't blame her. Everyone was standing, staring at her with the "aww" and "oo" sounds. Finally, she stood in front of me. With glistening eyes, she swallowed and bit her bottom lip to stop herself from sobbing. I, too, found myself a little damp in the eyes, so I could only imagine how much she held back.

After the pastor said a few words, Jenna's father gave me Jenna's hand, and then everyone took their seats. We nodded at the pastor to confirm we were ready and he began, "Dearly beloved, we are gathered here today to join this man, Maxwell Knight, and this woman, Jenna Mefferd, in matrimony."

After those words, everything else blurred as I gazed deeply into Jenna's eyes. She looked so content. I was more than happy to be able to put that huge angelic smile on her face. The time came to exchange our vows. We had told the pastor we would write our own.

Jenna handed her bouquet to Becky, then we both faced each other with our hands joined in front. With a big intake of breath, and setting my eyes on her, I began, "My dearest Jenna. Where do I start telling you how much you mean to me? It's been a long journey in a short amount of time. When I first met you, I knew you were the one. It hit me so hard, I didn't know what to do. I couldn't breathe. But everything fell into place. What I did and said came naturally, because that is how I feel when I'm with you, like I'm home. I feel so blessed to have found you. Many search their whole life for their soul mate, but I found you when least expected. Every second, every minute, every moment, you are on my mind. My heart beats only for you, babe. My life was like a blank canvas, but you painted it with your love. You made me a perfect painting. I promise, from this day forward, in front of all these witnesses, and under the heavenly sky, that I will honor, respect, and take care of you and our future family with my life. You are everything to me. You are my something great, forever."

Jenna's lips quivered and she gazed down for a moment. When she looked back at me, a teardrop came down from the corner of her eye. She blinked rapidly in an effort to keep her tears at bay. I wiped them with a smile and held her hands again. From my peripheral vision, I could see Jenna's mom and my mom in tears.

Jenna took a deep breath before she started, "My dearest Max. You came into my life like a true Knight. You made me see what real love is. You made me understand that I deserved better. You've shown me that I was worth fighting for. I'm beautiful when I'm around you. You bring out the best in me. The once insecure girl is gone. I've become more confident and wiser because of you. Ever since I met you, you lifted me up and never let me touch the ground. That is how you make me feel. I promise, from this day forward, that I will be the wife you deserve, because you have no idea how much you mean to me. I can't put it into words. I will honor, respect, and show you every day how much I love you. You are everything to me. You are my something great, forever."

Tears streamed down Jenna's cheeks, and before I had a chance to wipe them, Becky handed her some Kleenex. She was crying, too. I wanted the pastor to hurry. It took every ounce of my energy to stop myself from kissing Jenna that moment. If I could, I would have carried her back to our hotel room, stripped her naked, and made sweet, passionate love to my wife.

After we exchanged our rings, the pastor spoke again. We were near the end. "We have come together in this place and heard the willingness of Maxwell and Jenna to be joined in marriage. They have come of their own free will and in our hearing have made a covenant of faithfulness. They have given and received rings as their seal of the promises. By virtue of the authority vested in me under the laws of the State of California, I now pronounce you husband and wife. You may kiss the bride."

Carefully wrapping my arms around Jenna, I tilted her body just enough to make a show and gave her a kiss everyone would talk about. Clapping and wolf whistles erupted around us. After I helped Jenna steady, I guided her arm through mine and we headed down the aisle. What an amazing experience.

CHAPTER 31
JENNA

Relief washed over me when the wedding was over. I cried but maintained enough control not to sob like crazy. What an amazing opportunity for Max and me to show our love in front of our family and friends. As we proceeded down the long, white aisle, I noticed what a fabulous job our wedding coordinator had done with her staff.

The tower Max and I had stood under in front was draped in lavender material that looked like curtains. Long, grand vases stood on either side, filled with the most beautiful colors of flowers I had ever seen. They looked so perfect that I would almost have thought they were fake. White lace and small bouquets of flowers hung from one chair to the next in the center aisle. I was so busy making sure I wouldn't trip and locking my eyes on Max that I hadn't enjoyed the beauty of the set until afterward.

Our reception area was set outside of the restaurant called Amaya, on the deck adjacent to the area where we had exchanged vows. White linens covered the tables. On the center of each table was a vase of uniquely decorated purple, pink, and white flowers. Each place setting included a party favor filled with Godiva truffles in a silver paper box with purple and white ribbon. Everything was color coordinated to the tee, and I had to give big thanks to my mother-in-law.

Clink, clink, clink. Matthew hit his wine glass with a fork, standing up. The mic was right next to our table, so it was easy access for him. "Welcome everyone. For those of you who don't know me, shame on you."

The crowd laughed.

"Just kidding," Matthew chuckled. "My name is Matthew Knight, the younger brother of the groom. I'd like to make a toast, but not the kind you would eat."

The crowd laughed again.

"You can tell from my jokes that I'm the jokester of the family, and the better looking one. Just kidding again," Matthew said, chuckling. "Okay, but seriously. I'm not going to bore you with what a great guy Max is, because all the wonderful stories you hear about him are true. And I'm not going to bore you with what a great brother he is, because everybody knows he is.

"I want to share a story that will touch your heart and is why we are here. When Max was in high school and I had no idea what falling in love was, I asked my brother what love meant. He said he wasn't sure, but when he knew, he would let me know. Time passed, and I asked him again in college. He said he didn't know. To which I would say, 'With all of the women you've dated, you don't know?' He simply said he would let me know.

"I asked him again after we started working with our parents. The answer was the same, until Jenna walked into his life. He spotted her at a restaurant and hadn't officially met her yet. Max called me that day. And do you know what he said?" Matthew paused. "Max told me that when he saw Jenna, his heart thumped so hard that it felt like it was going to jump out of his chest. And when she left, his heart had stopped beating. The reason why Max says his heart only beats for Jenna? Because it's true."

My heart expanded with bliss. Max said that to Matthew? If I'd known how he felt, I could have saved us a lot of heartaches. Max squeezed my shoulder. His arms were wrapped behind me. When I gazed into his eyes, he pressed his lips on mine softly and tenderly, as if to confirm Matthew's words.

Matthew gazed directly at us. "Let's raise our glasses and toast this amazing couple, who couldn't be more perfect for each other." He waited to see more glasses up in the air. "To Max and Jenna, may you have a fruitful life together with a minivan full of kids. And may your heart thump hard for each other for the rest of your lives. Here is to something forever."

Clink, clink, clink. The sound of glasses echoed in the air. Max's parents, my parents, Matthew, and Becky all toasted their glasses. It was easier since we all sat at the same round table. Then Becky stood up.

"Hello, my name is Becky Miller. I'm the maid of honor. The instant I met Jenna, I knew she was special. And I knew we would become best friends for life. Her innocence and genuine heart were what stood out for me, and I had to make her my friend. Just like Matthew, I'm not going to bore you with stories of what a great person Jenna is, because she is. I want to share a story that will touch your heart. Jenna was always the safe one. She hardly took any risks, but when she met Max, her whole world became a huge mess. She couldn't breathe. They were soul mates destined to be, because no matter how hard Jenna tried to stay away from Max, she couldn't.

"I remember telling Jenna that if she didn't take a leap of faith with Max that she would never know. After finally making her decision, she told me whatever happened, she would be okay. You see, Jenna always prepared for the worst. A part of her was expecting something to go wrong, but their love for each other was too strong."

When Becky took a moment to catch her breath, Max kissed me on the cheek. "So," Becky continued, "Max...you are simply Jenna's air. You make her world spin. To Jenna and Max. Love you both very much."

Clink, clink, clink. Matthew started hitting his glass, then the rest followed.

"I'm going to make your world spin, babe," Max said as the clinking of glass rang louder and louder. What was he doing? He helped me up, leaned me back, and gave me a passionate kiss.

The wolf whistles echoed, indicating everyone was satisfied with that kiss.

After dinner, we had the father-daughter dance and mother-son dance, then Max and I slow danced together while the harpist played. The cake was delicious and many pictures were taken. It couldn't have been more perfect. Just as the reception ended, the sun started to set in splashes of pink and purple. Never had I seen such beautiful colors in the sky. And never had I seen and felt so much love and support as I did that day.

"Mrs. Jenna Knight. Let me do the honors." Max opened the door, swooped me up in his arms, and carried me over the threshold.

"We did it. I can't believe it's over," I said, feeling my back touch the bed. Max dropped next to me.

"Yes, we did. It's official. Tomorrow, we'll be heading to Paris, then Rome. By the time we come back from our honeymoon, we'll be able to sleep in our new home."

"Really?" I turned on my side to him.

"I forgot to tell you. The movers are moving everything out of my apartment to our new home. Matthew is going to direct them."

"You're so lucky you have Matthew."

Max kissed the back of my hand. "Yes, I am." Max caressed my cheek and looked lovingly into my eyes. "I'm so happy, babe."

"Me, too," I said sincerely. "I can't believe I'm Mrs. Knight. It's going to be hard to get used to."

"I understand. You've been Jenna Mefferd for so long. Thanks for taking my last name."

"I wouldn't have it any other way. It's all or nothing."

"Good, because it's all for me." Max's eyes turned dark and greedy. I knew that look too well. My body had already started to tingle. "I love you, Jenna Knight," Max said, unzipping the back of my dress. Then he carefully took off my veil and undid my hair. Max hovered over me. "I'm going to show you all night just how much." His hot breath rushed down my neck, then lower to my shoulder. His kisses traveled downward as he tugged my dress down, exposing my strapless lacy bra. "Beautiful," I heard him mumble against the base of my breast.

I drowned in pleasure when Max circled his tongue around my nipple. "Oh...Max," I murmured softly. He didn't stop there, he continued to glide his tongue down the middle over my exposed skin. When he got to the base of my stomach, he rubbed and kissed my belly as if he was kissing our baby. His touch was different in that area.

Max had undressed me past my waist, and let the dress fall on the floor. With the dress out of the way, Max took his time and kissed his way up my white stockings, to the garter, and to my lacey white G-string. When I heard a low growl, I knew Max liked what I was wearing.

I gasped as he ran his tongue over my clit. The sensation shot up to my core, expanding fast and hard. I wanted more.

"I want to undress you," I said, out of breath. It was my turn.

After Max helped me up, I kissed the side of his neck while I undid his bow, his vest, his shirt, and helped him out of his tuxedo jacket. I slowly ran my hands across his firm chest, feeling every curve of his tight muscles as his chest rose and fell. Max groaned and shuddered from the warmth of my tongue. As I continued to taste him, I unbuttoned and unzipped his pants and let everything drop to the floor.

Max was hard, big, and ready for me. Down on my knees, I licked his dick from base to tip, then sucked and stroked the way he liked. "Jenna," Max hissed and made the pleasured sound I loved to hear. Max started to rub my shoulder, and then threw his head back with his eyes closed. He needed to touch me. He yanked me up and kissed me, full of passion, desire, and want.

I couldn't recall how my bra and all the extra lingerie I had on vanished, but that was what Max did when his hands ran all over my body and he kissed me like there was no tomorrow. He was so smooth and graceful with his hands and his lips that being completely naked always surprised me.

After what seemed like an eternity of foreplay and me begging him to be inside of me, he finally entered. The shot of pleasure coursing throughout my body made my head spin. I was lost to his touch and the pleasure he was giving me. There was no sense of time or reality. Only Max and I existed. Sometimes Max would look into my eyes and ride me slow. Sometimes, he would rock faster, causing me to expel short, gasping pleasure sounds. Max always made sure my needs were fulfilled, but he gave me more than I expected that night.

Our wedding day was by far the longest we'd explored one another. I didn't know what time it was and I didn't care. I was beyond exhausted. He wanted to make our wedding date memorable. There was no doubt in my mind that he had done what he had set out to do. I felt desired. I felt wanted. I felt his love in every kiss and every touch.

CHAPTER 32
JENNA

After we had brunch together with our family and friends, we said our good-byes. Mom and Dad decided to stay a few extra days with my in-laws, and Matthew and Becky drove to Los Angeles airport to catch a plane to take the flight to San Francisco. I had no doubt that Becky's parents would adore Matthew.

"Mrs. Knight," I heard. "Mrs. Knight."

I looked up at the pilot and realized he was calling me. I was Mrs. Knight. It felt so strange to be called that name, even though it belonged to me now. It would take some time to get used to. "Yes?" I smiled.

"Please tell Mr. Knight we can take off now."

Just as he finished his words, Max entered. He had been checking the back of the plane. "We're good back here."

"Put on your seatbelt sir, we're clear to go." With that, the pilot closed the door behind him. I could never get used to the idea that I was riding on a private plane.

"You comfortable, babe?" Max asked, making sure my seatbelt was fastened.

"I already did it, Max."

"Just making sure, babe." Max kissed my forehead. "If you're tired, take a nap. And if you're hungry, let me know. Our lunch is already prepared."

"Thanks." Max was so good to me and always catered to my needs. He held my hand as the plane took off. Looking out at the beautiful clouds, I wondered how on Earth I was so lucky to find someone like Max.

After we landed, we got into a car with heavily tinted windows. Max had hired a driver for the duration of our stay. The time difference didn't bother me much since I'd slept most of the time on the plane.

"We're going to take a quick detour, then we'll be on our way to the hotel," Max informed.

"Why?"

Max kissed the back of my hand as he held it and grinned widely. "You'll see."

What did he have up his sleeve?

When our limo driver pulled over, Max helped me out of the car. We were both dressed in casual wear so I knew we weren't going any place fancy, but I never would have imagined that we would stop by a bridge.

"What are we doing here?" I asked, observing the people around us. Many couples were holding hands. When I turned to Max, I first noticed the countless locks on the bridge. Holy cow! "What is this place?"

"This is where couples come and declare their love forever by writing their names on the lock, then they toss the key into the river."

Then it dawned on me. Becky had mentioned what they had done in our conversation. "Becky told me about this place."

Max pulled out something from his back pocket and dangled it in front of me with an irresistible grin, like he was about to do something naughty. The lock was the biggest one I had ever seen. It was bigger than my hand. I was pretty sure that no locks on this bridge could compare to the size of ours. "That's huge."

Max chuckled. "Yup, mine is. That's what you said."

"Oh my God, Max. I didn't mean..." I decided to play along. While I caressed his chest and pressed my body on his, I spoke with a sultry tone. "That's true. Yours is huge. And I want to lick it." Sometimes I surprised myself.

Max chuckled again and his grin told me he liked my comment. "I can show you later, but let's do this." Max wrote my name, then his with a permanent pen.

"Where should we lock it?"

"Right here." Max pointed.

Becky had told me they'd hung their lock at the start of the bridge. I didn't think we would ever find it because I couldn't visualize what she meant, so I was surprised when Max found it. "Did Matthew tell you about this place?"

"He did, but I also knew about it. I had planned to bring my wife here when it was time. And here we are."

I smiled at Max, knowing I was his first. "Are we going to put ours next to Becky and Matthew's?"

"That's the plan." Max handed the lock to me.

Matthew and Becky's lock was big—it stood out from the others for sure—but ours was bigger. "Theirs is silver, too."

"Ours is platinum, babe. Heavy duty. I had it made by a locksmith."

Why did that not surprise me? "Platinum, Max? Seriously?" I laughed.

"Nobody is going to be able to break it. Let's put it on together." After I looped it through, Max helped me press into the hole until it clicked. "On the count of three, we toss the key together. This is forever, babe." Max pressed his lips on mine. "One...two...three."

Max's hand that was already cupped behind mine gently pushed forward. The key flew just high enough to plop into the river. I jerked with a scream. Max had slapped my ass. "Come on, Mrs. Knight. Let's go have some fun."

Our honeymoon was an amazing experience to remember. Max and I took a lot of pictures to show our family and friends. Though we were gone for two weeks, it seemed like a dream. It went by too fast.

Just like Max said, all of our belongings were set when we got home. Max also paid for them to put everything in its place so I didn't even have to hang anything in my walk-in-closet that looked more like a room. Even the furniture we had agreed to purchase was placed in the correct position: the crib, dresser, the rocking chair, and little baby fixtures.

"The painters are coming by tomorrow. You can ask them to design the nursery however you'd like." Max slipped his arms around my waist from behind and kissed my cheek. "My parents, Matthew, and Becky are on their way."

"I can't wait to see them. I also have a doctor's appointment next week."

Max's hand fell down to my stomach. "You mean *we* have a doctor's appointment." Suddenly, Max jerked away. "Did you feel that?" he asked excitedly, his eyes wide. "I felt our baby move."

"I did," I said with exhilaration.

"That was incredible." Max got down on his knees and placed his hands on my belly. "Come on, baby, move for Daddy." He leaned in closer and his expression told me he was consumed with joy. Max kissed my stomach, stood up, and gave me a kiss. "Was this the first time?"

"Yes it was. Our baby knows we're home."

"Our baby is smart."

The sound of the doorbell broke our conversation. "Let's go down together." We started down the stairs. "Should we tell them the sex of our baby?"

"Nah," I laughed. "Not just yet."

Max swung the door open. "Jenna!" Becky practically jumped on me. She was really starting to show. Then it was Matthew's turn. He looked down to my stomach. "You sure ate a lot in Paris."

We laughed out loud from his teasing comment. "You know how Max is. He loves to feed me. Let's go to the family room."

"Matthew already gave me the tour of your house when the movers moved you in. I made sure they placed everything where I thought you would like it," Becky explained as we sat on the leather sofa. "You have a beautiful home."

"Thanks, Becky. You shouldn't have. It's no wonder everything looked right in place. So, how are you feeling?"

"So far so good. I have a doctor's appointment every other week. Enough about me. Tell me all about your trip."

Max and I shared as much as we could. We even told them about the lock, but we didn't mention that ours was bigger.

"Mom and Dad are coming, right?" Matthew asked.

"They're on their way," Max replied, placing his hand on my stomach again.

"They live down the street. You'd think they would get here first," Matthew chuckled. "What are you doing?"

"We felt our baby kick for the first time today."

"We did, too." Matthew grinned, gazing at Becky. "Do you know if you're having a boy or a girl? We'll tell you, if you tell us."

We all laughed and stood up when there was a knock on the door. "Here they are," Max said. We followed behind.

Becky stopped me. "I don't know if Max told you, but we're moving down the street. A house went up for sale. We loved it so much that we put in our offer and they accepted it."

"Becky. That's wonderful." I embraced her tightly. "We can help each other."

"That was our thoughts exactly. And before I forget, Nicole and Kate want to throw a dual baby shower for us. Is that okay?"

"It's perfect."

The door opened, but before Robert and Ellen could see us, I asked Becky a quick question. "How did your parents take it? And what did your sister think of Matthew?"

"My parents adored him, and Rachel, too. They loved Matthew. And Ellen and Robert were beyond excited," Becky said quickly, smiling. Ellen and Robert had spotted us. I would ask her more questions later.

"Welcome," I greeted, giving them hugs. "Max had dinner catered. Let's head toward the family room."

"Babe, it's for you." Max handed me the phone. "It's your mom."

I excused myself to our bedroom. "Mom?"

"Jenna. How are you?" Mom's tone immediately gave me   comfort. "Is everything okay?" I had called my parents the day we got back from Paris, so to get a call from her this soon worried me.

"Everything is fine. Dad and I wanted to say thank you. We received the big statue of the Eiffel tower and the various chocolates you mailed. It was a nice surprise."

"Max and I wanted to thank you and Dad for coming."

"You don't have to thank us."

"I know, Mom, but we wanted to. I'll see you in a couple of months, right?"

"Yes. Dad will finally retire. We also agreed to take Max's old place, but only if he let us pay the rent. We can't stay there for free."

"I think he paid it off."

"Regardless, we're not staying there for free. That is our deal."

"Okay. I'll let him know."

"I can't wait. I'll help you with the baby in any way I can. I wasn't able to be there much for your wedding, but now it will be easier."

"Don't worry about it. I didn't do much either."

"Well, I'll let you go. Drink lots of fluids and eat healthy. Do you know the sex of the baby yet?"

Oh God! I wanted to tell her so bad, but Max and I had made a promise to each other. "Not yet, Mom. Our baby is stubborn. The legs were closed. Maybe on the next visit we'll find out."

"I'll call you soon. Love you. Bye."

"Love you, Mom."

M. Clarke

CHAPTER 33
2 MONTHS LATER

BECKY

"I could eat everything off this menu," I said through the hunger.

"Me, too," Jenna added. Jenna looked like the ideal pregnant woman. You couldn't tell she was pregnant, except when you saw her stomach. Her face glowed with a flush of pretty pink, and you could tell how happy she was. As for me, my feet, my hands, and my face looked puffy, mostly from fluid retention.

"Well, I'll be joining you all soon," Nicole stated, looking at her menu.

There were no movements from the three of us, except for Nicole's eyes flickering back and forth on the menu. We were waiting for her to clarify her comment, but she offered none.

"What did you say?" Kate asked after a long period of silence.

Nicole dropped her menu on the table. "I'm pregnant."

"Oh my God. Congratulations," the three of us squealed.

"When did you find out? When is the baby due? How? I mean, forget the how," Kate snorted. She rambled so fast she tripped over her words.

"We haven't announced it to our families yet. So you're the first. It's only been two months. Our baby is due seven months from now, in June."

"That's awesome. We can have play dates," I said.

"Did you have morning sickness?" Jenna asked.

"No. I'm hoping that I won't get it." Nicole shrugged. "After seeing what you had to go through, I hope it never happens to me."

Kate crossed her arms on the table and gazed at all of us. "I'm just glad that I won't be the only one with a child. Now you'll understand what if feels like to be a parent. I love Kristen and I wouldn't want anything different, but it can get crazy frustrating at times. But at the same time, there's a lot of joy and wonderful memories you wouldn't trade for anything."

When the waitress came by, we ordered our food and drinks.

"How are you feeling?" Nicole gazed at me. "We're praying everyday that your baby and you are safe."

"Thank you. I'm tired and bloated." I looked at my hands. "But I'm thankful that I've been steady. My kidneys are functioning, but not to their full capacity, and my blood pressures have been normal. I've been very lucky. I just need to hang in there for another month and a half." Suddenly, my body flushed with warmth. I took a sip of my water, hoping it would help me cool down.

When the waitress came back with our food, we ate and held small conversations about Jenna's honeymoon, the baby shower Nicole and Kate were hosting at Jenna's house, and what items to register for.

"Isn't this strange?" I asked, looking at my friends. "We used to talk about the guys we were we dating, our jobs, and our sex lives. But now...we're talking about marriages and having babies."

"We're at that age," Jenna sighed. "And pretty soon, we'll hang out at our kids' birthday parties, graduations, and I hate to bring up the morbid topic, but funerals as well."

"The circle of life," Nicole added. "It's never ending."

"I'm glad that we have good friends to share all of the happiness, and even the sadness, because the sadness isn't so bad when you have friends to talk to," I said, taking another bite of my big, fat, juicy hamburger. It oozed with a satisfying sensation. The warmth that spread so quickly in my body disappeared. Maybe I just needed to eat more, but I wasn't as hungry as I was with the first bite.

"It sure isn't." Jenna smiled at me, then at Nicole and Kate.

"Let's make a toast," I suggested, lifting up my glass of water. "Not the kind you would eat." We all laughed, recalling Matthew's words. I laughed lightly and said, "Sorry. I had to say it. Anyway, here's to Nicole being pregnant, having safe deliveries, and our lifetime friendship."

With a clink, we toasted. After Jenna placed her glass down, she got up. I immediately knew what she was up to. Not wanting her to pay for the bill, I followed after her. "Jenna. What are you doing? I told you I got this."

Jenna turned to me and looked surprised. "How do...Becky. No. I'll get it."

"It's too late, Jenna. I already gave the waitress my credit card the second I walked in the door."

"No you didn't," she argued, opening her purse.

"Want to find out?" I challenged with a smirk. "I didn't bring my purse up here, did I?" My expression faded into a scared one when the room started to spin. Everything around me seemed to move in slow motion. Hot and cold feelings alternated quickly, flashing through my body. The sudden change of temperature hit me fast and hard. My heart was pumping in overdrive, and it got worse when I felt like I was losing my breath.

"Jenna." I tried to get her attention, but I didn't know if she heard my desperate call for help. All I could think of at that moment was my baby and Matthew. Oh God. Please don't let anything bad happen. When I felt myself losing control of my muscles and the day started to turn to night, I knew I was in big trouble.

Jenna

I got worried when Becky's smile disappeared so quickly. Did I say something to offend her? But I knew that wasn't it. "Becky, are you okay?"

When she didn't answer, I thought maybe she was in deep thought at first, but she showed signs of stress. Her eyes stared into space and her face lost color. Becky mouthed a word, but no sound escaped her.

"Becky!" I reached for her just in time and stopped her from collapsing to the floor. My tone caused a lot of attention. Nicole and Kate must have heard me, too. They were on the floor next to us.

"Call the ambulance," I shouted at the waitress standing over us. I didn't give her a chance to ask questions. I was so scared. I didn't know what else to do or how to help Becca. With my trembling hands, I made sure her head rested on my leg. Please don't let anything happen to the both of them, I prayed to myself. "Hang in there,

Becky," I pleaded, moving the strands of hair away from her face, then holding onto her hand. Feeling her hand so cold, I started to massage it. I had no idea what I was doing, but I had to do something. I was going out of my mind.

The store manager dashed to us. "We've called the ambulance. Is she breathing?"

"Yes." Her chest rose and fell slowly. "How long will it take them?"

"They said five minutes or less."

"Okay." My eyes swam with tears as I reached into my purse. "Call Matthew and Max." I handed the phone to Nicole or Kate. I didn't know whom exactly. I didn't want to take my eyes off Becky. I was too afraid that her condition would worsen if I did. "Everything is going to be fine." I had to let her know that, had to hope she could hear me. I also wanted her to know that I was right there. Realizing I had a cardigan on, I took it off and placed it on her.

"Matthew is on his way," Nicole said.

"No," I snapped. I didn't mean to. "Tell him to meet us at the hospital. By the time he gets here, we'll be gone. Did you get ahold of Max?"

"No. He's in a meeting, but the secretary said she'll let him know."

Five minutes felt like forever, especially because we were desperate. I released a long breath when the sound of the siren rang loudly. Thank God! When the sound stopped, I knew they were just outside. The rush of cool air brushed my face when the door opened. Fall had kicked in. Though it wasn't that cold, my senses were heightened from being in panic mode.

"Ma'am, you need to move over so we can help your friend." The gentleman helped me up. "Was she injured?"

"No. I caught her just in time."

"Good. How many months is she?"

"She's due in a little over a month. We're due around the same time."

I saw the other two men placing Becky on the stretcher. It ripped my heart to see her with a breathing mask on and so still.

"Have you notified her family?"

"Yes." I realized that I didn't call her parents, but I would wait and ask Becky or Matthew. I wanted to tell him that I was her family, too. I was her best friend, her sister, her everything, just like she was mine.

"Is this your sweater?" He placed it in front of me.

"Yes, thank you."

"We'll take care of her from here, ma'am. You did a great job."

The gentleman was sweet and polite. As I watched the stretcher go up the ramp, tears fell down my cheek. I had to hold it together and be strong for her. There were no guarantees in life, but there was hope, and that was what I needed to hold on to.

Nicole and Kate placed their arms around me as we watched the ambulance take off.

"I have Becky's purse," Nicole said. "I can drive us to the hospital. Did Becky drive here?"

"Yes. I'll speak to the restaurant manager about allowing her car to be parked here over night. Don't worry about me. I'll be fine. I can drive to the hospital."

"Okay, we'll meet you there," Kate confirmed. "Don't worry, Jenna. Becky is stubborn. She won't let anything happen to the both of them, but we'll still pray."

After I gave them both a hug, I went inside.

CHAPTER 34
MATTHEW

When I heard Nicole's voice on Jenna's phone, I immediately knew something had happened to Becca. Blood drained out of me before she could complete her sentence with Jenna's name. I was pissed off at myself for not being there for her. We were at the tail end of the pregnancy; I should have forced her to stay home.

I hated going to the hospital. It was where everything bad happened in my life. All I could do was pray that my Becca was safe. If something happened to our baby, we would be devastated, but we would get through it. We could adopt. Many people did it.

After inhaling a deep breath, I entered. Becca's eyes grew wide with happiness to see me as tears streamed down her face. She looked so worried and fragile. "Becca." I reached over carefully and hugged her with a sigh of relief.

"Everything is fine," she started to say when I released her, "don't worry." Her tears kept coming. I pulled out some Kleenex and wiped them for her. "I was so scared...so scared that I'd lost our baby. They need to do more tests, but the doctor said the baby's heart rate was strong. He even showed me on the ultrasound."

I held her hand as she told me the rest. "The doctor will come by to explain everything to you. He wants to talk to you, too. He told me that I'm going to be on bed rest and will most likely have a cesarean. He's hoping that the baby will hold on till at least two weeks prior to the due date, so I need to be on bed rest for about a month. He's going to let me know what dates are available."

I kissed Becca's hand. "Don't worry about a thing. I'm going to take care of you. I'm also going to hire someone when I have to go into the office. I can do most of the work from home, but I'll have to go in for meetings. We have the New York Fashion Show to get ready for, but I won't be going."

Becky nodded with a smile. It was the first time I'd seen her so vulnerable. My Becca the firecracker was scared, and though I needed to be strong for the both of us, a part of me was scared, too.

"Should I call your parents?"

"No. Let's see what happens. I don't want to worry them. I'll call them later."

"Jenna, Max, Nicole, and Kate are waiting in the waiting room. Do you want to see them? You don't have to if you need your rest."

"I do. I think Jenna stopped my fall. It could have been worse."

"Yes, it could have, but it's all good. Let's be thankful for that." I said those words more for me, because the thought of Becca hitting her head, or hurting any part of her body—or worse, something happening to our baby from the fall—drove me insane. I had to think of something positive. "I'll go get them."

Becky

Matthew tried to hide how scared he was, but I saw right through him. Never had I seen him distraught before, except for the time he found out about Amber killing Tessa. I knew why. He was most likely blaming himself for not being there. Although I hated the idea of being on bed rest for a month or so, I had to do it for the safety of our child and for me. At least this would force me to catch up with all of the submissions deadlines.

My friends didn't know how to act around me when they first entered the room. Their smiles were plastered on their faces, somewhere between genuine and forced. When I let out a snort, they laughed with me.

"How are you feeling?" Jenna asked, standing in front of Max, who offered a warm grin. "You gave us a big scare."

"You had to make a big scene so Jenna couldn't pay the bill," Nicole scolded playfully, narrowing an eye at her.

"That was the plan." I shrugged. "You know me. I like to win."

"Next time, use a different tactic," Kate added. "We're so relieved you're fine."

"I'll make sure to do that. I'm not planning on doing this again." I glanced over to Matthew. After raking his hair back with a soft sigh, he finally took a seat. At least his serious face softened. He appeared a bit more relaxed than when he'd come in. Looked like Matthew and Max were either discussing work or me.

"What did the doctor say?" Jenna asked, rubbing my arm. "What happened to you?"

"My blood pressure was too high," I answered, feeling bad for causing all of this trouble.

"I didn't call your parents. I didn't—"

"I'm glad you didn't. I'll let them know what happened. My parents will be coming to visit soon. They want to see their grandbaby after all. Meanwhile, I'm going to need lots of visits from my dear friends. I'm stuck at home." I frowned.

"Don't think of it that way. It'll be a great excuse to get together. Party at Becky's," Nicole said.

"Which place?" Jenna asked.

"It'll have to be at my new place. The lease on the apartment where Jenna and I used to live ended several days ago." Stupid pregnancy hormone was making my eyes teary, or that was my excuse. "You'll have to excuse the mess, though. There are still unopened boxes." I looked at Jenna when I said those words. It saddened me that the place where we made memories was officially the past. We created a lot of happy and sad memories there, memories that molded our friendship and made us the people we had become.

Jenna took a deep breath and blinked rapidly as she smiled at me. She was holding back her tears. We had a deep level of friendship that we didn't have with Nicole and Kate. I loved them dearly, but Jenna and I had been through growing pain wars together. We cried. We laughed. We argued. Pretty soon we were going to be sisters-in-law. Pretty soon we were going to become mothers, whether we were ready or not.

"That sounds like a plan," Nicole said. "We should probably have the baby shower at your new house."

"That might be a good idea."

"Great. Let's do that. It will work out perfectly. I'll call our guests to let them know that we've changed location. Kate and I just need to take care of a few things. And...oh, I informed everyone that we didn't know the gender of both babies."

"Okay." I yawned and closed my eyes a bit.

"I think we should get going so you can get some rest."

Nicole was right, but I would never ask my friends to leave. My eyes felt heavy and I floated into a peaceful state of relaxation in which I knew that everything would be fine.

After they left, Matthew took my hand. There was so much I wanted to tell him, but my eyes were closing and my body felt limp, hopefully drifting into a peaceful rest. "Matthew," I mumbled. Matthew leaned closer to my mouth. My voice was hardly audible. I wasn't even sure if he could hear me. "I'm ready."

Matthew brushed his fingers through my hair, making me even sleepier. The feel of his touch and the serene feeling his care produced made me fall deeper. "After the baby is born and the doctor says all is good. I'll be ready to officially be your wife." I wasn't sure if those words left my mouth, but for sure that was what I wanted to tell him. I figured I was successful even though my eyes were closed. Matthew pressed his lips on mine and whispered the sweetest words. "I love you, Becca."

I love you, too. Those were the words I wanted to say, but I couldn't. I was already knocked out.

Chapter 35
Becky

I couldn't believe the day was finally here. My baby and I did great. We held on until the cesarean date. I looked like a balloon and my body felt so heavy to move, but that would disappear in time.

After the doctor gave me an epidural shot on my spine, which I couldn't believe I felt no pain from, I started to go numb below my waist. When I saw the size of the needle, I was glad I hadn't seen it before. I probably would have refused it.

"My family, your parents, Jenna, and Max are in the waiting room. Do you feel anything?" Matthew asked, walking in. The doctor had asked him to fill out more forms in addition to the ones I had already signed.

It had been so long since Matthew and I had sex, I wondered how he was holding up, because all I could think of when I saw him were perverted thoughts. He looked so delicious, all dressed up in blue scrubs — just like the doctor — I wanted to strip them off him. "I feel something. I want something," I said in my most seductive voice.

Matthew chuckled. "Don't say that, Becca. You're flat on your back with an easy access hospital gown on. All I have to do is just pull that string and I could see all of you." His hand slipped down to my breast, causing me to gasp. He gave me a slow kiss that would have produced all sorts of funny tingles down my legs; however, I couldn't feel anything now on my lower half.

When the sound of footsteps approached, Matthew made sure I wasn't exposed and stepped aside.

"We're all ready for you," Dr. Frances said. He was dressed the same as Matthew. More people came in and pulled the bed I was on. "Matthew, since this isn't an emergency situation, you may be in the same room."

"Don't worry, Doc. I don't plan on missing a thing."

Matthew

I had no interest in seeing Becca's gut, so I held onto her hands, gazing into her eyes while hovering at the side. She would open and close her eyes, sometimes squinting them. "Are you in pain? Do you feel what they're doing?"

"No. I'm just anxious."

"Me, too." I wanted to keep her mind occupied. "I think I'm going to steal your gown and mine so we can play doctor and patient. What do you think?" I got a loud snort out of her.

"I think that's a great idea, 'cause I want to do a whole bunch of nasty things to you, Doctor Knight. I'll be a good patient and do whatever you've been dreaming of and wanting to do for the past couple of months. You've been so patient and enduring."

That sounded way too hot to my ears. Whispering to each other and flirting had my dick straining in my pants. I had to turn off my emotions or we would be that couple the doctor and nurses would remember forever.

"It's a—" I heard a voice begin. Becky's eyes grew wide. I stood up and turned to the sound. That was fast.

"You have a beautiful daughter, Mr. Knight."

I knew I was going to have a daughter, but seeing her in front of me was a whole different, amazing feeling. I didn't know what to do until the nurse handed her to Becca.

"Hello there, little one," Becca cooed.

All I could see was her face, but that was enough to break me down. Whatever I had been feeling, this depth of happiness filled me completely. Since they had just taken her out and hadn't cleaned her thoroughly yet, she still had some smudge of white stuff on her face that looked like white cream.

"She's beautiful," I said softly, afraid that if I spoke any louder I would scare her. Her wide eyes glistened chestnut brown. She was alert and staring back at us.

"We're your mommy and daddy. And we love you so much. Your two sets of grandparents, Auntie Rachel and Jenna, and Uncle Max are waiting in the waiting room. They can't wait to meet you." Becca paused. "You did it. You held on for us. I'm so proud of you." A teardrop fell from Becca's eye and my eyes teared up, too. I couldn't believe what I was seeing in front of me. She looked like a little angel sent from Heaven just for us. She was healthy and perfect.

"I love you," I said to Becca, and kissed her check. "I love you, too." I kissed my daughter's cheek. "Thanks for being so strong."

Becca and I froze there, unable to stop staring at our miracle, the miracle that had a slim chance of surviving, of making it through as far as she did. She was a fighter for sure.

"It's time to clean her up." The nurse took her from us.

Like a child, I wanted to pout and give a million reasons why I needed a minute longer, but I gave in. I had no choice.

"What's her name?" Dr. Frances asked.

"Addison Marie Knight," Becca said proudly. "She's named after Matthew's grandmother."

"That's a beautiful name."

"Seven pounds, twenty inches," the nurse said.

"Perfect." My lips locked on Becca's, then we both shifted our gaze to Addison.

While the doctors stitched Becca back up, I held both of her hands. Thank you for second chances, I prayed. Thank you for keeping both of them safe.

My mind drifted back to Tessa and our unborn child. I wondered if Tessa and I would've had a baby girl. Whatever the reason why they were taken away, it only led me to believe that they weren't meant for me. It was funny how things turned out in life. Things happened for a reason in their own time and place, and helped people to learn and grow. Though I would always love Tessa and our unborn baby, and would keep them close to my heart, I was looking at my future, my purpose, my reason for living. And I couldn't have been happier.

CHAPTER 36
JENNA

A wave of pain coursed through me. It was light at first, but it got stronger. My body shuddered from trying to contain the ache. The pain expanded and deepened and it made my muscles weak. It felt hot, cold, then hot again, alternating as sweat sprang out across my forehead.

I moaned, alerting Max to look at me. He didn't say a word. He was waiting for me to speak. "I'm okay. I feel cramping." Rubbing my stomach, I turn to the side. When that was uncomfortable, I shifted upward.

"Are you in pain?" Max asked, looking down where the needle stuck in my arm. Two types of liquid flowed through me, IV and Pitocin. At a week past my due date, the doctor had suggested that we induce labor. Though Max and I didn't like the idea, the fact that being so late could cause stress to the baby made us decide to do it.

"Let me check your dilation," Dr. Howard said, walking in with a nurse.

Max smiled and turned away. He still had a difficult time with another man seeing me naked.

"Looks like only two centimeters. We're making progress. The baby's head is in good position, too." Dr. Howard pulled my gown down. "Hang in there and let us know if there is any discomfort or if you have any questions."

Before I could ask him a question, the monitor started beeping. Was something wrong with me? I turned to the sound, then to Max. He moved to the side for the nurse to come around. At that point, my heart was pumping on overload and I waited breathlessly. The sound died as quickly as it had come.

Dr. Howard's shoulders relaxed. "The sound you were hearing was a warning that the baby was not getting enough oxygen."

"What do you mean?" I asked. The doctor's words were simple and understandable. I just needed a moment to take it in. Max grabbed my hand when the nurse gave him a space to move in.

"It could be many factors, but one of the common ones are too much straining on the baby's heart during induced labor, or the cord being wrapped around the baby's neck, cutting off the oxygen."

"What can we do about it?" Max inquired. My poor Max, he looked so worried, like he was the one having a baby.

"Right now, nothing. All we can do is wait. If it happens again, we'll have to prep Jenna for the possibility of a C-section. We'll give her an epidural. An epidural is a shot that is used to numb the pain from the waist down, which I know you are aware of. The nurse will be right outside. I have to check on another patient, but I'll be back. Don't worry. I have a pager. They can contact me any time."

"Thank you," Max said, watching the staff walk away.

Another wave of pain hit me. I took in deep breaths and exhaled slowly, just like they'd showed us at the Lamaze class. Max, feeling the squeeze of my hand, knew I was having another round of cramping pains. Like a good trooper, he breathed with me.

It wasn't that long, but time seemed to drag during the pain. "How are you doing?" the nurse asked. She lifted my gown. "I'm going to check your dilation. Can you lift your legs for me?" I did as instructed. "Hmmm...still only two."

"Only two?" I let out a huff. With all of the pain I had been enduring, I'd thought I would have at least expanded a bit more.

"Don't be discouraged. It takes time, but two is better than none."

It was easy for her to say it. She wasn't the one in labor. "Ahhh," I cried softly, holding my stomach. I wanted to scream, but I contained myself by biting my bottom lip. Women had said being in a labor was like having really bad menstrual cramps. My cramps never got bad, so I had no idea what I was in for. And no one could truly understand what it was like to be in labor unless they'd experienced it.

Max dragged his hair back and took a forceful step toward the nurse. "Isn't there something you can do for her pain?"

"She'll have to hold on. It's too soon for an epidural."

"Okay. That's right." Max nodded, looking disappointed. He had forgotten what we learned in Lamaze class. I couldn't blame him. In fact, I was surprised that I remembered to breathe.

The nurse checked my vital signs when the beeping noise that I'd heard before rang in the room. This time, knowing the reason for the sound, I panicked. "The baby," I whimpered.

Max stepped aside again for the nurses and Doctor Howard. The beeping sound was faster this time. "Let me try shifting the baby's position." I had no idea what he meant, but what he did next made me cry out in pain. This time I couldn't hold it in.

I wasn't sure what he was doing, but something pushed inside of me. I cried out with no control. "Look at me, babe," Max directed, holding both of my hands. Focusing on Max's loving face helped somewhat, but when my back arched in pain, I turned away. It took two turns, but whatever the doctor did, the beeping noise stopped.

Doctor Howard released a long sigh, looking relieved. "Sorry, Jenna. I know you didn't like the idea of having a cesarean, but I'm afraid there's going to be no choice. You haven't progressed. You're still at two and it's been a couple of hours. The anesthesiologist will give you an epidural and get you ready. The baby's heart rate dropped stronger this time. I don't want to take any more chances. We need to deliver now." He turned to Max. "Mr. Knight, you are welcome to join us in the delivery room, but you'll have to put some protection on. The nurse will bring them to you."

"Yes, please. I want to be in there with my wife."

While Max was putting on the scrubs, I got my epidural. I held my hands tightly in a ball, ready for the pain on my spine, but nothing came. "There, done. You did great," the anesthesiologist said. "Pretty soon, you won't feel a thing."

I did great? He was awesome. "I didn't feel a thing," I praised him. "Thank you."

"That's what I'm good at, painless as possible. We want to make sure you're comfortable. You're all ready. Everything is going to be fine."

"Thank you." I smiled. There was peace and assurance in his tone. Whatever the worries I had before about things going wrong during birth, they vanished. His words soothed me like an answer to my prayer.

Max stretched his arms and strutted to us. "How do I look?"

Delicious, I wanted to say, but instead, I offered a soft laugh. "You look like a doctor."

When the anesthesiologist walked away, Max hovered over me. "You look so cheerful. I'm assuming the drugs are working?"

"Yes." Some sensations wavered through me, and now it felt like having a baby was going to be a piece of cake.

Max's gaze on me turned heated. "Now that you feel better, how do I really look? What did you want to say, Jenna? I could see in your eyes that you wanted to say something else."

I tugged him closer so I could whisper in his ear. "I want to fuck you wearing one, Doctor Knight."

Max's lips pulled back in a huge grin. "Maybe I can buy one, but only if you'll wear that gown."

We started to laugh when we jerked back from the sudden sound. The nurses and doctor were already halfway in the room, but the sound started increasing, faster than the last time.

"Code blue," I heard one of the nurses yell outside of the room.

Another bed was reeled in. It took two men to switch me over, one on each side. It happened so fast that I had no time to register what was happening to me. It was the strangest feeling to have my body being lifted like that. Having no sensation to my lower half, I felt as if half my body was missing.

"We need to get her in now," Dr. Howard demanded. His tone shot up my adrenaline. Fear flushed through me.

My baby was all I could think of. What if something terrible happened? "Max!" I cried out loud as they started to wheel me.

"I'm right here, babe. Don't worry about a thing. Everything will be fine." Max sounded calm, but fear lurked in his tone.

"Everything is fine, Jenna," I heard one of the nurses say, but stared at the white ceiling above me as they wheeled me into the room.

"You can't come in, Max," someone said.

"What do you mean?" Max sounded agitated. Then I heard the door close.

My heart pounded with no mercy, and I was scared out of my mind. I didn't care what happened to me, I just wanted my baby safe and well. Please God, I prayed. Please don't take my baby. Max and I will take good care of our baby. Please. Tears slid down the side of my face on both sides.

A warm hand touched my forehead. "Can you feel anything? I just gave you an extra dosage of epidural just to make sure."

"I'm okay," I replied, wiping my tears.

"Max is waiting outside. We don't let the husband in during code blue situations." I gazed at the door. Max was just outside it. I could see his face, but he couldn't see that I was looking at him. I wanted him with me. He should be with me, I wanted to demand, but the baby came first.

Max

Damn it! The nurse blocked my way and fuckin' closed the door on me. How could she do that? Jenna needed me and I couldn't be there for her. It was the most frustrating thing. Pacing back and forth helped me relieve some tension and frustration, but that only lasted for a few seconds.

When the nurse yelled out code blue, my heart dropped to the floor. Knowing what that meant had me scared for both of their lives. I told Jenna everything would be fine even though I wasn't sure. Guilt consumed my heart. When Jenna told me she was pregnant, a huge part of me wished she wasn't. I was even upset about it, but the possibility of losing our baby devastated me. How could I have ever wished the baby wasn't conceived at all? Tugging a fistful of my hair with both of my hands, I took deep breaths. Please don't let anything happen to our baby or Jenna, I prayed.

Unable to control my curiosity and needing to know that everything would be fine, I plastered my face against the small window, but it was frosted. I could hardly see a thing. Damn it! I had to pull myself together. This was not how I should be acting.

Just before my pulse shot up again, the door opened.

"You may come in now. Everyone is fine," the nurse said, swinging the door wider.

"Thank God," I huffed under my breath, and went straight to Jenna.

Jenna

"Is my baby okay?" I asked with hesitation. I was afraid to know. Oh God! What if my baby came out all blue and couldn't breathe?

"They are working fast...almost done," the anesthesiologist assured me.

I looked beyond the blue long cloth that blocked me from seeing what they were doing. I could understand why. I probably would have fainted from the sight of my guts all hanging out.

"And there...we are done."

"That was fast," I sighed. It was over within a few minutes.

"Yes, we're fast. We have to be. Every second matters."

"Is my baby okay?" I was so scared to know...so scared to see.

"Why don't you see for yourself?" The anesthesiologist looked up with a smile. Just as I was about to see whom he was smiling at, Max called my name.

"Jenna."

"Max." I turned my head and more tears streamed down. I couldn't help it. He was my comfort, my husband, and the father of our child. Max's worried face made me frightened. "You did great, babe. I'm so proud of you." His words made my heart pound faster and I prepared to hear the worst. Before I could ask anyone what was going on, I saw a white and blue blanket lying on my chest.

"Congratulations," Dr. Howard announced. "Here is your precious baby boy, but you already knew you were going to have a boy. Twenty-two inches and eight pounds."

My mind was filled with millions of thoughts, and they were swimming around with so much joy that I couldn't even fashion them into words. "Hi there." It was all I could say as I stared into those beautiful, brown, shiny eyes filled with wonder...filled with curiosity...filled with love. As joyful tears ran down my face, I smiled at everyone and thanked God for keeping our baby boy safe.

"Mommy and Daddy promise to take good care of you. You come first." I couldn't help myself. I wasn't sure if I was allowed to touch him due to possible germs on my finger, but I did it anyway. I was his mother. He lived inside of me for nine months. We shared a bond that only mothers and babies could understand. Nobody was going to tell me what I could or couldn't do. With tiny strokes, I caressed his cheek. "Ahhh," I sighed softly. I melted into his softness and into the newborn baby smell.

Max kissed my cheek. "I love you." Then he kissed our baby's forehead tenderly. "I love you very much. You gave us one huge scare, little one."

"What's the baby's name?" the nurse asked.

"Connor Maxwell Knight. He's named after Max's grandfather," I said proudly.

Max

"Are you comfortable, babe?" I asked, helping her adjust the bed with the remote control.

"I'm drugged up. I'm all good." Jenna rewarded me with a faint smile. She looked so drained. "When is the nurse going to bring Connor?"

Right on cue, the nurse walked in. "Would you like to hold him?"

I stared at her for a brief second before I answered, "Sure." Folding my arms in the position I was taught in Lamaze class, I waited. An overwhelming sensation coursed through me when she placed his precious small body in my arms. At that very moment, another level of happiness filled me up. I loved him the moment I heard his heart beat, but this was beyond what I had prepared for.

Standing there, I stared at his round chubby face. His eyes were closed, but that didn't stop me from studying and memorizing every inch of his face. With his cute little nose, perky little mouth, and full head of hair, he was my son.

"I'm your daddy, Connor. We're going to have a lot of fun together. I'm going to teach you how to catch a ball, how to ride a bike, how to swim, and how to pick up girls." Jenna giggled. "There's so much I want to show you and teach you. You're going to be so loved. Every day will be filled with precious memories. Everything I am, everything I have belongs to you." My muscles became relaxed. I hadn't realized how tense I was. Connor and Jenna were safe, and it hadn't hit me until I held my baby son.

Placing Connor in Jenna's arms, I wrapped my arms around them. After planting a kiss on Jenna's cheek, I said, "I love you both."

Jenna couldn't keep her eyes away from him, just like me. Her smile brightened the room. I could feel her love and happiness from the way she was holding him. It came so naturally to her.

"When you're ready, you can try to breast feed him," the nurse said.

"Okay." Jenna sniffed his scent. I could understand why she had done that. There was something pleasant about the smell of a newborn child.

CHAPTER 37
JENNA

A huge "Welcome Home Connor Maxwell Knight" banner was spread across the foyer when I walked through our front door.

My eyes were wide and excitement filled me to see my parents, my in-laws, Nicole and Keith, Kate and Craig, and Becky and Matthew surrounding us. Looking beyond them, I saw blue balloons that floated almost to the ceiling, and vases of red roses were everywhere. I knew those were from Max.

"Welcome home," someone said. I was so overwhelmed to see a welcome home party that I didn't recognize the voice. Though my parents and in-laws were at the hospital the day of Connor's birth, it was nice to see them again. After we had lunch, we gathered in the family room.

"Becky, I would have understood if you couldn't come," I said. It had been a month since she gave birth.

"We only drove a few blocks. And plus, I had to come see you and Connor. He's such a great looking baby."

"Of course he is," Max said proudly with a curve of his lips. "He's got mine and Jenna's genes."

Everyone laughed at his humor. "I'm glad you're here. And Addison looks a little bit bigger." Addison was dressed in an adorable pink dress with a pink bow in her hair. I couldn't help but stare at her delicate facial features.

Her tiny fingers were wrapped around Becky's pinky. It was the sweetest thing to see. It was difficult to tell who she looked like, but for sure she had the same color eyes as Matthew.

"She grew an inch in one month," Matthew informed us proudly.

"They grow up so fast, especially the first year," Ellen said, admiring Addison. "Anyway, want some coffee or tea?"

"I'll help you," my mom insisted. After they took orders, they left the room.

"Ellen is right. They do grow up too fast," Kate said, gazing at her daughter. Kristen had turned three recently. What a difference a year made. Her hair was longer and she acted a little bit more mature than the last time I had seen her. She sat quietly between Kate and her dad with an iPad.

"Not only that, they are technologically advanced, too," Robert commented, observing Kristen.

"They are learning things a lot faster these days," Dad added. "I see junior high school kids with cell phones. Jenna didn't have one until she was in college."

"I'm sure there are other things kids these day are advanced from. I don't even want to think about it," Robert added.

Nicole leaned over my shoulder. "Connor is so adorable. Look at that face. He's going to break some hearts. It will be cool if I have a boy. Then at least when we have a play date, one won't get left out."

"Well, even if you don't there might be another chance," Kate threw in.

All eyes flew to her. "Are you?" I asked.

"Yes, I'm pregnant with our second." Kate's lips pulled back so big that I could see so much happiness in her smile.

"I didn't tell you, but we had been trying for a year. And it finally happened."

"Congratulations," we all said.

Connor started turning his head while his lips were searching to latch onto something. "It's feeding time," I announced. I said it more for me, but the men cleared out as if the room was on fire. I had to laugh at that. Max left and came back with the nursing pillow that helped support Connor during feeding. He also placed a cushion behind my back, then left.

As I unbuttoned my shirt, I could feel Connor squirming under my arms. His little mouth started to tremble and his facial muscles twitched. A hungry cry was soon heard.

I pushed my nipple into his mouth just as it opened. "There you go." Milk gushed not only from where he drank, but from the other breast as well. A sensation shot through me and I could feel it dripping. Thank God for my pad, which would stop it from leaking out.

"Will you look at that?" Becky said. "He's a great drinker. Addison was a bit stubborn at the beginning."

"Hmm, I wonder who she takes after," Nicole teased.

"What?" Becky exclaimed, laughing. "I'm not stubborn...sometimes."

"Both of you are lucky. I had a difficult time feeding Kristen. She had a hard time latching on. It also took me some time to produce milk. Wait till your nipples get sore. I hated that part."

"My nipples are already sore," Becky sighed.

I had read about the possible difficulties of producing milk and babies having a hard time latching onto the nipple. Little things like that made me feel so grateful. A loud sound erupted.

"Oh my God," Nicole squealed. "Was that from Connor or from you, Jenna?"

The four of us started to laugh. "It's not me." I couldn't stop laughing, but I had to remain still. Connor was still drinking. When he drained one side, I patted him on the back, then switched him over to the other breast. The bulge from his diaper indicated he'd let out a big dump.

"Well, he's a boy for sure," Becky murmured, sniffing Addison. "I think I need to change her diaper, too."

"Jenna must have eaten a lot of beans. Connor sure smells like it," Kate joked, placing Kristen on her lap.

"Great, this is what I have to look forward to," Nicole laughed, laying the diaper mat for Becky.

Becky started to change Addison's diaper when she looked up. "This is silly, but did you think the same as me? I thought when I delivered Addison that I would get my body back. I mean, I knew it wouldn't be back to the way it was right after I delivered her, but what the hell...I still looked pregnant."

"I did, Becky," Kate said. "I delivered naturally. You think all that stuff would come out of your body after you deliver and your stomach would be flat."

"Let me help you. This is good practice for me." Nicole pushed Becky aside and finished changing Addison's diaper. "It's God's way of making sure you don't get pregnant right away. I mean, let's face it. I sure wouldn't want sex if I still had the muffin tops. I'm going to assume you haven't in months."

"A baby came out of me. Hell, there was no way I was going to let Craig back in even with doctor's approval for a long time."

"See?" Nicole shrugged. "Well, those are my thoughts."

"I guess that's one way of thinking of it," I agreed.

"Maybe I did feel insecure with my body. It also took me a while to get my body back to the way it was," Kate said.

"I don't think our bodies will ever be the same," Becky added.

As I waited for Connor to finish, I absorbed our conversation. As we had progressed in our stages in life, our conversations had shifted. It was wonderful to have friends you could share your thoughts, sorrow, happiness, and experiences with. Many friends entered your life, but the truly worthwhile ones stayed. As I gazed upon my friends still talking about how our bodies had changed, I couldn't stop smiling. These were the moments I wanted to capture and remember forever.

"You did what?" I heard Matthew's voice from the kitchen, and the sound of loud laughter. "Becca, we're going Paris. No way is my brother's lock going to be bigger than mine."

Oh boy!

Two months later

When Max went to work, it was just Connor and me. After I placed him down for an early morning nap, I went downstairs to get a bite to eat. As I ate a yogurt, an egg, and some blueberries, something caught my eye in the family room. On the coffee table was a letter and a single red rose. My heart jumped with excitement. What was Max up to?

I picked it up and read it.

Mommy,

Daddy wants to take you out to dinner
with Uncle Matthew and Auntie Becky.
I'll be okay with Grandma Paige and Grandpa
Jonathan. They are going to come over by 5:30.
They are going to take good care of me.
I'll be safe, so don't worry. Check inside your closet.
There is something Daddy wants you to wear.
You will look beautiful in it.

Love,
Connor

With a huge smile on my face, I texted Max. *You are amazing. I can't wait for you to take me out to dinner.*

Surprisingly, I got a text back right away. *You have it wrong. You are amazing. I'm not sure what I can't wait for, you in that dress or me taking it off you.*

It had been a while since Max and I had flirted like this or even had sex. And it had been a while since my face flushed with warmth.

Maybe I'll let you watch me take it off myself.

I like the sound of that. Get some good rest. You won't be getting much sleep tonight.

My stomach did a funny twist and wetness spread on my breasts. Darn Max, he made me wet in more places than one. Max's text had aroused me. Before I could text him back, Becky's named flashed.

"Hello, Becky."

"Did you get a letter from Max this morning by any chance?" She sounded very hesitant to ask.

"Yes, I did."

"Oh good. Then I didn't spoil anything."

"Don't worry. You didn't. I know we're going out to dinner together. So, what does your note say?"

Becky laughed. "Those boys are too cute. Mine said, 'Dear Mommy, Daddy wants to take you out to dinner with Uncle Max and Auntie Jenna. Grandma Ellen and Grandpa Robert will be coming over to take care of me at 5:30. Check inside your closet. Daddy wants you to wear something special. I know you will look beautiful in it. Have a great time and don't worry about me. Love, Addison'."

After we compared notes, we hung up as our laughter lingered. Walking up the stairs, I couldn't wait to see what Max had in the closet for me. At first I couldn't find it. Off to the side was a white box with a large red ribbon on it. I'd missed it in the massive walk-in closet. After I untied it, I opened the box and pulled out a silky black dress. With spaghetti straps, the dress was simple, yet elegant.

As I admired the dress, I draped it on my body to take a look in the mirror. My body wasn't back to its original weight yet, but I was fine with it. Instead of being insecure about it, I decided to be bold, and I would make sure Max wouldn't be able to keep his eyes off me. The sound of Connor's cry got my attention; so did the weight of my full breasts.

"You look stunning, beautiful, and edible." The way he said those words came out slow and seductive. Max was leaning against the wall, watching me slip into my black heels. He wore a dark silver suit, but the way he looked in it had my heart pounding and made me feel aroused tingles. Max wore suits so well. It was hard not to stare, and it was hard to look away. We hadn't even kissed and he was already making me want to rip off my panties for him.

"So do you," I said, trying not to tip over as I finished the last strap of my heels. Max was making me nervous from the way his eyes were dark and greedy. "There. I'm ready now." I casually moved one step at a time toward him, trying to look as seductive as I could.

"I can watch you do that all day, Mrs. Knight. I'm going to be thinking of you doing that during dinner." Max's hot breath brushed my neck. "I might not make it past dinner."

"Max." I ran my hand across his chest and another wave of want coursed through me. "Why wait for after dinner when you can have dessert first?"

Max growled at the same time as he gripped my ass. "Don't tempt me, Jenna. I'm really considering taking your offer, but we'll be late. I want to taste and savor every single space of your body."

I moaned, feeling Max press his groin into me. I wanted him now. Cold air took his place when he stepped away. "Your parents are waiting downstairs. We should get going. I'm not going to be able to resist another touch from you."

"When do you plan on coming back to work?" Matthew asked, taking a bite of his pasta. "Not that I'm rushing you. Or is my brother making you stay home?"

Max placed his glass down and raised a brow. "I'm not making Jenna do anything. She can speak her mind. Right, babe?"

I peered up, seeing both of them waiting for my answer. Lost in deep thought for a second, I twirled my spaghetti noodles with a fork. Max and I had discussed this issue several times. Max wanted me to be a stay at home mom, but I had other plans. I reassured him that everything would be fine. My parents would watch Connor three days a week. We finally compromised on me working part time. Also, we agreed not to hire a nanny, but we would have a housekeeper instead. As for Becky, her job allowed her to work at home fulltime. That was the beauty of our schedule. We got the best of both worlds.

"Max doesn't make me do anything, or else he knows he'll be sleeping in one of the guest rooms," I confidently said with a smirk.

Becky nudged Matthew with her elbow when he started chuckling. "Don't laugh. I tell you that all the time."

As laughter rang in the air, I recalled the days when Becky and I lived together. We were so scared to date our husbands back then. We guarded our hearts because we thought they would hurt us, that they weren't the ideal husband types. How wrong we were. They are the perfect model of what ideal husbands should be. Just because they were good-looking and successful didn't mean that they were like the other playboy types. We had to give them a chance. Becky and I had found our true loves, and we both found what we were looking for.

During dessert, our topic changed to Connor and Addison. Though I knew he was home safe with my parents, I missed him. As I thought about him, I felt my breast pads dampening. It was feeding time. Luckily, I had pumped before I left.

Matthew slid his chair out. "We should get going home. Becky and I hardly slept last night." Matthew paused. "No, that's not what I meant. Get your mind out of there," he said to Max, chuckling. "Addison woke up too many times. She's teething."

"It's not fun." Becky closed her eyes. She did look a little out of it, but she was still gorgeous in her black dress that was similar to mine.

"We should get going, too," Max said, standing up. "I'll get the bill this time." Max pulled out my chair and helped me slip into my sweater.

"After the stunt you pulled in Paris, you'll be paying the bill from now on," Matthew joked. "That was my idea."

"If I recall—and I do recall correctly because I'm never wrong—it was *my* idea," Max retorted.

I knew they were playing around by the sound of their tone, but enough was enough. Becky and I looked at each other and started walking away together.

"Becca," Matthew followed behind like a lost puppy. "After we get married in Paris, we're swinging by China before we come home."

"Where do you think you're going without me?" Max whispered, whisking me into his arms. Then he turned back to Matthew. "Why are you going to China?"

Becky offered a huge smile as the four of us walked out the door. "We didn't want to tell you guys until it was final, but we got approved. We're going next month to check out their adoption facility. We're trying to decide which country to adopt our second child from. We're not planning to adopt until Addison is at least three, but we were told that it could take years, so we're planning ahead."

"That's wonderful, Becky." I squeezed her tightly. "I can't wait to be a part of your wedding, and I can't wait to plan your bridal shower."

"I did this all backwards, didn't I? Baby shower before bridal shower."

"No one said that was the way it had to be. We go with the flow."

"When did you become so wise, Mrs. Knight?"

I looked over to Max. "When I met Mr. Knight."

CHAPTER 38
BECKY

I was tired as hell, but it had been a while since Matthew and I were intimate. He had been trying, but my lack of self-esteem from gaining weight and being tired had turned me off. Matthew had been so understanding, supportive, and loving that I wanted to show him how thankful I was for having an amazing husband.

Matthew plopped on the bed. "Addison is finally asleep. Are you out of the shower or shall I join you?" He snickered under his breath. Matthew was positioned with both of his arms tucked under his neck, showing off his well-defined muscles. I walked out of the bathroom to see him half asleep.

"Matthew," I said softly. I believed it was the way I said his name that made him flash his eyes open with a grin.

"You're going to take off your robe for me?" He twitched his brows with a hungry look.

"Maybe, maybe not." I threw my head back slightly to allow the towel that was wrapped around my hair to drop. Slowly, I untied the robe and let it glide off my shoulder, but not all the way. The wetness of my hair felt cool on my skin, but the way Matthew looked at me caused me to shiver. His eyes were like hands, undressing me, touching me, and I could already feel him.

Before I could let it fall, Matthew stood up and opened it up just enough to expose my breasts. Another shiver coursed through me. It felt as though Matthew was seeing my naked body for the first time. When he licked my shoulder, I shuddered again. Oh God! Just that one lick did crazy things to me. I wanted more.

Matthew continued kissing and licking down to my breasts, then further down. It was a good thing I had just fed Addison or milk would have poured out of me. I closed my eyes and threw my head back, enjoying every second of pleasure he was giving me. With a flick of his hand, the robe dropped.

Matthew gently laid me down, spread my legs, and continued where he'd left off. The sensation of his wet tongue right next to my clit made me explode. Needing more, I shifted my body. I moaned loudly when Matthew's mouth fell perfectly on my clit. Oh God that felt so good. "Matthew," I screamed.

"You like that, Becca?" he asked as he moved up and pressed his dick against me through the material of his briefs.

I gripped a fistful of his hair. "Yes, I want you inside of me, now. But go slow."

Matthew put on a condom. "I'm going to have to go slow. It's been so long. I don't think I can be inside of you too long. I want to make you feel good. Let me make you come with my fingers."

Holy shit! My head spun in ecstasy. Matthew brought me to the edge with his fingers. The way he licked, teased, and flicked my clit, I was beyond ready for him.

"Matthew, please. No more. I need you inside me." Shuddering with pleasure, my body squirmed and ached for him. He didn't give me a warning. The most pleasurable sensation shot through me when he entered me. "Oh, God, Matt. Yes."

As Matthew continued to make love to me, he cupped my face and gazed at me with tenderness, with respect, and with love. I loved this man more than I could have ever imagined. He was not just my husband-to-be, he was my soul mate, my best friend, and my everything. "I love you," I murmured under my breath, erupting from this beautiful feeling that only Matthew gave me.

"I love you more." I knew he meant it...I saw it in his eyes, felt it in his touch, and heard it in the sounds he made as he made love to me. Matthew loved me. It had taken me a while to accept that someone like him could truly love someone like me. I was no longer an asshole magnet. I was Matthew's magnet. We would stick together through thick and thin, and in my case in sickness and in health. I couldn't wait for what life had in store for us, because I would have the best husband that was made perfectly for me.

Jenna

Max and I were on the same page that night. He wanted me as much as I wanted him. It was difficult to control the heated feeling when Max kept on sliding his hand up my dress during dinner. I had to slap it away without making a scene. I had to admit, it wasn't entirely his fault. My spaghetti with sausage dinner was making me think perverted thoughts. The sausage was as big as Max's dick, and I couldn't stop thinking about licking it. A couple of times I purposely placed my hand on him. He coughed and sat taller so he wouldn't make a scene. I had a few laughing moments.

"Do you like what I'm wearing, Max?" I leaned against the doorframe, looking as seductive as I could. I was still shy at times, but knowing Max loved to see me in anything I wore made it that much easier to show him my naughty side. I had put on black lingerie I'd bought online recently. It was a low cut, see-through lace. It even came with garter stockings and a long black silk robe to match the outfit. I looked like a high-class hooker.

Max turned as soon as he heard my voice. He had just laid Connor down for the night and walked into our bedroom. His eyes darkened with greed, taking in the vision of me. "Jenna," he growled, coming for me with that slow, seductive walk. He yanked his purple tie off and twisted it around his hand. By the time he reached for me, his shirt was unbuttoned all the way. "You look like you want to be fucked, Mrs. Knight." It was amazing how much I had changed. Max would never have used the word "fuck" with me before because I would have cringed, but now it made me more aroused.

"Yes, I do, Mr. Knight."

There were no words after that, Max claimed my mouth in hunger. His stubble felt achingly good against my skin as he continued to kiss and lick my neck and shoulders. "I'm going to tie you up and make love to you until you scream my name," he said, placing his hands tightly on my ass.

Oh how his words did erotic things to me. The next thing I knew, he had tied my hands to the bedpost at the foot of the bed. "I'm going to kiss every inch of you."

Max did just that. I was drowning in his touch, his love, his wet licks that drove me to scream his name. "Max." I heaved a deep breath. As he licked and sucked my clit, his magic fingers did wonders to my body. Pleasurable sensations traveled through every vein, every bone, and every muscle. Quivering, I lost all sense of reality, of time.

When Max took a moment to take off his clothes, I watched him as I panted, out of breath. Max was beautiful, inside and out. He was the epitome of what a man should look and act like. He was the epitome of an ideal husband. And I was lucky that we had found each other.

"I love you, Jenna," he said, purposely grazing his stubble down my body. Oh God! I arched my back. I wanted more, yet it was too much. It was painfully pleasant, and he knew it did crazy things to me. Tiny electric sparks shot through my skin. I wanted to touch him so badly, but I was tied up.

"I love you, too, Max," I said as our eyes met. When I felt his knee spread my legs, I gasped sharply from the pleasure of feeling him inside of me. Max untied me as he continued to rock slowly.

"Oh, babe." Max rolled his eyes back with an intense groaning sound. "I don't think I can last. It's been so long."

Max pulled out to make sure my needs were fulfilled. I didn't know how long he played with my body, but I knew it was getting close to feeding time when I felt my breasts getting full.

"I feel so guilty when I touch your breasts," he murmured against my nipple. "When do you stop breast feeding?"

I was at a loss for words when Max entered me again. "I don't..." Moaning in pleasure, my hips moved in unison with Max's. "Max..." Out of breath, out of my mind, my body felt so weak. "Max!" I screamed when I felt myself climaxing.

"That's it. Come for me, babe." His hot breath scorched the side of my breast. Max avoided my nipples as if they were off limits, but I wanted and needed for him to touch me there, too. As he continued to pump faster, I guided his hand to my breast. It was as if I had released a beast. He hissed with excitement. Max's eyes grew greedy and dark, and he fondled them roughly. "Oh, Max," I panted, releasing short, quick breaths, and sounds I don't remember making blurted out of my mouth.

"Jenna...I need to...I have to..." he continued to say, rocking faster and harder.

"I want to be on top," I said.

That got his attention. I shoved him over so fast that he was in shock. I became the wild beast. I flung the tie around my neck and licked and kissed him all the way down.

Max squirmed. "Jenna."

"I want you to scream my name, Max," I requested as I continued to taste his long, thick dick.

Max rewarded me with that sexy, cocky grin. "Sit on me."

I pushed onto him and rode him hard and fast.

"I've created a sex monster," Max groaned, taking in the pleasure. I could tell he was beyond his limit. "Jenna," he screamed my name. His hands on my hips moved to my breasts. I leaned lower, wanting to have my naked body touch his, to feel his warmth, to feel every part of him.

Max lifted his hips and bent his knees to thrust deeper. That put us both over the edge and I screamed. "That's it, baby. I'm coming, too." The bed rocked to the rhythm of Max's tempo, and I actually thought the bed was going to break. It felt like we were going to drop to the first floor with the bed. "I have to...I want to..." Max growled, and his mouth went straight to my nipple.

Immediately, the sensation shot through my breasts just like it always did when Connor started drinking. Oh shit! As we both exploded from intense pleasure, Max's face was getting a shower from my nipples. Milk squirted over his face. We both laughed like crazy. "Oh my God, Max. Get a towel."

It was the most hilarious thing to watch. Milk dripped on me from him. Instead of getting a towel, Max carried me to the bathroom and turned on the water. "We need a shower, babe. A nice warm shower. Let me wash you up."

Max held me tenderly under the warm running water and kissed me gently, taking his time with long, soft strokes. "I love you, babe. Thank you for giving us a chance. Thank you for giving me a son. Thank you for making me so happy."

I leaned into him, touching his body with mine as much as I could. My heart expanded to its fullest from his words, from his caresses. "Thank you for making me believe I was worth fighting for. That I was worthy of your love."

CHAPTER 39
JENNA

Five years later

"Surprise!"

I gazed around to see my family and friends gathered in a private room of the restaurant called Jazz Kitchen in Anaheim. A large square table was set in the middle of the room; a bouquet of beautiful flowers in a tall glass vase was set on the table. And lavender and white balloons were tied to the back table for decoration.

"Happy thirtieth, babe," Max kissed my forehead.

"Thank you," I thought I said. Standing there, stunned and silent, it felt like a dream as I smiled at our guests. Hopefully my smile didn't look dorky, because I felt my lips tugged too close to my ears.

"Jenna," I heard a voice call. "I'm going to take Cassie from you."

"Mom." I finally snapped out of my confusion. Feeling her arms around me, she took my six-month old daughter out of my arms.

Oh my God! It hit me. Max had thrown me a surprise party. "Jenna, Happy Birthday." Becky, Nicole, and Kate gave me a hug all at once.

"Thanks for coming?" I said, looking down. Christopher had let go of my hand. After he turned two, all he ever wanted to do was follow Connor around.

"It was so hard to keep it away from you," Becky exclaimed. "I was so afraid that I was going to slip."

"Well, you did a great job because I was completely clueless. Max told me that he had planned a special dinner for our family for my birthday and that we would spend the night at the Disney hotel, since it's in walking distance. We also planned to go to Disneyland the next day. Wait." I paused. "Are you going to Disneyland with us?"

"They sure are." Max placed his arms around me.

"I can't believe it. It's going to be so much fun," I squealed.

"Let's see how long we can handle standing in line with all of these kids," Matthew added.

"Before we discuss our itinerary, let's eat first," Max suggested. Taking my hand, he led me to the buffet that was set up just for our room. "Birthday mommy needs to eat. I already told Connor and Christopher to eat lunch. My mom helped them with their serving."

"Did I tell you how much I love you?" I asked, taking a plate that he offered out of his hand.

"As many times as I tell you that you're beautiful."

"That many?"

"I still don't think it's enough." Max winked; the one that sent all sorts of shivers through me.

"You're too good to me, you know that?"

"I have to make sure Mrs. Knight is happy." Max scooped a spoonful of vegetables and placed it on my plate.

"Balloon, Mommy," Christopher whined, tugging my dress.

"You can have it after lunch," Connor said. "I told him to stay with Grandma, but he wouldn't listen."

"Would you like to sit with Mommy and Daddy?" I asked Christopher.

With his head tilted back, his brown eyes were wide open. Christopher nodded with the most adorable pouty face.

"Can I sit with Addison and Shawn?" Connor asked. "We want to play super heroes. I'm Superman. Addison is Supergirl. And since Shawn is younger than me, he's Superboy." Connor lifted both of his arms to show us his muscles.

Max chuckled lightly. "Yes, you may, but we need to see how much you ate before you throw your plate away."

"Okay, Dad." Connor took off with his hands in the air.

As I watched him dash off, I gazed upon my mom and Ellen doting on Cassie while they ate and the dads talked about golf. It was such a sweet sight. I'd heard horror stories about in-laws unable to get along, but not in our case. Thank God!

"Mason is so cute," Kate said, taking a bite of her fish.

"He's such a lucky boy to finally have parents who will love him," Nicole added. "How old is he again?"

"He's almost two," Matthew replied, spoon-feeding Mason, who was sitting next to him. "He's still getting used to us speaking English. We hired a nanny that speaks Chinese to help us through the transition. It's only been two weeks, but he's adjusted pretty well. It took us longer to adopt than we had planned. We were still deciding which country to adopt our child from, but we finally decided on China."

"Did you name him after a family member in your family?" Keith asked, placing his cup down after taking a sip.

"Actually," Matthew started to say, chuckling. "He's named after a paranormal young adult character Becky likes to read about."

That got everyone's attention. "Really? That's awesome." Keith grinned.

Matthew's tone rose with excitement. "He's named after a descendant of a God. He can shoot lightning bolts out of his fingertips. He's badass, I tell you."

We all burst out in laughter. "Seems like someone read that book. What's it called?" Max teased.

Matthew shrugged his shoulders. "*From Gods*. But just the part where he did things with his bolt of energy to make Skylar go crazy for him. You know...I have to make Becca happy."

"Oh God! Matthew!" Becky lightly punched him. I totally understood the reason for that slap. Becky was not the shy type, except around her in-laws. Sex was one topic that was off limits with parents for the both of us. Becky looked at me and cringed.

Kate glanced at her husband. "What are you laughing about? You should read that book."

Everyone started laughing again. "Let's change the subject. We have kids here," Max murmured, gazing at Addison and Connor. They were staring at us with wide, curious eyes.

"Wow. Mason can shoot lightning?" Connor asked.

"No, no, no," I said quickly while we continued to laugh, but now it was from Connor's question. We had to start being careful of what we said. Connor was more observant about what we discussed these days. "Uncle Matthew was joking."

"Oh," he chuckled. And just like that he picked up his fork to eat again and turned his attention to Addison and Shawn.

"Excuse us for a moment," Becky said out of the blue. "Jenna, Kate, Nicole, I need to talk to you."

We followed Becky to the back. It was the first time I'd seen my birthday cake. Max had it made from my favorite bakery. It was decorated Louisiana-style to match the atmosphere of the restaurant. It even had a beautiful mask on the top.

Becky placed a box in front of us. "I was originally going to get it for Jenna as her birthday gift, but I couldn't help myself. I had to get it for all of us."

"Becky, you didn't have to do that," Kate scolded playfully.

"Open it." Becky looked so excited. She was practically holding her breath. "I can't wait for you to see it."

"It's beautiful. Oh, Becky." I hugged her tightly with tears in my eyes.

"I love this," Nicole added. "It has my baby's names. Shawn and Sarah."

"Mine, too." Kate held hers up. "Kristen and Kelly."

Becky reached into her shirt and pulled something out. "See. I was trying to hide it. I got one, too. It's sterling silver, so make sure to take good care of it." The names of her children were imprinted on the bottom of the circular pendants that were layered from small to big, Addison and Mason.

Placing the pendants on the palm of my hand, I reflected on the years when Becky and I first became roommates.

"How many children do you want?" I asked Becky as we sat on the sofa, sipping our tea on a cold winter night.

"I think two. I don't think I can handle more than two kids fighting together," Becky snorted. "My sister and I used to fight all the time. Drove my mom crazy. How about you?"

"At least three. Two boys and a girl. But I'm a bit afraid that I may take after my mom and will have a hard time conceiving."

Becky snapped out of her thoughts and started laughing. I knew she was thinking dirty thoughts. "Well, think of it this way. You can have lots of sex trying."

I had to laugh at her humor. "I hope sex is good."

"If you meet the right husband it will be." Becky blew into her cup and took a sip.

"If that ever happens." I ran my finger around the rim, wondering whom I would end up getting married to.

"You will, Jenna. You have a beautiful heart. I have no doubt you will marry a man with the same heart. I'll make sure of it," she stated and winked.

"The same goes for you, Becky."

"I hope so," she sighed. "With my luck of men these days, who knows?"

"Someone great is waiting for us out there."

"I hope they're wonderful."

"Yeah...I hope one day we'll get our something forever."

"Jenna, are you okay?" Becky's voice snapped me back to reality.

"Yeah. I was just thinking about what we said to each other when we first became roommates.

Becky nodded with a small smile. I could tell from her expression she knew exactly what I was talking about.

"Could you help me with this?" I asked.

After Becky put on my necklace, she swung her arms around my shoulders. "Group hug."

Kate and Nicole squeezed in as we held each other tightly. From my position, I could see Max and Matthew smiling at us. Their faces were full of love, care, and understanding. Then my vision shifted to all of the children. Thinking about them always warmed my heart. I thanked God for my life. So much had happened in the past seven years for Becky and me.

This once insecure girl, who wanted everything to be safe, had changed. I had become the woman I was meant to be. The confident Jenna needed a man like Max to show me that I could trust and love again with all of my heart and soul. He made me feel beautiful. He made me feel desired. He showed me I was worth fighting for. And that alone made me believe in us.

Life was full of surprises. Sometimes the surprises were not so good, but the good ones made my life even better. Like Max and the unexpected pregnancy. At the end, those unexpected surprises were the ones that brought the most joy in my life. I could not imagine my life without Max and my children. As I looked at them, my heart expanded with so much happiness that it couldn't possibly get any fuller.

I didn't want to think about "what if I had never given Max a chance?" The truth was, Max and I were meant for each other. One way or another, we would have found each other at the right time and place. This I knew for sure from the bottom of my heart. I couldn't imagine my life with anyone else and I never would. He was my something great. My life was something wonderful as I gazed at my family and friends. And now...we would live for something forever.

Something Amazing Available NOW

M. Clarke

About the Author

International Bestselling, Award Winning, Author M. Clarke resides in Southern California. When she started reading new adult novels, she fell in love with the genre. It was the reason she had to write one-Something Great.

Made in the USA
Columbia, SC
18 September 2019